In the sheltered world of a No
manor, young Catt's life seem_   _____ ____ hopeful.
Despite her humble background, she is taught to read
and write by the son of the house – a Catholic priest –
and has the prospect of becoming the personal maid of
Lady Anne Leyton herself. But then she accidentally
stumbles upon the shameful secret of her birth and is
sent away from the house forever – to suffer a life of
misery and humiliation.

Rescued by a shy young shepherd, Catt's story shifts to
the wilds of North Yorkshire. There, the challenge of life
on the bleak and cruel moor and the love of a good man
give her the strength and purpose to succeed. Then, in
one defiant gesture she abandons her faith and embraces
the superstition of the Bridestones – the great brooding
stones standing high on the moor above her home –only
to find that there is a bitter price to pay . . .

A tale of lost faith and enduring obsession, Audrey
Butler's moving and dramatic story of a young girl
battling against the prejudices and pitfalls of Victorian
England is inspired by the life of her own great-
grandmother.

Audrey Butler was born and went to school in Yorkshire
and can trace her North Yorkshire ancestry back to the
reign of Elizabeth I. She wrote her first book – a best-
seller about war-time Czechoslovakia – when she was 14.
After graduating in Modern History at Oxford, she
worked in publishing, translating historical and
children's books from French and editing reference and
non-fiction books. She has edited five editions of the
Dictionary of Dates (the latest, in 1996) and written
another children's novel, about the Spanish Armada, for
her own five children. With her husband she is the co-
author of a book on churches in Suffolk – where she now
lives. She has contributed to magazines and radio and
writes a weekly column in her local newspaper. At
present she is working on another Yorkshire novel,
inspired, like *The Bridestones,* by her research into her
family background.

THE BRIDESTONES

Audrey Butler

The Book Guild Ltd
Sussex, England

This book is a work of fiction. Although based on fact, *The Bridestones* has been enhanced with imaginary characters and incidents.

The Book Guild Ltd
25 High Street
Lewes, Sussex

First published 1996
© Copyright Audrey Butler 1996
Set in Baskerville

Typesetting by Southern Reproductions (Sussex)
Crowborough, Sussex

Printed in Great Britain by
Athenaeum Press Ltd
Gateshead.

A catalogue record for this book is
available from the British Library

ISBN 1 85776 115 4

FOR MY GREAT-GRANDPARENTS
Thomas (1842–96) and Alice (1846–1918)
– together now in a moorland churchyard,
– much of this is their story.

The hope I dreamed of was a dream,
Was but a dream; and now I wake,
Exceeding comfortless, and worn, and old,
For a dream's sake.

. . . Lie still, lie still, my breaking heart;
My silent heart, lie still and break;
Life and the world and mine own self are changed
For a dream's sake.

CHRISTINA ROSSETTI

1893

There had not been a funeral quite like this one in Pickerby for years. It was particularly surprising, folk thought, because Catherine Halliday, though clearly, albeit somewhat mysteriously, comfortably off these days, had never been one for ostentation or overtly extravagant spending.

As for her husband Luke, whose funeral it was, he had always seemed so quiet and unassuming – why, you scarcely noticed he was there, most of the time! And he had slipped out of life equally quietly . . .

And now this! Maybe there had been another secret legacy – like the one Catherine had implied she had a dozen years back, when she and Luke suddenly rose from virtual rags to the relative riches of Townend, their own farm – or had the bereavement turned her brains to water? For there was no doubt she had always been something of a puzzle, strangely remote and sprung from nowhere – there were persistent rumours of a workhouse upbringing . . . Certainly, she was no Yorkshirewoman, with that clipped, flat accent of hers! And all this ceremonial had been paid for in advance, in gold sovereigns, no expense spared: the undertaker's boy, who could always be relied on for background information, had been quite specific on this and had spread the word accordingly.

Luke had been well-liked, for all his shyness, more approachable and open by far than his wife. Nevertheless, many of those turning out to see the cortège pass were motivated by curiosity as much as sympathy. The funeral carriage was the best obtainable, the black horses that drew it were extravagantly bedecked with black plumes and ribbons. Behind the hearse – the coffin itself seemed almost out of place in all this splendour with its single spray of white heather from the widow, and not a wreath to be seen – was Catherine's carriage.

Alongside her sat her married daughter and her twelve-year-old son, another Luke – the only children still living when there had once been four – five, if you counted that first poor little stillborn boy, but few of those here now knew anything about that one. But they did remember the two pretty little girls who had coughed themselves into the grave even before their father. *Their* funerals, now, had been almost unnaturally subdued and modest affairs. Why, Catherine herself had not even been present.

In the next carriage followed the son-in-law, together with the Pickerby parson who was to conduct the funeral service. This was not to be here at Pickerby, of course, but at Gelling, up on the moor's top. Luke had been born there. Now, in death, he was going back. The only remaining family mourners were John Briggs, the Pickerby blacksmith, and his wife Susannah, Luke's sister – they who had befriended Catt and Luke in the days when the Gelling Hallidays shunned them.

But now it was Catt's turn to do the shunning: the Gelling Hallidays had not been invited to today's affair.

As the cortège swung ponderously past the Melchester junction, turning out of Pickerby to start the long, slow climb out of the vale, with its lush fields and comfortable clusters of houses and up onto the bare, lonely moor, Catt wondered how in the world she would manage to survive the next couple of hours, let alone the future that lay beyond. The emptiness weighed down on her like a massive rockfall: she felt crushed beyond endurance.

I am only thirty-nine, but my life is over, quite over, she thought. Without Luke, there's no meaning in it any more. Everything I've done, everything I've dreamed of doing, everything I've sacrificed – it all counts for nothing, now. I ought to be dead, too . . .

Then her pale, sharp little face shattered into a grim smile. But at least I've seen to it that Luke gets this moment of triumph at the last! And I have a share in it, too – and how glorious it's going to be!

For there, at the Gelling graveside, she knew beyond any doubt whatsoever would be those uninvited Hallidays . . . Catt could picture them now, shrinking back in shock and envy at the sight of their Luke – poor, despised Luke, the unloved, outcast son with the stammer, who had been bewitched by the Papist woman and made the laughing-stock of his father's will – finally coming back in such style!

Oh, the pleasure Catt would soon be taking in ignoring them completely! She could see herself sweeping by in her Melchester-made black taffeta and velvet while they shuffled miserably in their rags. Would Luke's brother Will have managed to stay sober long enough to get there at all? she wondered. And what about Will's Betsy? Would her employers have allowed her time off from the washtub? That same Betsy who in times gone by had stood over her, impassive and merciless, and in finery that, cheap though it might be, was more than she then seemed likely ever to posess, while Catt scrubbed and sweated through a pregnancy which Old Will had made finish in a premature labour with one of her twins stillborn, the one that she'd wanted the most . . .

Well, God – if God there was – who had treated her so badly so often seemed at least to have shown some fairness at the end. For all Will and Betsy's children had died within days of their birth, and High Moor, the Halliday home which Luke had loved so dearly and hopelessly, had never done Will any good, even though he got it. So, never mind the heartbreak! At least I have a son, a living son, sitting here alongside me. And, thought Catt, trying to blot out the misgivings that kept surfacing despite all her attempts to crush them, though Luke always wanted High Moor so much, there was bad luck in its very stones. He was better off without it. Townend, the Townend I got for him, was – is – so much, much better! And yet the doubts would not go away . . .

Though it was December, the day was crisp and clear. The sky was a harsh icy blue. It cut like steel into Catt's very heart, even as its brilliance caught the dead heather covering the open moor around, transfusing it with a strange, almost unearthly glow. Now, for the next mile or so, that was all there was to see – the hard sky and the shimmering heathland with only the raggle-taggle sheep wandering among it, wild, scrawny sheep like those Luke had once tended with such loving care and had always longed to possess again. And never did. For I wouldn't let him, God forgive me! They were a part of that world I hated so . . . Catt cried to herself. But it was too late, much too late, for any excuses now.

At the fork by the Horseshoe Inn, just before Gelling village, the cortège turned off towards High Moor. There, the horses were halted. Catt stepped from the carriage, trying to tread with a firmness she was far from feeling, her drawn face even more ashen than before. She forced herself to look up at the gaunt, grey stone building. Memories overwhelmed her.

The farm was abandoned now, part-shuttered, and the unshuttered windows had lost their glass years back. It looked even more uninviting than when Luke had first brought her here as a bride more than 20 years ago, she thought. Here, Luke's father had cursed her and struck her. Will and his wife had exploited and mocked her and maybe even tried to poison her. In the end she and Luke had had to run away at dead of night, along with their newborn daughter. She had never been back, and Luke but rarely . . .

Then Old Will, Luke's father, had died – and there followed that wicked, cruel will of his that made such a scapegoat of Luke. Young Will – idle, feckless, drunken Will – took over High Moor, of course. Things went to the bad very rapidly after that; Will was soon evicted, the farm joined to High Hall, the house turned into a store and over a hundred years of Halliday occupation ended. If only Luke had been the eldest son and not the youngest, how different things might have been! Well, Will was a day-labourer now, when working at all, and the haughty Betsy a washerwoman, and the pair were nigh on penniless – while she, plain, nameless Catt, who had come to High Moor with nothing, was a farmer in her own right, and a prosperous one. Oh, it was wonderful to contemplate, until – and Catt caught her breath and felt a fresh stab of pain at her heart – until you remembered that Will and Betsy still lived and Luke, dear, darling Luke, was dead. And so, despite all she had tried to do, he and she were still the losers, right to the last . . .

Catt pressed her lips against the wall of the deserted house, kissing it through her mourning veil. For Luke had loved this place as fiercely as she had come to hate it. Despite all that had taken place, Luke's passion for High Moor had endured till the moment of his dying. It was for Luke that Catt had come here, to make his final farewells. Never again would she venture near this accursed place.

Then it was back into the carriage, and on to Gelling and the church. As Catt turned and glanced behind her, for one last, ritual look, she saw the Bridestones rearing up on the horizon beyond the farmhouse, seeming to taunt and threaten still. And she shuddered.

But the moment passed. Soon they were recrossing the Whitcar road and ahead was the village, and in its centre the squat, grey Norman church. Catt could make out the clutch of people hovering around the lych-gate. She fancied she could even pick out Will, fat and blotched (or was she imagining it?) and reeling slightly, and the scraggy, scrawny figure of the once flamboyant Betsy.

Catt swept from the carriage like a queen, all her confidence and vigour flooding back. In the midst of her terrible grief, she could still savour to the full the astonishment on the faces of the assembled company at the sight of the lavish cortège. People fell back to let her step forward.

Will came shuffling towards her and plucked at her silk sleeve, 'Betsy and I . . .' he muttered.

Catt halted, stared through him, said not a word. There was a sudden hush, nothing but the murmur of her rustling skirts.

Her son-in-law leant forward, thinking that in her misery

she had not realised what Will was trying to say, perhaps not even remembered who he was.

'Mother, I think this is –'

Catt flicked Will's fingers from her gown, imperiously contemptuous. She might have been swatting a particularly repulsive fly. She turned on her heel and stared resolutely at the coffin, which was now being transferred from the hearse onto the village bier that had carried generations of Hallidays on their final journey.

Her voice rang out, clear, firm and utterly pitiless. 'No, Harry. I do not know this – person!'

Everything was ready now. Catt looked calmly at her son. He was trembling slightly, biting back his tears. She too desperately wanted to cry and yet she could not. She rested her hand on his arm, took a deep breath and prepared to follow her husband's body into the heretic church.

1

For as long as she could remember, Catt had been following her mother, Mary Jane, about the Hall on her daily work-round.

Mary Jane's sphere of responsibility was strictly limited. She 'did' the Long Gallery, hung with the family portraits that went back even beyond the days of 'bad' Queen Bess, and Lady Anne Leyton's private rooms and oratory, and, of course, the main Hall chapel itself. Mary Jane was a superb polisher of silver and brasses and somewhat surprisingly, a special confidante of Lady Anne's, even though, being illiterate and totally unschooled, she was not qualified to be a proper lady's maid.

And as far back as she could remember, Catt had realised that her mother was very pretty and that she was not. Mary Jane's hands might be red and rough, but her face, with its apparent open innocence, made Catt think of the face of Our Lady on the chapel statue. Not that she ever dared voice the comparison, of course. That would have been dreadfully sinful!

(But it was surely no sin to wish to be beautiful, too! 'Please make me look just a bit as pretty as Mamma!' beseeched Catt, and waited for the miracle that never came. Years later, she would mark it among the first of her many unanswered prayers . . .)

Mary Jane was externally extremely devout, and Catt followed her example unblinkingly. Generations of Youngmans had been servants at Leyton Hall and, like the Leytons, had clung to the Catholic faith regardless of the

1

Reformation that had turned most of England Protestant centuries ago.

For centuries past, Leyton Hall had been all but isolated from the world outside its walls by its religion; only now, in the second half of the nineteenth century, was this isolation gradually withering away. Past squires had stuck to their religion and kept their heads well down. The fines they paid for their devotion meant that, bit by bit, the Nottinghamshire estate grew smaller and poorer. The Leytons tended to marry within a narrow circle, in an attempt to preserve both their faith and what remained of their fortune, cousin often marrying cousin. After the religious persecutions ended, Leyton Hall still survived – shabby, inward-looking and dull. By the early 1800s its brand of religion was not easy to distinguish from that of its Protestant neighbours. Priests were treated as servants – except when, as at Leyton Hall in the 1860s, the younger son of the house was the family chaplain – so following the Protestant squires' habit of making younger sons into parsons, whether they were really suited to the task or not . . .

The Leyton son had been chaplain at the Hall since returning from his studies in Rome when Catt was about eight – and she worshipped the ground he walked on. For Catt, life at Leyton ceased to be dull the moment she first set eyes on Charles Leyton – tall, handsome and distinguished, with his black curls and patrician nose. She was so entranced that she was grateful for the slightest scrap of attention he gave her. Even at the age of eight, it was love at first sight.

Charles first noticed her soon after his return from Rome. Mary Jane was sweeping the chapel, and Catt had been given a duster and put to polishing the pews. But books had always fascinated her, and this was why Charles Leyton happened upon her that day, curled up in a corner with an open Mass book, trying to decipher words she did not know . . . She looked up at him, grey eyes locking into grey eyes.

'I wish I knew what this meant!' she said.

Charles burst out laughing. Intrigued by her forcefulness, he set about teaching her simple reading and writing. 'After all, when you're grown-up, my mamma may want a new maid – and you'll need to read and write to be that.'

Up to that moment, Catt had always thought she would like to be a nun. Little though she was, she had stared long and hard at the Leyton portraits in the Long Gallery, at those long-dead Leyton daughters in their nuns' habits who had ended their days as prioresses in Cambrai or Bruges. Never mind that Mary Jane had insisted this was impossible; she and her husband could never provide the dowry Catt would need before a convent would accept her.

From then on, however, everything changed. There was no more talk of convents. Catt threw herself into working for the future Charles had opened up to her: for she knew that if ever she were to be maid to Lady Anne, she could spend the rest of her life near the person she adored. She devoured any book that came her way, however boring, however little she could understand it; she practised her handwriting, copying endlessly from those selfsame devotional books; she learned to embroider vestments even more expertly than her mother. If only she were not so plain! As she grew older she would stare dolefully into the mirror and ruefully rub the pointed nose in the pale, pointed face in the almost unconscious hope that it would somehow manage to shrink a little . . . But at least Lady Anne was not interested in beauty on its own account – and Charles, she knew, had not the slightest interest in her appearance.

That is, until the day when, entering the chapel unexpectedly and seeing the sixteen-year-old Catt arranging the flowers in front of Our Lady's statue. Charles glimpsed her profile – his own – and knew, for the first time . . .

*　　*　　*

For a moment, Charles stood at the door, unable to move, shocked beyond bearing. Then, overwhelmed by a torrent of remorse mingled with overpowering affection, he rushed over to her and, turning her to face him, kissed her on the brow.

'Why, Catt, dearest little Catt, I had no idea, no idea at all! God knows – I am so very, very sorry.'

Catt's world shattered suddenly into a thousand searing fragments. She felt herself ablaze with shame and unbelief. Here in the chapel, she was burning as if in Hell itself! A priest – her childhood idol – the person she loved and respected most in the whole world, whom she had considered almost a saint, trying to make love to her!

Appalled and terrified – of her own emotions, as much as of those she believed he was expressing, she later realised with even deeper shame – she tore herself free from him and, somehow, stumbled from the chapel, slamming the heavy door behind her. Once outside, she ran, almost unseeing, home to the lodge – and cowered there in her bedroom, shaking and weeping uncontrollably until her mother returned. And then blurted out the whole story in a flood of hysterical tears.

'Father Charles – he tried to . . .'

Mary Jane stared at the swollen puffy face. She was as shocked as her daughter, but, as it transpired, for quite a different reason. She shook her still pretty head. 'No, no, Catt! It isn't what you're thinking – it's not like that at all! How could you be so wrong – so' – and Mary Jane's voice hardened – 'so wickedly wrong? Don't you realise he would never have touched you so, he couldn't have, not in a month of Sundays. It's wicked of you to think such things . . . for, don't you see, he's your father!'

So the nightmare went on, becoming more awful by the minute. Numbed with shock, unable, and then unwilling, to believe what she was hearing, Catt listened to her mother's faltering, tearful explanations. She heard of the fifteen-year-old scullery maid being 'taken up' by the family's young son. It had all been so sunny and innocent, Mary Jane insisted. He wasn't a priest then, and they were both young and lonely. Nothing really wrong in it all, to begin with, but then came those forbidden meetings in the coppice . . . Well, of course, Mary Jane had always known in her heart of hearts there was no future in it. Their worlds were miles apart, and on his side it had been just a young man's passion, even though he'd always been kind. But she'd loved him, couldn't help herself . . . Then one day, she had found she was pregnant. By then, Charles Leyton had gone to Rome to train to be a priest, and by the time he returned to the Hall, several years later, Catt was seven years old. He had had no idea – not till today – that she was really his daughter, and no thought any more, beyond simple friendship, for Mary Jane, either. Those fateful tumbles in the Leyton meadows were long forgotten . . .

Only Lady Anne had guessed – early on, even before Mary Jane's pregnancy had begun to show. But the secret had remained between her and Mary Jane. There had been Mary Jane's marriage, swiftly arranged by Lady Anne, to Joshua Youngman, son of one of the estate gamekeepers – kindly, slow, bumbling Josh. If he ever suspected the baby that followed so swiftly upon the marriage was not his, he never said so. Stolid and dependable, he took his sudden promotion to lodge-keeper as a kind of act of God, likewise his fortuitous possession of the lovely Mary Jane, whom he had loved silently and hopelessly for years. Catt's birth was a difficult one; Mary Jane had no more children. Josh seemed not to worry. He could lavish all the more of his heartfelt, inarticulate love on little Catt and his wife.

After Catt's birth, Mary Jane returned to a rather more select set of duties than she had had before. Her silence on the subject of Catt's birth was well rewarded, but Lady Anne was careful not to mark Catt out in any special way. The gold cross and chain she had was the present that Lady Anne gave to all estate workers' children on their First Communion. Indeed, though her mother and Lady Anne seemed to enjoy a certain intimacy, Catt herself found Lady Anne – an angular, sad-faced woman, burdened now with the management of a run-down estate for a son and heir away in the army in India – unapproachable when not actually terrifying. Despite her ambition of one day graduating to being Lady Anne's personal maid, Catt had so far usually felt slightly uncomfortable when her ladyship offered her the odd word. This despite the fact that Lady Anne was considered almost a saint – she spent hours in her private oratory, heard Mass every day and numbered the year in religious feast-days and not according to the ordinary calendar! But from babyhood, Catt had sensed that, for some reason, Lady Anne disapproved of her. Now she knew why. And knew, too, with sickening certainty, that she could never have become the lady's maid at Leyton Hall, however hard she might have tried. All that effort and dreaming had been for nothing . . .

Still, who would have thought that Catt's world could end so suddenly? For end it did. No sooner had Mary Jane disclosed her relationship to Charles Leyton than she left her still sobbing daughter to hurry back to the Hall. There she would have to face Lady Anne with the fact that she had been obliged to tell Catt the secret she had promised never to reveal . . . Mary Jane shrugged. Catt was nearly grown-up now; she would have to stand up for herself. The important thing was that she and Josh should not suffer on account of a hysterical girl . . . Behind Mary Jane's endearing features lurked a ruthless survivor.

To Catt, half-demented by events, it seemed no time at all before Mary Jane was back, white-faced but resolute, to announce that Catt had been forbidden to set foot again in the Hall as long as she lived.

For the first time since Charles's kiss, Catt recovered some of her spirit. 'But *I've* done nothing wrong . . .'

Mary Jane set her jaw firmly. 'It's all arranged. Lady Anne is seeing to it. And in spite of it all, what do you think? She says she'll find you a place elsewhere, though it won't be easy.' Mary Jane smiled triumphantly. 'She's a real saint, her ladyship, as I've always said, but never more than now.'

And Mary Jane rattled on, impervious to Catt's reaction. Until Lady Anne reached her 'solution', it seemed, Catt was forbidden to venture outside the lodge door or speak to anyone except her parents. But it would not be for long – her ladyship was always so clever at sorting things out . . .

Catt could hardly believe her ears. She, the innocent result of a long-dead affair, was now being turned into some kind of leper. She could sense Mary Jane distancing herself from the

6

embarrassment that was her daughter with every word she spoke, and in the days that followed, the distance widened. Catt felt hurt and spurned almost beyond endurance. Not even Josh was allowed to come and talk to her.

After three terrible days, which seemed to Catt, shut away in her room, to have lasted three years, Lady Anne herself came to the lodge – and alone, without even the maid who usually accompanied her everywhere. Catt was summoned to the parlour.

Lady Anne refused to sit down. To the cowering Catt, she seemed taller and more forbidding than ever as she handed a long white envelope to Mary Jane and proceeded to conduct a conversation as though Catt was not present at all, directing her gaze to a point somewhere well above the victim's head.

'I am here,' said Lady Anne, speaking with funereal solemnity, 'because I have now heard from my cousin in Melchester, a Miss Fredericks.' Her face cracked in a ghost of a grim little smile. 'I am relieved to be able to tell you that, as an act of quite remarkable Christian charity – and on account of her affection for me, of course – she is prepared to give the – girl – a place in her household.'

At this, Mary Jane began to gush and curtsey, but Lady Anne raised her hand sharply. 'Kindly remain silent, Mary Jane! Your daughter will get board and lodgings. In view of the – exceptional circumstances – Miss Fredericks will provide her with caps and aprons and so forth in lieu of her first six months' wages. If she proves satisfactory, there may be a small wage after that. Very much later, perhaps, the whole situation can be re-examined.' Lady Anne nodded towards the envelope, took breath, and then, speaking in tones which implied a very great favour indeed was being imparted, she continued: 'In this envelope, Mary Jane, is a single railway ticket from Brigham to Melchester. Your husband will see that the girl boards the train which leaves Brigham at halfpast nine tomorrow morning. He is excused his usual duties for this purpose. Miss Fredericks is arranging for the train to be met at Melchester. After that' – Lady Anne's tone reverted to the reproachfully sepulchral – 'after that I shall receive regular reports from my cousin and I shall keep you informed. There will be no further mention of the chapel – incident – or of your subsequent disclosures to your daughter by anyone in this room ever again. I know I can rely on *you,* Mary Jane, but' – and here Catt *was* permitted a direct stare, of such cold ferocity that she felt almost physically hurt by it – 'should your daughter ever even think of defying my orders, Miss Fredericks will, of course, dismiss her instantly, and we shall disclaim all further responsibility for her – and for you and your husband too. Is that quite clear? Do you understand what I am saying?'

Mary Jane had been weeping quietly throughout. Now she nodded dumbly and bobbed automatically. The old woman thawed slightly and rested a skinny hand on her shoulder, but – after that single, chilling stare – again quite ignored Catt. More gently, she said: 'You may return to the Hall as soon as tomorrow is over. I am prepared to forgive you for breaking that first promise. You were overwrought, It was understandable – I know I can trust you in the future. Perhaps I was foolish to think that things could have turned out otherwise than they have,' she admitted sadly. 'Still, no permanent damage has been done, and once the girl is safely away, we can put it all behind us . . .'

Catt had listened to all this, first with astonished disbelief, then with fear. She had never been further from her home than the village. Brigham, the nearest big town, was rapidly spreading towards the Leyton boundaries, and its smoking factory chimneys and gypsum workings were visible from the Hall windows, but Catt had never once been there, not even to the Goose Fair. Now and then she had seen trains – though they were still relative novelties in this part of the county – passing the end of a distant field, but she had never travelled on one, nor thought of ever doing so. She had no idea where Melchester was. It was clearly a long way off, and sounded as though it was at the end of the world.

Suddenly, she realised how sheltered her life had been for all her sixteen years – the thought of being pitched headlong into the outside world, virtually without warning and all alone, filled her with rising panic. I shall never manage . . . not possibly . . . not without Mother and Father, she thought. And then remembered, with sickening clarity, that dear, loving Josh who had always been closer to her than Mary Jane, was not her father at all. Her real father was Father Charles. She felt ashamed, somehow dirty. She was a priest's bastard daughter! Catt shuddered. She was beyond the pale of civilised people, utterly disgraced . . .

And then it came to her, in a blinding flash, how unjust it was – all this shame that was being piled upon *her,* laid at *her* door – and yet she had had nothing whatsoever to do with it. She was the *result* of sin – if sin it was – not its *cause.* Even so, she recalled bitterly, there had been not a single mention of Father Charles throughout the whole of Lady Anne's speech, which had also implicitly exonerated her mother – the very two people who had brought her to this. 'It's not fair!' she muttered. But no one seemed to hear her.

However, the burning resentment gave her new vigour, did something to drive away the terrors of the unknown future. Catt began, from this moment onwards, to see herself, and the world around her, in a new light.

While she was gathering her new-found thoughts, Lady Anne had swept from the room. Only Mary Jane remained, weeping more noisily now.

So it was left to Catt – a new, more determined, independent Catt – to take the initiative. She shook her mother gently but firmly by the shoulders, 'Don't, Mother, please! You know quite well you will be better off without me, as things have turned out! And at least you and – Father – are secure here.' She took a deep breath, to find the courage to spell out the truth. 'In the end I would have been an embarrassment to everyone – even you. And just think, some good may come of it! For I'll have the chance to see the world beyond Leyton – and one day, when things are different, I promise you, I'll come back, somehow . . .'

2

It was a misty, damp morning, still dark, when Catt and Josh set out for Brigham. Lady Anne had provided her own pony and trap, and Josh seemed under the impression that in some mysterious way this meant that a great favour was being done to Catt, despite all that had passed. For whatever Lady Anne and his wife might say, for Josh, Catt would always remain his own precious little daughter – and so he was determined to play down the disgrace of this parting, for his sake, almost as much as for hers.

'Isn't this grand?' he burst out, his red, simple face gleaming with excitement, as the trap rolled out through the Hall gates – then, remembering the present circumstances, dropped suddenly silent, covered in confusion. 'Oh, lass – I didn't mean – I just meant, it's not often we go in her ladyship's trap.'

Catt squeezed his arm sympathetically. She too had captured some of his initial excitement and felt for a fleeting moment that it was good to be setting off on a great adventure! But it didn't last. Her disgrace at leaving Leyton was total, she knew; the pony and trap couldn't alter that. And it didn't matter in the least that this disgrace was none of her making.

Despite the enormity of her mother's betrayal of her in front of Lady Anne, Catt had still clung to Mary Jane in one last embrace, and had been unable to stop the silent tears trickling down her cheeks.

Now she looked back at the lodge silhouetted against the dawn sky and tried to etch every line of it in her memory, so that she would never forget it. She breathed deep the lush grass of the Nottinghamshire fields; the scent would have to last her a lifetime.

From now on, tears and embraces would never come easily to Catt; Mary Jane's implicit rejection was to leave a permanent emotional scar. And though she had assured her mother and Josh that she would return to Leyton one day, she knew with sickening certainty that it was highly unlikely she ever would.

'Look – here's the start of Brigham. Why, it'll be reaching out to our lodge before we know where we are, and that's a fact!' commented Josh, as the countryside began to peter away into a landscape of wasteland and the lean-to shacks that housed the workers in Brigham's new gypsum mines. Then the mineworkings were behind them too, and they were plunging into the maze of crowded streets that was the new Brigham of the stocking-makers and the laceworkers. The sweet smell of grass and meadow turned to the reek of smoke and filth and sewage. Catt felt sick. Was this really the world outside Leyton? It seemed more like one of the paintings of Hell from the Leyton chapel books!

Old Brigham lay ahead of them, less of a nightmare – the ruins of the old castle on a hill to the left, some graceful church spires and the beginnings of a great new building which Josh said was to be the new town hall. 'And bigger than the one in London, they say – the factory owners are paying for it. It's them has the money now, not old families like the Leytons . . .'

But too soon they were back in the warren of dark little streets that led to the railway station. Catt stared, mesmerised, at the great new building, all brick and glass and soot, feeling as if it was the place of her imminent execution. The crush of people around was frightening, the noise deafening, even so early in the morning.

She clutched her shabby cloth bag – another item donated by the Hall, and which Mary Jane had said showed once again what a loving and bountiful mistress Lady Anne really was – and she held very tightly to Josh's arm as he elbowed his way

11

through the crowds. She sensed he was really as confused as she was, that appearing his usual stolid self was a real effort to him, and she wished she knew how to thank him for it. Nothing seemed quite real: she had the feeling that everyone on the station knew exactly where they were going and how to get there, except Josh and herself.

Impossible to hear oneself speak: amid the din, a porter mouthed some instructions and pointed to a platform on the far side of the concourse. Catt's train was already standing there, belching furious smoke.

'Lord save us! We must be only just in time!' Josh's voice had an edge of panic.

He wrenched open a door and Catt almost fell into the carriage, only to find herself, so it seemed at first, surrounded by almost as many people as there had been outside. There was a spare place, however, on the wooden seat near the window. She squeezed herself into it and peered miserably through the dirty glass at Josh on the other side. Any feelings of adventure she still retained about this journey collapsed abruptly. She felt suddenly very frightened and, among all these people, very alone.

Josh was grinning bravely, but wiping his eyes with his neckerchief; Catt guessed he was near to tears. She felt a desperate longing to hug and kiss him as she had done as a child. Oh! If only *he* were her father – instead of Charles Leyton!

Josh opened the door again, and pushed a tiny package into Catt's hand. 'Be a good girl, Catt! God bless!'

Then a porter came between him and the train, slamming the doors to. A whistle blew and they were off, away from Brigham, away from Leyton, away from Mary Jane and Josh, away from Lady Anne – and Father Charles – and from everything Catt had ever known.

As the train gathered speed, her trembling fingers undid the wrapping around Josh's present. It was a rosary, made up of crude blue and red beads, scratched and faded. Josh's own, she knew. For a brief moment Catt held it to her cheek, then dropped it into her bag.

Lady Anne might have graciously lent her pony and trap, and her mother might have shed tears by the thousand. But only Josh had thought to give her a leaving present.

*   *   *

Never again, thought Catt, even before the journey was half over, will I travel on another contraption like this – not if I live to be a hundred!

Seen from a distance, across the sweep of fields from Leyton, the pasing trains had held a certain mysterious allure in their steaming magnificence; but as a passenger in one of them, she felt trapped in a nightmare where everything had the inconsistency and awfulness of a bad dream.

The carriage groaned and rattled at a seemingly breakneck speed. It panicked her, simply looking out of the window, because the landscape rushed by so fast she was swept by a wave of nausea. It was even worse when they plunged into a tunnel: then there was sudden pitch-blackness, with the badly fitting window at the same time letting in a cloud of acrid, choking smoke, so that when they came mercifully out into daylight again her eyes were red and her throat raw and rough.

But at least she had an elderly woman beside her, even though her clothes stank of stale sweat. Opposite, Catt was acutely conscious of the bold glances of a lanky young labourer. Every so often he would stretch out a leg, and his shoe would touch hers; she was afraid that in a really long tunnel he might reach for her skirts . . . Warnings of the moral dangers of the Protestant world outside Leyton, remembered from long-ago chapel sermons, came flooding back.

Fighting her sickness and panic, Catt said a series of silent Hail Marys. In the far corner, a baby wailed. The young man's travelling companion chewed tobacco and spat on the floor with monotonous frequency. A notice over the window forbade spitting, but Catt guessed the offender could not read it and probably cared less. She felt as if she was in some kind of dreadful mechanised Purgatory.

13

So she hardly noticed how the rich, rolling Midland landscape was gradually giving way to bleaker, rockier hills, and the red brick buildings changed to grey stone. From time to time there were stops; the mother and baby got out. Now there was no wailing, only the regular hawking and spitting. Catt gritted her teeth to stop herself screaming with pent-up irritation.

Then the clouds came up, and the rain came streaming down. They were passing factories now, with chimneys belching black smoke, and mean, narrow streets of mean little houses made meaner still by the pouring rain. It beat on the carriage window, cutting white gashes down the grimy pane. It was all so grey and dirty and hopeless. Catt felt grey and hopeless too.

Her misery must have been obvious, for she was given a dig in the ribs by her pungent but kind-hearted neighbour. 'You look worn out, lass. But we're almost at Melchester now – and isn't that where you get out? Look, over there, you can see the cathedral. And I do believe the rain's giving over.'

The tall, graceful spires meant nothing to Catt. But as she glanced at them obediently, assuming them to be part of some big Protestant church, she remembered, with yet another twinge of homesickness, that the village church in Leyton –she had never been inside it, of course – had a spire, too, though many times smaller than this one. She peered down at the huddles of red- and black-roofed houses and the white wall that snaked its way through them – the city's Roman wall, though she did not know that – and the next thing she knew, they were rattling across a wide, muddy river.

Then Catt's heart was in her mouth again. The train seemed so close to the edge, surely it would topple in . . . Once over, the pace slowed, there was a squeak of brakes and a great outrush of steam. Like a sighing giant, the engine lumbered into Melchester station and ground to a noisy halt.

Catt stepped out shakily and stood forlornly on the platform. The crowd milled all around her. She felt even more lost and desolate than before. Suppose there was no one to meet her? Whatever should she do then? But even as the panic and dizziness hit her yet again, a sharp voice impinged frostily.

'You're Catherine Youngman, I suppose?'

There stood a tall, severe, middle-aged woman, clad in sombre black from top to toe. 'I'm Mrs Braithwaite, Miss Fredericks's housekeeper. Your train was ten minutes late' – this last remark was spoken in particularly accusing tones, somehow implying that Catt was personally responsible for the delay – 'and Simpson doesn't hold with being kept waiting.'

So saying, she took Catt's arm in a grip of iron and swept her rapidly through the ticket barrier and into a forecourt crammed with every combination of carriage and cart and attendant horses.

Mrs Braithwaite cast a withering glance at Catt's bag. 'Is that all you've brought with you? My word, a real charity child for Miss Fredericks! Best keep it with you, then . . .' as they clambered into a small trap waiting near the station entrance.

'Here she is, Simpson,' announced Mrs Braithwaite gloomily. The driver nodded, said nothing. He did not bother to turn his head. It had been made very clear that Catt's arrival was not an occasion for even the smallest word of welcome.

They were off, clattering over the cobbles, a more familiar rhythm to Catt than that dreadful train. They passed the cathedral, then went under an arch in the great white wall and down an avenue of elegant Georgian town houses. Turning off, the trap came to a stop beside a large stuccoed building set back a little amongst trees and lawns, which resembled a small country manor despite its being so close to the city centre.

Catt was hustled round to the servants' entrance at the side of the house. A girl of about her own age let them into a big, beamed kitchen. It was not as big as the kitchen at Leyton Hall, but much warmer and a good deal more modern. Mrs Braithwaite and another formidable woman, whom Catt later found out to be the cook, proceeded to look her up and down, discussing her – just as Lady Anne had done, the day before

15

– as if she were not there at all.

'You found her all right then, Mrs Braithwaite?'

'Yes, Cook, I did indeed, but the wretched train was late, needless to say, and the station as cold and dirty as usual. I've never thought it a place for respectable folk . . . I'm worn out with all the standing and waiting about, I can tell you! Why, as you well know, it's not a part of my duties to fetch and carry for foundlings, even those with good character – and this one doesn't offer much cause for hope, does she? Not a very cheerful countenance for a start, considering all that's been done for her.' And then she spoke brusquely to Catt, as if realising for the first time that she was there, listening. 'Best put a better expression on that plain face of yours, my girl, and be sharp about it! Miss Fredericks, your benefactor, she who's saved you from the workhouse, if not worse – she'll be expecting proper gratitude, not some picture of misery.'

'Madam's waiting for you,' cook chipped in. 'In the withdrawing-room. She said you and this – person – were to go in to her as soon as you got back.'

Without further ado, Mrs Braithwaite took a further vice-like grip of Catt's arm and steered her out of the kitchen. 'Remember to curtsey when you meet Madam – I suppose you know how to do that – and be sure you only speak when you are spoken to,' she hissed.

Catt found herself being rapidly propelled up a long, dark staircase intermittently lit by flickering gas-lamps. Was it simply her terrible tiredness, or were the shadows beyond the circles of light really waiting to swallow her up forever if she stumbled? She felt so exhausted, so nervous, she neither knew nor cared.

She blinked as they entered the brightly lit drawing-room. Her feet sank into thick carpeting; there was none of the genteel poverty and shabbiness of Leyton Hall here. And yet, despite the sparkling chandelier hanging from the ceiling, the dark maroons and mauves of the furnishings made the room seem only marginally less gloomy than the stairway. But there was the same warmth that there had been in the kitchen; a blazing fire burnt in the elegant grate, and seated close to it

16

was a very old lady.

She was dressed in luxuriant purple. A huge jewelled cross hung around her neck, together with ropes of graduated pearls. There was a lace bonnet on her grey, old-fashionedly ringleted hair, and a set and sombre expression on her face – in perfect harmony with everything that Catt had seen of the house so far.

From the time she could first walk, Catt had been taught to curtsey to Lady Anne – and now, tired though she was, she made a specially deep sweep as a private act of defiance to Mrs Braithwaite.

'Well, at least she's been taught to show *some* respect for her elders and betters!' her new employer remarked approvingly. Then, more coldly: 'Stand up straight, child. Let me see what I'm making all these sacrifices for.' And: 'You're not much of a beauty, which is just as well, in view of your sinful ways. But you're not particularly well-formed, either – I trust you aren't too skinny to be able to work hard. For work in this house is never done with, I am happy to say. After a few days, you should have got over all your wild imaginings and wicked thoughts . . . now, what can you do?'

Flushed with embarrassment, Catt was inwardly seething. 'Most things, ma'am,' she volunteered shakily: 'Scrubbing and polishing, and I've been taught fine sewing and mending, and I can read a bit.' Here the old lady's eyebrows shot up disapprovingly. 'My writing is less good, though –'

'Enough of this!' Miss Fredericks raised a clawlike hand. 'More than enough!' She frowned. 'Mrs Braithwaite here will be in charge of all your duties . . . As for reading and writing, I am quite astonished that my dear cousin should have permitted it. No wonder there was such trouble at Leyton! I do not approve of the lower orders playing with words. That way lies the path to heresy and revolution. So you will make quite sure to forget every syllable of every word you ever learned.'

Miss Fredericks's mouth snapped shut. It was clear that Catt's interrogation was at an end. With relief, she started to make a farewell bob – but Miss Fredericks's arm was lifted once again.

'Just a moment. I should warn you that Mrs Braithwaite will be keeping me informed of your progress. You should remember, at the slightest sign of wrongdoing I shall have no hesitation whatsoever in returning you forthwith whence you came – and then it can only be the workhouse for you! So take care. You have been given a most generous chance to redeem yourself after your unbelievable ingratitude – my cousin at Leyton is indeed a saint! So make up your mind to be sensible and virtuous, obey your orders to the letter, work hard, be punctilious in your prayers. Put yourself in the hands of Our Blessed Lady, and implore her aid in avoiding further temptation.'

As Catt was led from the room, she tried to fathom yet again what it was that *she* had done that was held to be so unnaturally wicked. Here she was, cast out from Leyton Hall, even out of her own home – barred from them forever. Her mother, her own flesh and blood, seemed no longer to want her, either.

3

Catt looked forward to the blessed relief of being able to retreat to her own bed. At least she had only to share the room with Annie the timid girl of about her own age who had opened the door on her arrival at the house, even if it was a little bigger than a cupboard under the eaves, barely able to take two truckle beds and a chest that doubled as a washstand.

But first Catt had a further humiliation to undergo. She had to suffer the agonies of trying on her maid's clothes in front of an unsympathetic cook and Mrs Braithwaite. There was further biting criticism of her skinny figure and pale complexion and frequent allusions to her charity status within the household.

'What a fortunate young person she is indeed,' sighed cook.

'Out of favour where she comes from for the *unmentionable,* as you know,' responded Mrs Braithwaite with undisguised relish, so it seemed to Catt. 'And yet, given a place here! Can you credit such charity?'

'Let us hope and pray that Miss Fredericks's trust won't turn out to be misplaced – the Devil is very powerful!' contributed cook pessimistically.

At Mrs Braithwaite's sonorous, 'Amen to that!' Catt longed desperately to shout and scream, even to lash out physically at her tormentors.

You've no right to talk so! I've done nothing to be ashamed of, she wanted to cry. But of course she held back, hanging her head, biting her lip till it bled to prevent hasty words spilling out.

The threat of the workhouse was a real one: all her life she had heard such tales of it that its mention was enough to fill her with genuine terror. But all the while, the resentment smouldered deep down inside her. And this same resentment would grow and spread, as time passed, like a suppurating, incurable cancer. It was fuelled by the guilty realisation which Catt tried to hide even from herself, that until that fateful moment in Leyton chapel she had in her heart regarded Father Charles in the same romantic glow which had led, all those years before, to her mother's pregnancy and her own birth.

Well, her mother's sin had been bad enough, she supposed, but it paled to nothing beside that of falling in love with one's own father, never mind that he was a priest, too! The very thought made her shudder. She must surely be in the most dreadful state of mortal sin and destined for the eternal fires of Hell of which the Church so often talked . . . Resolutely, she pushed the subject to the back of her mind, trying to crush it out of existence – and yet it came back, back and back again . . .

That first evening in Melchester ended with Catt being taken back to the drawing-room yet again, now properly dressed in her maid's black gown and muslin cap, for the household's night prayers. These were conducted by a gaunt, grim-faced priest, a nephew of Miss Fredericks's who was now, Catt learned, in charge of St Agatha's, the new Catholic church in Melchester, largely paid for from his aunt's fortune, which stood at the corner of the street. The prayers and readings seemed, to the overtired girl, to go on interminably. All the servants were present, every one of them a Catholic of sorts: Miss Fredericks made it a rule never to employ 'heretics' as she called all non-Catholics. And they were all much older than Catt, except for Annie, the little undermaid, who had no living relatives at all, having been 'rescued' by Miss Fredericks from an orphanage.

That night, as she lay in her cold hard little bed, high up in the attic of the house, Catt could still not see why she should be held to blame for the fact that her mother and Charles Leyton had been young together, all those years ago, and fallen in love with one another. She had been the innocent result of that love; yet she was the one who was now being punished for it, for something quite beyond her power to control or change.

In a way, Lady Anne's rejection appeared even more hurtful than her mother's passive acquiescence in her banishment. After all, her mother had always been desperately anxious to please her 'betters' – it was a simple matter of submitting in order to survive, when all was said and done – and indeed, wasn't that attitude one of the reasons for her own unwanted arrival in the world? Gradually, it began to dawn on Catt that Lady Anne – proud, aristocratic, fastidious Lady Anne – was actually her grandmother! Somehow, this seemed harder at the moment to comprehend than the knowledge that her real father was a priest . . . but then the thought of Charles Leyton began to arouse such a hotchpotch of emotions within her that Catt could only bury her burning face in the pillow and pray for sleep to blot out those dreadful images that had recently begun to haunt her . . . Perhaps, after all, she had become as sinful as everyone said she was.

* * *

In the long days and weeks that followed, it was Annie alone who could take some of the edge off Catt's black and utter despair.

Catt was on her feet from five in the morning until ten at night, sometimes later, with scarcely a break. Laying the fires, her first task of the day, was the one she liked best. For then she was all alone. As she knelt by the chill grates, under the light of only a small candle – for Miss Fredericks, though wealthy, strictly forbade the costly waste of newfangled gaslight in the small hours – she could whisk herself back in her imagination to the higgledy-piggledy of old-fashioned Leyton Hall. She remembered how she had admired Lady Anne's calm serenity – in the time before 'that scene' had revealed her as a cold and empty shell; she thought of Josh, the father whom she now knew was no father at all, and of all his kindness and little foibles; and she pictured the soft voluptuousness of the Nottinghamshire countryside that lay spread out beyond the lodge gates.

And all the time, she tried desperately not to think of that other father, her real one, because, as she saw it, it was he who had been the origin of this dreadful calamity which had befallen her. Yet in her heart of hearts she had to acknowledge, too, that he had always been kind to her. Was it not Charles Leyton who had taught her how to read, and in so doing opened up a whole new world to her? But that was as nothing, any more, beside the terrible experience in the chapel and what had come after – an experience which had turned to ashes her lifelong love of her church and its saints and the Mass which she could now see only in terms of her own dreadful deprivation.

No matter that the Church remained physically suffocatingly close to her; mentally, she became determined to separate herself from everything it stood for. Every Sunday and Holy Day the entire Fredericks household went to the redbrick church on the street-corner. Every Saturday the servants were expected to go to Confession – though even for this, Catt was not allowed out of the house or its grounds alone. Mrs Braithwaite accompanied her.

If ever I manage to get away from here, Catt would promise herself, I shall never go inside a church again as long as I live! Nevertheless, despite all her efforts to the contrary, her faith continued to reach out and its images to draw her. Even as she vowed she had disowned it, even after she had mumbled formalised and petty sins insincerely in the Confessional, she would find herself praying: 'Jesus, Mary! Please help me! Help me get away from here – anywhere – only away!'

Yes, anywhere! For Catt was under no illusion that she could ever return to Leyton, no matter what soothing words she had spoken to Mary Jane on the subject. In retrospect, she realised that she and her mother had always lacked any close bond. There was something secret about Mary, something which Catt had never penetrated, dating back, perhaps, to the

22

circumstances of her birth, she now supposed. Whatever the cause, from the moment of Catt's hysterical outburst and Mary Jane's revelations, this sense of remoteness had deepened.

'Josh was sorry to see me go – but I think Mother was really quite glad – never mind all the floods of tears, they were nothing but show,' Catt told herself. After all, had not Mary Jane been quick to tell her that a condition of being 'found a place' in a 'good Catholic house' in Melchester was that she must never visit Leyton Hall, or anyone in it, again? On this, Lady Anne, for all her good works and constant prayers, – Lady Anne who had been a kind of living Virgin Mary to the child Catt, had been quite implacable.

As for Father Charles – though she had not set eyes on him since that fatal day, Catt assumed him to be the prime force behind everything that had happened to her since. She smiled grimly to herself. Strange, or perhaps not so strange, that the priest who preached so movingly about love and forgiveness should also be the man pushing his mother into getting rid of this living reminder of his past shame. Whenever Catt thought of this, waves of nausea broke over her again, and she wished him dead. Yet, even as she did so, those confused but erotic images kept intruding, pushing in again from the recesses of her mind where she had tried to hide them. And the passing of time made them more, not less, urgent.

Of course, Catt made no mention of any of this when telling Annie about her past life. Annie knew as did everyone in the Fredericks household, that Catt had left home because of some unspecified but dreadful disgrace. No one ever asked her any questions about this; Catt guessed thay had been ordered not to do so, under threat of instant dismissal – which would apply to her, also, if she divulged anything approaching the full story. Never mind that there was no fear of her doing that: she was far too ashamed!

So Catt held back, and in the few moments she had a chance to talk to Annie, mostly at night, when they were in bed and about to fall asleep, she simply described her life at the lodge – with the fields and the flowers and the songbirds, and the Hall with its chapel and the stained glass and the statues . . . All quite past and done with, she knew, But just talking about it eased some of the pain of its loss.

Annie was enraptured. 'How lucky you must have been!' she would say – and then go on to describe her memories of a seaside town to the north-east of Melchester, where her father had been a fisherman. When he drowned at sea, her mother had gone with the baby to relations in Melchester, but died soon after. Little Annie had been put in an orphanage run by nuns until 'rescued' by Miss Fredericks.

'Don't you ever long to go back?' asked Catt, fascinated by the description of a sea she had never seen, and all this talk of Whinborough growing fast, so Annie had heard, from fishing town into fashionable holiday spa. 'After all, there'd be lots of work there for people like us, wouldn't there? In the boarding-houses and suchlike? And we'd be so much freer . . .' She sighed wistfully. 'Here, we're in a kind of cage. And its door never opens – at least, not for me.'

Annie was unimpressed. She, after all, got a tiny wage and some hours a week off from the house. There was a 'follower' from a respectable family whom she expected to marry one day. Her childhood memories were fading fast and meant little to her any more. 'Housework is much the same wherever one does it, I reckon,' said Annie, philosophically. 'And the easiest way of getting out of here is to get married – then I suppose there'll be even more housework, but at least it'll be my own.' She blushed and giggled. Catt envied her her placid practicality, her security.

Still, much as she might yearn for Annie's obvious contentment with her future as she saw it, Catt was not really convinced. Whinborough, with its sea and sun and open spaces, had begun to take its place alongside Leyton in her day-dreaming. The more so as time slipped relentlessly by and her Leyton memories began to dim a little. Cut off from all contact with her family there, Leyton grew more and more unreal. Sometimes she wondered if she had really ever had a life there at all.

Whinborough, on the other hand, became more and more a part of her, even though she had never seen it.

Determination to do so gave her a new kind of goal: and its very existence spelled hope. Catt saw it as an almost biblical place. 'That bit in the Bible – about the Holy City – where there's no more weeping' . . . she mused, as the days dragged by, one by slow one.

She lit the fires, blackleaded the kitchen range and polished the brass and silver; and then, the next day, it all had to be done again . . . There were tiny changes, though. Miss Fredericks so admired her silver-polishing that this became Catt's principal duty and there was much less blackleading, thank goodness! And almost all the time she was working, she was in spirit far away in the town she had never seen. She saw it perched like a magic place on top of the red cliffs Annie had described, overlooking a sparkling sea alive with bobbing boats. She pictured the new white promenades where parasolled ladies in gorgeous silks and satins strolled and chatted. And she ranged further, beyond the bricks and mortar, and on out to that great vastness beyond the town that Annie had called 'the moors' and which seemed to stretch on for ever – aglow with purple heather and golden gorse – empty except for a few lonely hamlets and isolated farmsteads. There, Catt imagined, one could cut free from the whole world.

The bustling seaside town – the wild, lonely moors – Catt dreamed alternately of each and was not sure which she wanted more. Both were equally beyond her reach in practice; for she was a prisoner in this cold, heartless house as surely as if she had been in Melchester Prison itself. She had no position, no money. She was never allowed out alone. And even if she did achieve the impossible and manage to get away from here – what would happen to her family back at Leyton? Though she herself was barred from all contact with them, she knew they were being told about her from time to time, and that their future depended on her 'good behaviour'. She was forced to conform here, or it would go badly for them. However dreadful her own life was, she could never do anything that might hurt Josh.

Winter turned to spring, but the long Lenten fast took all

the pleasure out of the budding season and St Agatha's dry formality and the all-pervasive gloom of the Fredericks household managed to rob even the Easter celebrations of their remembered joy. Catt heard the bells chiming from the great Protestant cathedral at the far end of the avenue and thought it the happiest sound she had heard since she came here, heretical though it might be.

She felt a momentary lift. 'Perhaps things may start to get better now – I've been here three months, after all, and they are getting to know me . . . Perhaps I'll be allowed out soon, maybe with Annie' . . .

But there was no let-up in her misery. Indeed, something was about to happen which would make it even worse.

*   *   *

Catt had been in the middle of polishing the silver in Miss Fredericks's little oratory when she was summoned to go to the drawing-room. Nothing like this had ever happened before. What could she have done wrong? As she tucked her hair more tidily under her cap and smoothed down her dress, she tried desperately to come up with a reason but could find none . . .

Miss Fredericks was sitting stiffly in her usual chair. In her hand she held a letter. 'This is from my cousin, the Lady Anne,' she announced. And then, with unaccustomed gentleness, 'I am afraid you must prepare yourself for a very great shock, Catherine. There has been a fire at the lodge – and it is all burnt down. Your mother and – your father – both perished in it . . .' She paused to cross herself. 'May they rest in peace. We must thank God they probably suffered little, for it all happened as they slept – and assuredly they are gone to a better place . . .'

'Dead? *Dead?* I can't believe it! There must be some mistake. . .' For a moment Catt heard her voice, her own voice, coming as if from very far away, quite separate from her. Then there was a great hissing and rushing in her ears, and the room tilted and turned on its head . . .

Miss Fredericks was still in her chair when Catt came to. But Mrs Braithwaite was slapping her cheeks and splashing her face with cold water. She realised Miss Fredericks had begun to speak again and tried to concentrate, but the words she heard seemed as unreal as before.

'I am deeply sorry, my child, but we must remember it is the Lord's will – He giveth and He taketh away . . . Mrs Braithwaite will see to it that you have some mourning clothes. Naturally, Lady Anne will be standing in for you at the funeral mass in Leyton. But I shall arrange a Mass for the repose of your parents' souls here at St Agatha's, and of course you will be able to attend that.'

So she was not even to be allowed to see Mary Jane and Josh buried! Not given the chance to give that final kiss before the screwing down of the coffins! Oh, Catt was not really surprised, when she thought about it; this latest cruelty seemed to follow quite naturally from all the others. Still, the pain of it was almost unbearable.

That night, she, who these days found it hard to summon up tears for anything, cried herself to sleep despite all Annie's efforts to calm and comfort. She cried for all she had lost: she cried for the times she had taken Josh for granted – dear, patient Josh, who had loved her like the daughter he thought she was. She cried for her vanished childhood, and for Leyton, and for the happiness she had had there until that dreadful day when everything had turned to ashes.

And *he* was to blame for everything! He, Father Charles, the priest who was her real father. Not content with ruining *her* life, he had destroyed those of Josh and Mary Jane too. In her hysteria, Catt convinced herself that had Charles Leyton, by his actions, not forced her removal from Leyton, the fire would never have broken out, certainly never taken hold, and her parents would still be alive today. Never, never would she forgive Charles Leyton, not if she lived to be a hundred!

Yet even while she was swearing perpetual hatred, something deep within Catt was inexorably turning her back to him, again and again. She was overwhelmed by this powerful physical longing which, try as she might, kept creeping back whenever she was at her most vulnerable, however much it shamed her, and, in its unnaturalness, terrified her . . .

Mrs Braithwaite duly produced a stiff black gown, somewhat old-fashioned, but grander than anything Catt had ever previously owned: it was for special occasions only, which in her case meant simply Confession and Mass, beginning with the requiem for Josh and Mary Jane. When the mourning year was out it would be returned to the household clothes-chest.

It had belonged to a long-dead servant, and Mrs Braithwaite viewed its preservation as a personal triumph. 'It nearly went to the missions – but I knew it would be useful here one day,' she declared to Cook. 'And no spills or snags, mind!' she warned Catt. Besides the dress, there were crêpe bands for Catt's straw bonnet and around the sleeves of her jacket.

For a few days after the tragic news struck, everyone was unusually kind to Catt. But she was too numbed with grief to notice, too wrapped up in herself even to appreciate it. The subsequent reversion to the old sharpnesses and contemptuous silences therefore held less sting than it might otherwise have done. Now she really was well and truly a foundling! No mother any more – not even a 'fallen' one!

As the raw anguish gradually subsided, the anger deep within Catt burgeoned. Anger towards the entire Fredericks household – save Annie – for the pettiness, the carping, the sheer misery of everything connected with it. The workload she did not mind – that was a relief, a distraction, in a way, from the all-pervasive atmosphere of disapproval and bigotry. Why, even at Mary Jane and Josh's requiem she had been made to feel the meanest of sinners for even being alive at all.

Then there was the anger she felt towards her real father – the revulsion she felt for him making her almost vomit, at times – and all the more dreadful since it so often went hand in hand with that nagging ache of desire. She quite forgot she had once regarded him as almost a saint, had worshipped the ground he walked on. And finally there was her anger towards God – this God of St Agatha's who seemed always to be on the side of the rich and privileged and to ignore the poor and the weak . . .

Even so, while she raged inwardly, Catt clung still to Josh's little rosary, telling her beads night after night, remembering Josh all the while and appealing in spite of herself to the Lady who had praised the God who had 'exalted the humble and the meek'. She might now be cursing Him as a God who did no such thing, but it was hard to throw off the habits of a lifetime that easily, and besides, telling the beads brought Josh back to her as nothing else could.

The days lengthened. It grew warmer. The grieving was a little less raw. Catt began to have fewer of those bad, frustrating dreams where she watched, helpless, as scarlet tongues of flame licked at the lodge walls and she heard the desperate screaming from within, knowing that nothing could be done about it.

Whinborough came back to her, more alluring than ever for being out of mind for a time – with the shimmering sea before and the wild, glossy moorland behind it. If she could but step into this Whinborough dream, she would be free, she knew it! Here she felt like a poor caged bird, slowly wilting and dying in this grim fortress of a house.

Then suddenly, when Catt least expected it, the cage door snapped open.

It was on a Saturday: Confession time, the time for Catt to go to St Agatha's, with Mrs Braithwaite as her guard, for the usual recital of household omissions – and never a word, of course, about her innermost thoughts and hates and fears. But as they were on the point of leaving, the housekeeper slipped on the newly mopped kitchen floor and lay helpless.

Her ankle was badly twisted, the ligaments torn. There was no possibility of her walking anywhere that day or for several days to come, for that matter. But Mrs Braithwaite was a conscientious observer of religious practices, if not of its realities, and therefore determined to see that sinful Catt should not miss doing her duty. No matter that there was no one else to escort her.

'After all, it's but a step down the road, and you've been there so often now. Madam couldn't possibly object, for once, and in any case, I can't disturb her afternoon rest . . .'

Catt was all ready, in her black mourning gown and crêpe-ribboned bonnet. Lady Anne's little gold cross and chain was round her neck, and Josh's rosary in her moneyless purse with the tortoiseshell handle.

She bobbed obediently and prayed that no one could read her thoughts, which had rushed in on her so violently she felt as if they must be imprinted on her forehead in scarlet letters. Keep calm, she said to herself, keep absolutely calm. Despite feeling madly, deliriously happy on account of the wild, daring idea that had suddenly come to her. She did not dare speak, in case her voice should somehow give her away. So she merely nodded, bobbed and walked as decorously and slowly as she could out of the back door, out of the garden, and back, back into the real, living world outside.

The garden gate clanged behind her. The street was empty, silent in the afternoon sun. The spire of St Agatha's beckoned. Beyond it lay the avenue, the broad avenue that led eventually to Melchester station – the gateway which would surely take her to Whinborough and that new, exciting life of her dreams!

Or would it? For Catt had not a penny in the world.

4

Catt forced herself not to run the length of the street to St Agatha's. Though she believed the house empty, except for the injured Mrs Braithwaite and the sleeping Miss Fredericks, she was still cautious, for bad luck seemed to cling to her like a leech, these days, and suppose Cook had returned early from her shopping and was tweaking a lace curtain to look at her this very moment? She knew she could be seen the whole way to the corner of the street; but once inside the church she believed – she had never had the chance to test it – she could walk right through and come out again by a side door into the main avenue, well out of sight of Miss Fredericks's.

For the moment she kept her head discreetly bowed and her hands clasped round her purse. Inside the half-darkness of St Agatha's, she paused. Although she had been walking so slowly, Catt felt breathless, almost sick with apprehension.

She was about to run away. With Josh and her mother dead, there was no longer anything to hold her here. She was truly quite alone in the world now, and free to seek to earn her living from anyone who would give her the opportunity. But the first thing she must do, she knew, was to shake the dust of Melchester from her feet, and as quickly as possible. It would not be long before she was missed.

Catt dropped her fingers into the holy water stoup and thought: This is probably the last time I shall ever do this. From the confessional came the murmuring of a penitent, but there was no one in the body of the church itself. She tiptoed across the nave towards the side door. Automatically, she genuflected before the high altar, glancing up at the tortured figure of the crucified Christ that hung over the transept.

How often have I begged for help from You – and got none? she challenged, silent and defiant. Prove You really exist! Help me now! Never mind that she was now taking on God as well as the Fredericks household!

She was through the side door and out on the main avenue, as she had hoped to be, and she started to walk very fast, almost running, towards the walled town centre. There, she remembered, was the square which fronted the railway station. Never mind that she had sworn not to ride those frightening trains ever again – it was the fastest means of escape. For that she could put up with anything!

As she half-walked, half-ran, she glanced at the shops along the way, but there was no sign anywhere of the three golden balls she wanted, for this was too prosperous and respectable a part of the city for a pawnbroker's shop. Still, it was vital she find one, and soon, or her plan would come to nothing. She had to have money to make her escape.

Then, as she neared the station square, genuinely breathless now and self-conscious about it, afraid a passer-by might notice her agitation and try to stop her, Catt saw the pawnbroker's sign down a side-alley and almost shouted with joy. Within the space of a few minutes she was in and out of it, a sovereign and a half-sovereign in her purse, and no gold chain and cross around her neck any more. Lady Anne's First Communion gift had been more valuable than she had ever dared think.

As when Catt first arrived at Melchester, in a time that now seemed an age away, the station was a confusing mass of humankind – noisy, assertive and sometimes rough. Catt clutched her purse tightly to her and struggled towards the booking-hall. She felt suddenly strong as a lion, able to accomplish anything. As she faced the clerk, the town of her dreams set between sea and moor flashed before her eyes, and the word 'Whinborough!' sprang from her lips like a triumphal shout.

She was brought down to earth again by the prosaic rejoinder: 'Return, miss?'

'No, no – just a single – the cheapest single there is.' And she longed to shout out, so that everyone could hear: 'For I'll never be back. I'm never coming back to Melchester, never! No matter what happens!'

'You want platform 3, due out in five minutes.' The clerk studied her pale, radiant face: it made taking this fare somehow out of the ordinary. 'Off to a job there for the season, are you? And all those –'

But Catt had gone, swallowed up in the crowd, pushing towards the iron bridge and over it onto her platform and into the train, with only seconds to spare. She sank back luxuriously against the hard wooden seat; it might as well have been velvet, she was so excited over her own achievement. The train gathered steam and slid out of the station. Soon, cathedral and town were left far behind.

It was a small miracle. Scarcely 45 minutes had passed since she was standing in Miss Fredericks's kitchen. Only about now, thought Catt, would people be beginning to wonder why she had not returned from Confession. Perhaps Annie would be back from her weekly afternoon walk with her young man by this time, and they'd send her to look. Dear, simple Annie, who had first put the idea of Whinborough into her head, but who would never, she was certain, imagine that that was where she had gone. Catt's brow wrinkled in sudden doubt. Wouldn't she? No, surely not – and even if she did, Annie would never tell. She had known how unhappy Catt was, even if she had not really understood why . . . Catt wished she had been able to say goodbye to Annie. She was the only person she had any regrets in leaving like this – it was sad to think she would never see Annie again, never be able to thank her.

Unlike the train from Brigham, on that dreadful journey of disgrace, this one was half-empty. That was a godsend, too, for all Catt wanted now was to be able to sit back, gather her thoughts together and try to work out the best thing to do when she finally reached Whinborough.

It would be getting quite late in the day by then – but at least it was May now, and the evenings were drawing out. The train would certainly get there in daylight. First she would need to find lodgings for the night – a thing she had never had to do in her life before. And then, next day, look for work . . .

But, oh dear! Next day was a Sunday. Catt shook her head, sighing. She could not possibly go knocking on doors for work on a Sunday – no respectable house would stand for that – which meant she needed to find lodgings for two nights, not to mention the food she would have to buy. More of her precious money would go! And she needed more clothes, too – a working gown and cap and apron, some undergarments, at the very least . . .

She closed her eyes. In the space of a few short weeks she had lost everything she had ever had – her family, her home, her security, her faith and, worst of all, perhaps, though she would not admit it even to herself, some of her innocence. Here she was, alone and friendless, journeying to a strange town, with no idea of where to go when she got there and owning nothing in the world except a gold sovereign and the clothes she stood up in. And Josh's rosary, of course . . . At least I look respectable, she told herself, and the mourning dress might make prospective employers more sympathetic and less inclined to ask awkward questions or seek references . . .

And, after all, she was her own mistress now, free from all the pettiness and jibes of the Fredericks establishment. Now was the moment when she could make a completely fresh start. No one here knew anything about her past life. Catt's spirits started to lift. She had so much to look forward to, from now on! She had burst out of that dreadful prison of a house and here she was, heading for the freedom of the open moors and the limitless sea . . . Surely, at long last, events were moving her way.

However, Catt felt a good deal less sure of herself as the train clattered into Whinborough station. The time had passed surprisingly quickly and the jolt of the stopping engine broke abruptly into her day-dreaming. Here was another swirling mass of people to face, as noisy and aggressive as on the Melchester concourse, and she was more tired now, more confused . . . Once again, panic gripped her; her isolation in the midst of all this hustle was deadening. And the chatter seemed to be in a tongue far removed from her own idea of the English language! Adding to the general mêlée was the pushing and shoving of the Whinborough donkey-boys, bawling out their offers to carry passengers to a particular hotel or boarding-house.

Catt's hand went to her aching forehead: it burned, hot and damp. She undid the clasp of her bag, reaching for her handkerchief – and then, almost before she knew it, there was a sharp jerk on her arm and her purse had vanished, and with it, all the money she possessed.

She was scarcely aware of her movements after that. She must have wandered along, sightless, almost like a sleep-walker. Though she imagined she was making for the town centre, she was in fact heading out of it. For how long she walked, Catt had not the faintest idea – minutes, an hour, more . . . On she went, past rows of new redbricked houses, shut-eyed and decorous behind their lace curtains and laurel hedges – for the station itself had been on the new outskirts of Whinborough. Then the buildings started to tail away and there was just greensward – and, in the distance, the blue haze of Annie's moors . . . Suddenly, she came to her senses and saw that the light was fading.

What in the world was she to do now? Lonely, frightened, her courage quite gone, Catt sank miserably onto the grass verge, covering her face in her hands, her whole body racked with tearless sobbing.

And there she stayed, until the cartwheels squeaked noisily to a halt on the track beside her. Till now, Catt had been unaware that anyone else had been within miles of her. A man's voice, with an accent more pronouncedly Yorkshire than any she had heard in genteel Melchester, intruded into her misery and set her shivering uncontrollably again.

'Now, lass, don't take on s-so! Wh-whatever's the m-matter? Are you h-h-hurt?'

Catt looked up into the fresh, tanned and extremely concerned face of a young man perhaps five or six years older than herself. He was wearing rough farming clothes – moleskin trousers and a kerchief round his throat. Tall and fair-haired, his thin, slightly drawn features were made almost handsome by the blue eyes that were faintly veiled as if by some deep, secret sadness. It was a good face; it shone with kindly innocence, and even in that first moment, Catt knew that she could trust the owner of it absolutely.

As for him – at the sight of this pale, frightened girl, his heart melted and the extreme shyness that his stammer concealed melted away too, as Luke Halliday fell, from that moment onwards, completely and passionately head over heels in love for the first and only time in his life.

*   *   *

Luke leant over from the cart and held out his hands. Catt grasped them, hardly realising she was doing so. She struggled to her feet, trying to smooth back her hair and stop this stupid shivering.

'C-can I h-help you? Are – are you l-lost?'

The events of the past few months had made Catt morbidly suspicious of almost everyone; and even before that, she had been brought up never on any account to speak to strangers – and particularly, needless to say, strange men. All her life that underlying distrust of the world was to stay with her, a permanent if invisible barrier between her and the rest of society. Even her own children would never be able to breach it fully. Luke alone – for the present, at least – was to be different. With Luke, in these first happy days, there were to be no barriers at all.

Now the words of Catt's story came tumbling out – not the whole story, of course; even Luke was to be kept ignorant of some of that – but the essential bones of it, as she saw it. She told him how she had been orphaned, and had run away from a house she had hated and where she had been mistreated, and how now, with her purse stolen, she was desperate – alone, penniless and friendless . . . She began to shiver again.

Luke put his arm round her shoulder. 'I know what we can do,' he said, speaking with a quiet confidence that was in fact

36

as much a surprise to him as it was to Catt. He felt suddenly so protective that his stammer quite disappeared. 'I'll take you to my aunt Nell!'

Catt stared at him, round-eyed, not understanding. But thankfulness for this totally unexpected kindliness gave her face a new radiance, transforming her, in Luke's eyes, into nothing less than an angel.

'Who –' she began.

'My aunt Nell.' He beamed triumphantly. 'She'll take you in – and be glad to. She has a little boarding-house near the old harbour. I've just come from seeing her – it's but a ten-minute ride back. Jump up!'

As they trotted back into the town, Catt perched, still only half-believing what was happening, beside her rescuer, Luke explained; there was the occasional stutter still, but all the same, he talked with a fluency that surprised even himself. And as he spoke, Catt began to feel less afraid of life, more at peace. For the first time for weeks, she was being given a look at a world outside her own immediate problems.

Luke was working on a farm belonging to a distant cousin – high up in the moor, five or six miles to the north of Whinborough. The relative was well-off but mean. There'd be no use him taking Catt there – there'd be no welcome and no work offered, either. 'But Aunt Nell – she's different . . .'

Catt noticed how his voice changed whenever he mentioned his aunt's name – and his expression changed, too, and became less strained. 'Nell's a really *good* person – just like Mother was,' he said. Besides which, she was a 'holiday landlady' in the summers, and now that the daughter who had always helped her had so tragically died not a month back, she was in urgent need of an extra pair of hands, as the main flood of visitors was starting to arrive . . . 'Not that she'll be able to pay you much,' Luke added anxiously, looking at Catt's neat black mourning dress. 'It wouldn't be like being a lady's maid, the work was rough . . .'

'Oh, I was no lady's maid,' Catt interrupted vehemently. 'I was the lowest of all the servants! In fact, I'd no position at all – no wages, either – and they kept me in all the time. It was like a prison – till today, when I got away from it – truly it was!'

'Not allowed out? No wages?' Luke jerked the reins in his astonishment, making the cart sway momentarily, and Catt to clutch his arm to steady herself. Hurriedly, as he righted matters, she released her grip, flushing self-consciously.

'It's a long story.' Catt shrugged, and he saw the bitter set of her mouth. 'I was being punished –'

'Punished? *You?* A bonny lass like you? No – you must be imagining things!' But as Luke spoke, he saw the hurt in her eyes, and knew he was wrong to doubt her. 'I'm sorry, but it sounded so – so topsy-turvy! What in heaven's name were you supposed to have done, to be punished like that?'

'I don't honestly know.' Well, Catt thought, I do know, but it makes no sense, and there isn't a sensible reason. 'I was being punished just for being born, I think – just for that!'

Here she managed a wan smile. With this new-found friend beside her she felt suddenly altogether more hopeful, and some of her old confidence was beginning to stir . . . All the same, she doubted if his pity would survive the revelations of the whole of her story, and in any case, she didn't really know where to begin the tale. Her heart almost sang with relief when Luke replied quietly: 'I know what you mean. I really do. You see, I've been punished, too. Just for being alive. We're two of a kind, you and I.'

He stretched out a hand, taking Catt's in his. This time she did not try to move away from him. So they remained, unspeaking now, simply content and secure in their presence together, for the rest of the journey into Whinborough. Catt's head was resting lightly on Luke's shoulder, and she was fast drifting into sleep, when she was roused by the jolting as the cart trundled down a steep cobbled lane and Luke halted the horse by a row of red-tiled fishermen's cottages within sight of the sea.

She gasped in delight. It was better by far than she had imagined it would be! In the onset of twilight the sea seemed like a gigantic bolt of grey shot silk. This first glimpse of it had an almost hypnotic effect upon Catt. She felt drawn towards it, as if by a magic force. Without realising it, she tightened her hold on Luke's hand. Aloud, she said with a tremble: 'So that's the sea! Someone at my old place told me of it, but I could never really picture what it would be like.'

'Aye – that's the sea!' Luke laughed at her transparent amazement, and Catt felt warmer than ever towards him. When he laughed, his whole face seemed transformed, all the cares vanished. 'But it's not always as calm and kindly as it looks now. It doesn't excite me much, I must admit – but my mother was born in sight of it, and she always loved it, never mind that it had taken half her family in its time.'

He jumped from the cart and handed Catt down with a flourish, then poked his head round the open door of the nearest house. A strong smell of baking wafted from it and Catt suddenly realised how hungry she was. But she hung back as Luke plunged inside.

'Aunt Nell! Aunt Nell! Come and see – I've found you a helper!'

Catt scuffed her feet, feeling uneasy and faintly ridiculous, acutely conscious of how peculiar her situation must look to an outsider. Surely Luke was going much too far in assuming his aunt would offer a total stranger like her bed and board and work!

But she was wrong. In no time at all, she had been swept inside and introduced to a tiny black-gowned, black-haired woman with eyes as blue as Luke's. Now they were sparkling with surprised amusement.

'Why, Luke, I never thought I'd see the day when you'd be so bold as to speak to a lass outside the family – let alone bring her here!' With that, Nell turned to Catt. 'You must have put a spell on him! But,' – her voice turned serious – 'you'd be a godsend to me, and that's a fact. That's if you don't mind hard work and shifting yourself to anything. My poor Clarrie's only been buried three weeks – she'd been in a galloping consumption for a month before that. But it's hard to believe that this time last year she was alive and well, and such a bonny, good girl and such a help to me – though it's not on account of the work that I'm missing her, you understand . . .'

Luke's arm was quickly round his aunt's shoulder as the

blue eyes filled with tears. Catt could not bear to see such pure, simple grief. It brought back all too vivid memories of her own – and she broke in, anxious both to comfort and to share the burden of the sadness.

'I know! I know just how you must be grieving! My mother – and my father – both died in a fire a few weeks back. I'm all alone, too. I was coming to try to find work in Whinborough when my purse was stolen at the station – so I've nothing, and no one to speak up for me! But I promise you I'm honest and I'm hard-working. If you take me in, I will do my very best.'

After this, it was not long before Catt was all set up in the room which had been Clarrie's and which still held the Valentine cards the dead girl had received only weeks before her death. Now her mother gathered them together. 'She was a pretty lass. There were lots of lads after her,' said Nell, with the ghost of a smile. 'Ah well – the minister says the Lord giveth and taketh, but' – she shrugged, bitterly – 'He has an odd way of showing His purposes. Now why should it be that He always seems to be taking from people like Luke and me – who have little enough to start with, while His giving seems to go mostly to those who scarcely need it, they've so much already . . . ?'

The words struck a chord with Catt. They mirrored the feelings she had had since being expelled so unjustly from Leyton; that they were shared by Nell gave them new life and strength. She was to hear more of this kind of talk later – much later, after she had struggled into one of the dead Clarrie's cotton gowns and started her new life by helping Nell serve an enormous high tea. Nell's first lodgers of the summer season were a family from one of the northern factory cities – a retired tallow-chandler and his wife and two spinster daughters.

By this time Luke had gone, back to the moorland farm of his Halliday cousin. So when the visitors' meal was over and cleared, there was a chance for Catt and Nell to have their own meal in front of the kitchen range, and talk – and talk. For Nell, alone now for three weeks, talking had become almost a luxury. Now, in telling her story to Catt, she was able to purge some of her pent-up sorrow; while hearing another's trials and problems gave Catt a more rational insight into her own.

Nell was a widow, the sister of Luke's dead mother. 'Our father fished out of Whitcar,' explained Nell. This was another fishing port 20 miles north of Whinborough, 'But he was drowned at sea like nearly all the Stanforths,' sighed Nell. But before that tragedy, Henry Stanforth had had a four-man boat, and a lad called Matt Wilson had trudged from his tailor father's home in Whinborough, desperate to go to sea, and not a skipper in Whitcar would take him on, for fear of offending the tailor father. But Henry Stanforth did – and that was how Nell had met her husband. Then Matt's father had died, and with the inheritance Matt had bought his own boat and married Nell and come back to Whinborough because Whitcar had such a dreadful reputation for freak storms and drownings . . .

'Not that it helped him. Whinborough harbour may be safer than Whitcar's – but my father and Matt both drowned on the open sea and in the very same storm – with my Tom and Clarrie only babies . . .'

For a moment Nell paused, memories momentarily silencing the chatter. Then she brightened. 'Still, I was luckier than my sister Susannah, though it didn't seem so at the time. She was the prettier of us two sisters, with her golden curls and sparkling eyes and winning ways. One day, at Whitcar fair, she met a farmer – Luke's father, Will Halliday. It must have been the one day in his life that Will managed a smile, for I swear I've never once seen him smile in all the years I've been unfortunate enough to know him . . . Mind you, the Hallidays are a strange lot – known for it, always have been, rags-to-riches and back again, and there are all sorts of black tales told about them, going back years . . . Anyway,' Nell continued sadly, 'William swept our Susannah off her feet. There was talk at the time about him inheriting some distant relative's farm, up on Gelling Moor – more than 300 acres it was. Well, Will inherited right enough, but it turned out to be nothing but bad debts . . . The farm had been sold over his head even while he was moving in – it was all he could do to raise the money to rent about 25 miserable acres from the new owner and he's been struggling ever since.'

'No wonder he turned bitter!' murmured Catt.

Nell nodded. 'I grant you that – but Will Halliday was soured already. He was ill-treating my sister long before he knew his inheritance was worthless – yes, and drinking hard, too. Which made his pittance even poorer than it might have been. And to cap it all, his eldest son is his mirror image, even to the drinking and the temper tantrums. It's *he* who'll inherit if there's anything left, yet it's Luke who loves that poor little farm and its moors with his very soul. But he's been turned off it since he was thirteen years old and had to hire himself where he could. Will says the farm can't support more than one son, you see. The middle lad – Robert – went off to Canada with my own Tom a couple of years back, looking for their fortunes there. Will's only daughter went into service and then married and never goes near High Moor now – but Luke can't seem to keep away from it, unwanted though he is there . . . First he stayed close because he couldn't bear being far from his mother – but his father let her die without ever letting Luke know how ill she was, and him only a few miles away. Some folk say a drop of poison even helped her on her way,' interjected Nell darkly, 'but I don't think even Will would sink that low . . . Well, Luke was always quiet and shy – but since his mother died he's been quieter and shyer than ever. But you, Catt – you've brought him out of his shell and no mistake!'

Catt smiled. 'He was so kind to me,' she said. 'But I believe he would have been just as kind to anyone. He didn't know me at all – he just thought I was in trouble and wanted to help. Like the Good Samaritan,' she added, almost thinking aloud. 'Most people would have passed me by – but he didn't.'

She could hear the tremor in her voice, and was angry with herself for letting her feeling show so; angrier still as she felt her cheeks turning pink and heard Nell remark, only half-humorously: 'It looks to me as though Luke wasn't the only one bowled over today!' Then Nell turned suddenly deadly serious. 'But be careful, Catt, please be careful. Don't tease

42

him. Luke has a heart of pure gold and he's so gentle – just like his mother was. I couldn't stand by and see him hurt any more. Why, when I think how Susannah was made to suffer in the hell-hole on the moors . . .'

Catt tossed her head defiantly. The conversation was turning far too intimate for her taste: she had become afraid of emotions and confidences laid too bare. But she assured Nell solemnly: 'I wouldn't hurt Luke for all the world – but I daresay he's forgotten about me already.'

She turned away and busied herself clearing their plates. She tried studiously to ignore Nell's knowing smiles and to put Luke right out of her mind.

But all in vain. She found herself thinking of him all the time.

5

As the weeks went by and there was neither sight of Luke nor any word from him, Catt began to fear that he had, indeed, quickly forgotten all about her. It rankled with her, how much this upset her. She tried, unsuccessfully, to put him right out of her mind. He was working on a farm only a few miles away, after all – had he been genuinely interested in her, surely he would have been in touch before now, however busy he might be this time of year.

She tried to keep her thoughts hidden from Nell. This was not as difficult as it might have been, for there was soon more than plenty to keep her busy here in Whinborough. She had arrived just as the season was about to get under way, so there was always fresh cleaning, cooking or washing to be done. Not to mention the shopping expeditions with Nell – to the big open market in the town centre or the fish dock at the bottom of their own alley.

It was a busy house, but a warm and friendly one. Catt realised with something of a shock how frozen in spirit she had become after the frigidity of Miss Fredericks's regime, while even in her own home at Leyton – Josh excepted – there had been little emotional airing.

Under Nell's affectionate wing, Catt slowly began to thaw, then blossom. She was most aware herself of this in the evenings, when the day's work was done and she and Nell would sit in the little front room high on the second floor – the guests had the best parlour on the first – watching the world go by beneath them. There they would talk and do the mending, or work on the rag rugs which Nell made and sold in order to

44

make a little extra to tide over the winters, when money was always tight.

'The guests are only here in summer – and the season's quite short,' Nell explained. 'Whinborough goes back to what it used to be – just a fishing port – in wintertime. It's far too wild and windy then for city folk! So the money runs down between September and Easter. I'd rather knit jerseys than make rugs but there's no call for them these days. They're out of fashion, and then they take such a time . . .'

Catt loved hearing Nell talk. But she was just as happy to sit alone and simply stare out of the window. The sea never stopped fascinating her. It had a personality all its own, changing from day to day, from hour to hour. Sometimes it was as sunny blue as Our Lady's cloak on the statue in Leyton chapel – next moment grey, sullen, grasping and turning through grey to a boiling black that emanated fury and treachery.

She liked going down to the quay, first with Nell, later more often on her own, to choose from the newly caught fish. There was a kind of magic in the sights and smells of salt and sea and fish, and in the market chatter, which, despite all the terrors the sea might hold, was always lively and cheerful. It was a new adventure, too, to walk into Whinborough centre, with its newly built rows of smart shops and the huge, gleaming white-stuccoed hotel now being built on the south cliff. The Prince of Wales had promised to come and stay once it was completed, said Nell. That would certainly put Whinborough on the map! Then there was the new promenade. On Sundays, in particular, it thronged with people, both visitors and locals, parading in all their finery. Catt had never seen such beautiful silks and satins. Some of the women were like beings from another world – exotic, brilliant birds of paradise in gowns, bonnets and parasols all colours of the rainbow.

At Leyton Hall, despite the family's social rank, Lady Anne's clothes had been far from brilliant: old-fashioned in style and dowdy. Catt was particularly thankful for her mourning dress when she went to the promenade, for she knew there was no way in which she could begin to compete with this arrogant display of luxury and wealth.

But its attractions were beginning to fuel her ambitions, to turn her dreams in new directions. One day, she promised herself, I will be someone who matters – and with some fine gowns, too!

Once she had heard the bare essentials of Catt's unhappy past, Nell had shown herself uninterested in prying deeper. Catt was perpetually amazed to be taken on trust so, especially after the authoritarian and punitive regime at Melchester. Gratefully, she knew that Nell had no wish to distress her by forcing her to relive painful memories; for Nell, present good was of far more importance than past ills.

At the same time, Catt was surprised to find she herself was able to look back – to that past before Melchester, anyway – with more serenity as time went by. She had been bitterly homesick while she knew that Mary Jane and Josh were still alive – and how much she had resented Mary Jane's apparent wish to get rid of her, after the scandal broke! But once she knew both were dead, and the first grief had faded, she ceased to pine. Josh, she was sure, must already be in Heaven, and, despite her new-found cynicism in religious matters, Catt hoped he was looking down at her now, and praying for her . . . She was less sure about Mary Jane. Recalling Father Charles's talks on Purgatory – that place which souls passed through for the cleansing of sins before being able to enter Heaven – Catt could not resist smiling at the thought of her mother at this moment polishing her way along and, on the way, she trusted, acquiring compassion.

Father Charles! As soon as his name came up in her thoughts Catt's new-found equilibrium would totter. And for all her efforts to wipe him clean out of her mind, he kept breaking back in. Even worse, this seemed to happen more, not less often, as time passed. In addition, since her meeting with Luke, these manifestations of her darkest imagination had become increasingly shameful. Sometimes, indeed, Catt wondered if she could even be going out of her mind. Surely no sane person would be experiencing what she was?

She had only to think of Luke for his face to fade into that of the priest. Then she would see Charles, just as he had been on that last, fateful day. His arm would come to rest on her shoulder, as it had done, only now it was not expressing fatherly concern and distress, but had become the preliminary for a lover's embrace. She found herself going on to visualise him clasping her yet more tightly, pressing his body against hers, covering her face and arms with hot, forbidden kisses . . . Her face would burn, she would feel physically sick, crossing herself in the fervent but, alas, unrealised hope that the devil which must surely be responsible for this would be crushed and never return to tempt her again.

I have to stop this nonsense, Catt thought. In her bitterness and rejection, she was gradually coming round to the idea that for her at least, there could be no God. That meant there could be no Devil either. Any God there might be had betrayed her utterly, she felt – and certainly she was going to have no further interest in one who held court in a Catholic church. That part of her life was over, gone forever. Had she not, as she walked through St Agatha's on the day of her escape from Melchester and genuflected that last time, sworn she would not set foot in a Catholic church ever again?

But the faith which had been so much a part of her continued to grasp out at her. In moments of crisis, Catt would automatically cross herself. Last thing at night, as she kissed Josh's crude little rosary, she had to make a positive effort to stop herself from going on to recite the prayers she had once loved so much. One day, out alone in Whinborough, she took a wrong turning which brought her face to face with a large Catholic church, overpowering in its redbrick newness. Like a sleepwalker, she found herself opening the door, staring through at the high altar, being dragged irresistibly forward into it . . . Then she managed to break away, turn and walk back into the blessed sunlight of her unbelief.

On Catt's first Sunday in Whinborough, Nell had enquired whether Catt wanted to go to church. 'I don't go much myself,' she admitted. 'Since Clarrie died, it doesn't seem the same. But on Sunday evenings, I sometimes go to the

Methodist chapel on the cliff . . .'

Catt's first reaction was to shake her head and hope the subject would quickly go away. But then, conscious of Nell's underlying loneliness, she said hesitantly: 'I could come with you if you wanted.'

Even as she spoke, she knew this was a terrible thing for a Catholic to say – even one like herself who had abandoned her faith. Catholics – even lapsed ones – did not attend these heretic assemblies, not on any account! What had Father Charles declared, time and time again: 'There is no salvation outside the Church.' And there was only one true Church, Catt knew, and it was Catholic. Then, realising how her thoughts were turning yet again to Father Charles, she set her jaw resolutely. Father Charles might say what he pleased; he had no power over her any more. She would go where she liked. All the same, the thought of attending a Nonconformist chapel scared her despite her new defiance of the old rules, and she was secretly relieved when Nell did not raise the subject again.

A few days later there was great excitement.

'A letter! From Tom! From Canada!' Nell was radiant. 'Well – now I'll *have* to go to chapel this Sunday and get the minister to read it and write me an answer.'

For the first time Catt realised that Nell was illiterate, just as her own mother had been. Without thinking, she burst out eagerly: 'You don't need to wait till Sunday! Let me read it for you.' Then stopped abruptly, hoping she had not said too much. The last thing in the world she wanted to do was to appear superior to Nell.

Nell, however, was as pleased as she was surprised. 'You can *read?* Really? Why Catt, how clever. How lucky you are.' And when Catt had duly read the half-dozen sentences from the Ontario letter, written, she could see, by someone less well-schooled than she herself had been, Nell was vociferous in her admiration.

'That must have been a marvellous Big House you were at, to have you taught reading! I paid for my Tom to go to a school till he was eight, for my father and my husband had both been able to read and write a bit. But I've never learnt, and Clarrie neither. There wasn't the money or the time for her. I can't even sign my name – and I'd like to do that,' said Nell wistfully. 'It didn't used to matter – but nowadays, with all the schooling there is about, most people seem able to sign their name, and I feel bad when I'm asked and I can't.'

'I can soon show you how to do that – and more!' Catt promised, setting down to write the answer that Nell dictated to her, glad to be so especially useful, but Nell demurred.

'No. I'm past learning – just my name, I'd like to be able to write that.' And under Catt's instruction, she could soon manage this. But more she would not do.

It was now that the matter of Catt's religion came out – for of course Nell wanted to know who had been responsible for all this 'book learning'. Literacy had something magical about it to Nell. Though she wanted little of it for herself, it fascinated her.

'The priest taught me. He was the son of the house – and a scholar. He caught me looking at a book when I was tiny, and said I ought to be able to read it. I learned to read, then write. He found it interesting, I think. There was not so much for him to do in a country house; he had no proper parish in those days.'

Catt spoke in a deliberate monotone, anxious not to let any vestige of feeling show through. 'In my last place, though,' she added bitterly, 'they wouldn't let me read and write at all. They seemed to think working people shouldn't.'

Nell seemed to ignore this, but Catt's religious revelation prompted her to say, a little apologetically, 'If I'd known you were a Catholic I'd not have asked you to chapel.'

'Oh, but I'm not a Catholic any more!' Catt took Nell's hand impulsively. 'I've done with all that! For it's all a sham. They thought they were such *good* Catholics at my last place – they were so particular about church attendance and church rules – but all that observance meant absolutely nothing! I'm never going back to anything which produces people like that!'

She found she was almost shouting, and was conscious that Nell was staring at her in amazement. She tried to calm

49

herself. And what I've said is only half of it, she thought, for you know nothing of Father Charles, of my 'disgrace' – of the hypocrisy, the injustices, all done in the name of faith . . . Aloud, she added, more quietly: 'You see, everything that has gone wrong for me seems to have started on account of that – terrible – religion.'

Nell stroked her cheek and smiled affectionately. 'Never fear, in this house no one's forced to go anywhere. I've no patience with these church quarrels! But you'll have to watch what you say to Luke,' she reflected. 'Some of his family were Catholic, a while back. Not badly off either. His father always blames the loss of that land he was expecting on the cousin who was the last Catholic among them. Will swore that if that bit of the family hadn't stuck so long to the old religion and paid so much in fines through the generations, they'd still have been rich now. And it's true, Hallidays once owned half Whinborough Moor. But there, I think there's more to it than Will says. That cousin of his and his father before him were just gamblers and bad husbandmen – however, it's made Will fly into a rage simply to hear the word "Catholic" mentioned . . . Of course, all the Hallidays are Church of England now, if they're anything at all.' Nell sighed. 'Luke doesn't need to belong to a church to be a good man, anyway – and I reckon that father of his would still be a fiend, even if he were an archbishop!'

With Luke suddenly back in the forefront of her mind, Nell prattled on, religion now forgotten. 'But there! Reading and writing! Why, how surprised Luke will be when he hears of it. He's no more a scholar than I am. I suppose Will can write his name. But he was far too mean to send any of his children to school. They were all put to work on the farm from the moment they could toddle. And to think that you, a girl . . .'

'Please don't tell him – that's if he ever comes by here again!' begged Catt in sudden agitation. 'Don't tell him – not about the writing, nor the religion, either. But especially the writing. I don't want him to take against me, just because I can do something he can't. For I'm not a patch on Luke – I was just lucky in this.'

50

In the midst of it all, however, Catt felt an enormous sense of relief. All this time she had been waiting for Luke to write to her and wondering why he had not. She was sure he had forgotten all about her, never thinking that the real reason for the silence was because he did not know how to put pen to paper! Now, once more, she could dare to believe that he would be back to see her one of these days, and then . . . ?

Nell must have been able to read the thoughts behind the sudden radiance. 'Why, Catt, looking like you do at this minute, you're quite a beauty,' she declared. 'And I know very well why you're smiling! But, of course, you – and only you – must tell Luke your secrets. When you're wed, maybe . . .'

6

It was quite soon after this that Luke came back to Whinborough. As if to celebrate, the day had dawned clear and sparklingly bright; the sea shimmered like blue satin and the pink roses were just beginning their struggle to flower in Nell's little backyard, despite its almost total lack of sunlight, owing to its position against the rising cliff face. Catt was busy making pastry. She heard the grinding of cartwheels on the cobbles outside the kitchen window and turned to see Luke already in the room, there behind her, grinning broadly. She squealed with surprise and pretended to protest as he pulled her to him, the flour spilling down over his best Sunday jacket.

They both laughed. Catt pushed him away, starting to dust the flour off. The action shattered any shyness that might have grown up between them during their weeks apart.

'I thought I'd never be able to get away – we've been so busy with the lambing these last weeks,' explained Luke. Catt noticed that his stammer had all but gone. 'Luckily, someone this side of Whinborough was wanting some of the weaned sheepdogs we had over, and I offered to bring them, and now the rest of the day's my own. So can I take you for a walk around the town? Or maybe you can take me – you probably know it better than I do by now.'

Catt demurred, thought secretly longing to accept. 'We're full of visitors, I've a load of things to do for your aunt.'

'Nonsense!' Nell appeared in the doorway, matchmaking uppermost in her mind. 'I can manage this once. Why, you've done half a day's work for me already, Catt! It doesn't do to

52

pass up a chance like this – Luke's cousin up at Farsyke isn't often as generous as this with free time.'

So Catt and Luke set out up the cliff, towards the new town, walking side by side, decorously and rather gingerly, a little wary of each other, each on their best behaviour.

The streets were still almost deserted. On Sundays, most of the shops in this part of Whinborough were shut and the morning services had just begun in the various churches. Occasionally the drift of a hymn floated out as they passed a chapel building. Their feet echoed on the empty pavements.

Catt glanced shyly at Luke from under her eyelashes and gently touched his arm. 'Oh, Luke, I've been so looking forward to your coming to Whinborough again!' she burst out, unable to contain herself any longer. 'Because I wanted to say "thank you" properly – I never did that first day. I hardly knew where I was or what I was doing then. You really saved my life, you know, and I can never thank you enough.'

As Luke smiled and shook his head, she stumbled on: 'Oh, but you *did* save me! What in the world would have happened to me if you had not chanced to come along? All my money was stolen, and I was in a strange place. I'd have had to beg, to be sure – and ended up by being sent to the workhouse, like as not.'

It was at this point that Luke summoned up the courage to link his arm in hers. 'We were *meant* to meet that day, lass. I'm quite sure we were. I've never been more sure of anything!' Luke paused to rub his nose nervously, and Catt caught a fleeting glimpse of the sad little boy he must once have been, and longed to put her arms around him and hug him. 'Up to now, you see,' he went on, 'I've never seemed to be there when good luck was being handed out. I don't know why, but there it is. And things have been hard for me these last few years – bad even before Mother died, but worse since . . . Maybe Nell has told you something of it?'

When Catt nodded, Luke went on: 'Nell is the only one who understands me. I don't know what I'd have done without her, and she's had her own share of troubles, more than enough, without having to bear mine as well. I've lain awake at night, more than a few times, wondering what I'll do for family when her Tom makes enough money in Canada to send back for her, as he's promised.' Then he smiled – that marvellous, almost ethereal smile that went straight to Catt's heart. 'But I don't need to worry about that any more – not now I've got you!'

I must be dreaming, thought Catt. Surely this isn't really happening to me? I'm plain, I'm almost penniless, and he scarcely even knows me! Is he really trying to tell me that he loves me? I certainly think I love him – or do I? She searched for an answer, but none came. Perhaps it isn't love at all – perhaps I feel happy and safe when I'm with him, simply because he is so kind and good and gentle, and as luckless as I am . . .

She looked straight into Luke's eyes, then, and gave a sudden gasp, as, for a fraction of a second, she seemed to see right through them – through to the handsome, patrician features of the priest, her father. And again she felt, to her shame, that forbidden surge of a passion that did not relate to Luke at all.

'Why, Catt, what is it? Y-you've t-turned quite p-pale! H-have I said anything t-to upset you? Y-you know I w-would never . . .' In his anxiety, Luke's stammer suddenly reappeared; once again, he looked like a small, neglected boy.

But, very quickly, it passed – that dreadful, unnatural feeling – for the time being . . . Catt squeezed Luke's arm, saw the worry in his eyes, and loved and pitied and wanted to mother him all at the same time.

'No, of course not! *You* could never say anything to upset me – you know you couldn't – I was just thinking about the past.' And she tried to repress a shiver.

They were in a little park, and there, seated on one of the elegant iron seats, Catt spilled out her story to Luke – or a part of it.

She told him of her childhood at Leyton lodge; of how she had been well thought of right up to the day when the priest who had till that moment always been so good to her had seemed suddenly to be wanting something more . . .

Luke was appalled. 'Could you not complain?'

'He was the son of the house; everyone thought I was the one at fault for saying such things. They thought they were being lenient in just sending me away – a long way away – to Melchester . . . My – father – was upset. I do believe, but by that stage my mother was quite glad to see me go, I think.'

So Catt stumbled on, hardly aware of the gaps and half-truths in the version of events she was offering. Of one thing she was quite sure: she could never reveal Father Charles's true relationship with her to anyone, not even to Luke. It was not a question of heeding Lady Anne's threats on the matter – it was simply that she was far, far too ashamed! And, blinded as she was by that secret passion she had for Charles Leyton, she would not for years be able to admit, even to herself, that his 'advances' had been made to comfort, and in a search for her forgiveness, and had not been the preliminaries of lovemaking.

'It was worse than a prison, that house in Melchester!' cried Catt vehemently, moving the subject on. 'I could not go out alone, not even to church; someone always had to be with me. I'd been so wicked, they said, so I couldn't be trusted . . . and they said my parents would suffer if I didn't do as I was told. But then my parents died, so anything I might do could only rebound on me – and then came the chance to run away. From that dreadful place – and its dreadful religion. For it was a religion with no love in it, no love at all – just punishment upon punishment.' Here Catt grew more solemn, less shrill. 'Still, it opened my eyes to the truth. I'd been such a good Catholic. I'd adored my Church – but not any more! I've done with all that! I had to pawn my First Communion cross to get money for the train fare when I ran away – I'd heard about Whinborough, you see, and thought if only I could get here, I could find work, be independent. But then my purse was stolen and –'

'I'd like to meet that thief – and shake him by the hand!' declared Luke, smiling. 'For without him, we might never have met! And I'd shake your Miss Fredericks's hand, too, come to that, for it was her actions that drove you to come here – and we might take it further back still, to that rascally priest . . .'

He was simply trying to soother, lighten her tale; Catt knew that. But such chatter jarred her and she wanted to make him stop.

'Please, Luke, don't let's talk of it any more! I can't bear to think about it. It was a nightmare – yes, and I dream of it still – I only told you because I thought you had a right to know.'

Catt's eyes swam with unshed tears and her cheeks burned, and Luke, who as Nell had so often remarked, was shy, even in the company of his own sister, leant down and solemnly kissed her, surprising himself as much as Catt. It was a loving but passionless kiss – cool lips on cool lips – and they started away from each other, like young, frightened animals, almost as they touched. But it held the promise of depths of passion yet to be plumbed.

Luke flushed, mumbling some kind of apology. But Catt, exhilarated by her tale-telling and relieved to find how easy it had been to cover up the worst of the story, flashed him a rare, brilliant smile.

'You are the kindest, gentlest person I have ever met,' she said softly. 'After my – father – died, I thought there must be no goodness left in the whole world; certainly none for me. And then I met you – and Nell – and since then, I've been so happy, so very happy, that I can hardly believe it.'

Luke took her arm and they set off again, crossing the new bridge that spanned the break in Whinborough's cliffs and connected the old fishing port with the new Whinborough, the fashionable seaside resort, with its big hotels, glass-covered Winter Gardens, squares and fountains.

Luke was a more than competent guide, despite his early claim that he knew little about the place. He pointed out all the landmarks – even the strange, caterpillar-like construction on the western cliff face, soon to be a funicular railway which would transport visitors from hotel to beach and back again for a penny a ride, and was due to be officially opened by the Prince of Wales himself the following month. Why, half the pretty women from London would be there, said Luke – not to mention all the hopefuls from Liverpool, Manchester and Leeds – and then he clapped his hand to his mouth. 'I'm sorry, Catt!' He grinned half-humorously, half-apologetically. 'That's no talk for a lady like you to hear. You can see I've been too long among the other farm lads!'

Catt laughed. 'Nell's house is full of gossip,' she said. 'There was a Birmingham family staying last week, and I wouldn't like to tell you the things the husband was saying about the Prince . . . But it will be grand to see all the fine clothes – and there's a London band coming to play in the Winter Gardens. I hope Nell and I will have time to come and see it.'

When Catt's eyes sparkled as they did now he found her utterly entrancing. And if she was now in her seventh heaven, he was in his eighth at least. His head was awhirl; he wanted Catt desperately, and for Luke, that meant that he wanted to marry her. It was far, far more than a matter of simply wanting to make love to her – he wanted her forever, body and soul. Already he was imagining her sitting opposite him as he sat at the head of the table, in the Gelling farmhouse of his childhood, just where his own mother had once sat . . .

* * *

But, of course, as Luke knew all too well, this could never be anything but a dream. The farmhouse was his father's, not his, and even when his father died it would be his brother William's, never his. He had been turned out of it when no more than a boy, for all his mother had wept and implored her husband to let him stay. When she had died, his father had not even summoned him back in time to see her.

For years now, Luke had been no more than a hired labourer, shepherding for anyone who would give him work. Often, that meant relatives, for, as Catt was to find out, the Hallidays ranged in varying degrees of kinship and prosperity all over the Yorkshire moors. In good years Luke was much in demand; he was a conscientious worker and a byword for his sheep-rearing skills. Yes – a good worker, well-liked, even

– but easily exploited when it came to money. For he was a man with no settled home. Everyone on the moors knew that his father and brother chose virtually to ignore his existence and had made it abundantly clear that they neither loved nor wanted him.

Since leaving home, Luke had been back only for his mother's funeral. Even that, he recalled, had been the occasion for yet another drunken outburst from his father – a diatribe against the relation who had left him such a pittance of a holding, when he had been led to expect so much. 'The only good Papist is a dead one! Liars, every one.' And, of course, there had been the inevitable reiteration that there was absolutely no place for Luke here at High Moor.

'You were always your mother's boy,' Will Halliday had sneered. 'Well, try going back to her family for a living. Ask them to find you something, for there's nothing for you here – nothing, that is, unless you come back with a wife who'll keep house for us. That might go some of the way to justifying your miserable existence!'

There had been hoots of derisive laughter, then, and Luke could still hear his brother's contemptuous follow-up ringing in his ears:

'A wife? For God's sake, Father! You're more likely to see our Luke coming back with the keys of Heaven!'

Their laughter had continued to haunt him long after he stumbled away down the track which led from the family home to the Whitcar road.

Since then, he had not been back. But, several times in the intervening years, when he'd happened to be shepherding on Gelling Moor, or doing some carting to Whitcar past the turning that led off to High Moor farm, he'd looked with longing towards the place where he was born and spent his childhood, and which he loved with every fibre of his being. Every stone of the house, every inch of those 20-odd acres seemed a living part of him.

Until his meeting with Catt, High Moor had been Luke's one and only love. Now, he wished more than anything to take her there, to join the one love with the other, newer one. But, as he well knew, this was only a dream: High Moor was quite beyond his reach, and without it, so it seemed to him, was Catt.

'A penny for them!' whispered Catt, disturbed by Luke's suddenly stricken expression – and he started, then smiled down at her, glad to be jerked back to the present from memories he knew were best forgotten.

As he rode back to his cousin's farm later that day, Luke could think of little else but Catt.

7

Summer peaked in a sunburst July, which gave the royal visit to Whinborough, and the fashionable whirl that it produced, added verve and piquancy. The excitement – and the profits – spread far beyond the smart West Cliff, reaching out to the older, staider parts of the town, too.

Nell's boarding-house trade flourished. Her visitors would no sooner be settled in than most would hurry westwards and take a vicarious pleasure in observing the goings-on of the rich there. Some were admiring, others, more puritanical, shook their heads and said the world was going from bad to worse, with all this concentration on money and luxury – but they all came to look nonetheless.

'If things keep going like this,' said Nell, 'you and I will be able to start a proper hotel one of these days . . . if Luke doesn't carry you off first, of course!'

That idea set Catt thinking afresh. The thought of running a business – if not exactly her own, at any rate a partnership, and maybe up there on the West Cliff – was an attractive one. It would give heightened status, not to mention the money to buy fine gowns, jewels and books . . . But a life without Luke was not something she could contemplate with equanimity these days.

By August, when the days turned close and thundery, the wealthy visitors had mostly gone. Now the working people started travelling up by train from the dark industrial cities in the west, and from the mining villages that pitted half the county. They poured into Whinborough in their thousands at weekends, shocking the local Sabbatarians by their cheerful, noisy abandonment; and shocking Catt, too, when she saw the poverty only too obvious in the pinched pallid faces, particularly the children's.

For many of the day-trippers, it was their first glance of the sea, their only holiday of the year. They would queue patiently for donkey-rides and shell fish dinners, and only a few would spend too long in the public houses and be left behind when the last excursion train left Whinborough late on Sunday night, some of them turning up penniless in the police court next morning.

Nell was not so booked up now, but at Catt's suggestion she had started offering high teas of fish and fried potatoes or the traditional Yorkshire ham and eggs to this new sort of visitor, and these soon acquired quite a reputation. So Sunday, previously the slackest day of the week, was now the busiest.

It was just as well Luke was obviously too busy to come and see her again, thought Catt, as she served meal after meal, and then helped tackle the never-ending piles of dirty crockery; Nell would have been hard put to it to give her much time off at present.

But she found herself longing for him desperately. She would never have thought herself capable of wanting someone so much. If Luke were beside her, Catt told herself, his actual physical presence would chase away these evil, erotic images of Charles Leyton which still haunted her. Luke was the only man she loved; so why was it, that when her thoughts turned to him, they were all too often distorted, then smothered by these dire, dark yearnings? It was as though some primeval beast was battening on her dreams of innocence, and turning them into monstrous nightmares . . .

If only she could write to Luke, something very simple and short, just telling him how she loved him and missed him! Surely he would come running to her, then, however brief his visit, and this torture might end . . . But since he would not be able to read what she wrote, even this avenue of escape was closed to her.

Then came the bombshell.

It came in the shape of a letter from Canada, from Nell's Tom. In it was an imposing piece of paper which neither Nell nor Catt could make head or tail of. But when Nell showed it to the minister at the chapel, it turned out to be something called a 'banker's draft'. Nell had only to take it to a bank in Whinborough – and this was an adventure in itself since Nell had never in her life been inside a bank, regarding such places as only for those she called her 'betters' – and she would receive in exchange money sufficient for her boat and rail fares all the way to Tom's farm in Ontario.

There was more. The money was enough to cover two fares. Luke was invited, too, for Tom and Robert's farm was thriving. Not only could they afford to have Nell to live with them, as they had always promised – 'And they'll be desperate for a few good Yorkshire meals and some clean shirts, I'll be bound!' commented Nell, remarkably prosaic in the midst of all the excitement – but they wanted Luke there, too, to help them. They had managed to buy more land and now they badly needed another pair of working hands to help farm it.

Nell clapped her hands, happy as a child. Despite all the blows life had dealt her, Catt had rarely seen Nell sad for long; now, as the full impact of the letter sank in, she was in raptures.

'Ever since Tom left, I've dreamt of this day – but I never really thought it would happen! Oh, I know he promised he'd send for me when he could – but I didn't think he'd ever manage it. I felt he was just saying these things to ease the pain of the parting . . .'

She turned suddenly wistful. 'If only Clarrie could have been here, too, to come with me!' Then Nell's face lit up, excited by a new idea. 'But *you* must come instead of her, Catt! Of course you must!'

And as Catt shook her head dubiously, Nell rushed on. 'Yes, of course you can come! For I'll have to sell most of my bits and bobs of furniture before I go – and surely they'll raise enough for one more ticket from Liverpool to Canada, especially when you take into account the extra money we've earned this past season. And even Luke must have a sovereign or two of his own put by somewhere.'

One of Nell's neighbours plied a donkey-cart between the station and the holiday hotels. Now he was cajoled into driving out to Farsyke farm, where Luke was working, to deliver a message that he was wanted on urgent family business and should come to see Nell just as soon as he could.

'Yes, Catt, I know,' apologised Nell. 'You could have done me a letter, and probably old Isaac Halliday could have puzzled it out and told Luke what it said, but I'm not keen on him knowing my business. I want to tell Luke all about it to his face, so a first message by word of mouth comes best. Once Jonah mentions urgent family business, even an old skinflint like Isaac will let Luke have time off to come! Besides' – and Nell smiled – 'I think it's high time Luke had a day to himself. Isaac pays him little enough – and he needs a day to talk to you, especially now . . .'

Catt felt herself blushing. It was quite clear what Nell was thinking – and what she herself was hoping – that Tom's news was the catalyst that would propel the shy, self-effacing Luke into tearing himself from his beloved moors and proposing to Catt forthwith. Then, when the three of them set off for this new life in a wonderful new world, he and Catt would already be man and wife.

It sounded so perfect, a new country, a clean break with the past – and a past that for Catt was dominated by memories of loss and shame and humiliation. All this would be replaced by a glowing future with Luke, who loved her so. The prospects of happiness seemed limitless. The whole scheme appealed strongly to Catt's innate love of adventure. If successful – as she was certain they would be – they could become well-to-do, even rich. Canada surely offered prospects far better than those connected with that earlier notion of one day joining Nell in running a Whinborough hotel. In any case, without Nell, that idea was already dead and buried. Not to mention the fact that everyone said that in these new countries, like Canada, inherited wealth and family status meant next to nothing – but vision and hard work counted for so much.

63

Could anywhere be more perfect for Luke and herself?

But then Catt came down to earth with a painful bump. Luke might indeed love her – she was sure he did – and want to marry her. Yet if she were absolutely honest with herself, she could not help wondering whether she could ever really be capable of love at all. Had those innermost secret feelings about the man she now knew to be her own father perhaps created an emptiness in her heart which no amount of loving on Luke's part would be able to cure?

And there was something else – something which raised an even more immediate threat to these rosy prospects. Those moors of Luke's – would he *really* be willing to abandon them forever, even though they offered nothing but drudgery and frustration, whereas Canada held out such promise of wealth and happiness?

Catt thought of Luke talking, with a depth of passion given to nothing else, of 'his' moors and 'his' home upon them. The merest mention of them seemed to give him added life and vigour. If he were parted from them, might he not simply wither and fade? She felt as if a cold, icy hand had been laid on her shoulder. Life had been so sweet and settled and certain these last months – and this latest revelation had seemed at first sight to fill the cup to overflowing . . . But, in fact, Catt knew deep down, today's events had thrown everything back into the melting-pot.

Nell was much too excited to notice the strain on Catt's face. As they went about their usual household chores – for the boarding-house, though three-quarters empty, could not be ignored, even at a time like this – Nell's tongue never ceased wagging.

'What a mercy that you can write, Catt, for there's so much we've got to do and not much time to do it in. There's the landlord to be written to, to give up the lease of this house, and my things to be sold, and then there's the bank to be dealt with, the tickets to see to, and' – here came Nell's triumphant finale – 'there'll be the wedding arrangements to fix. We'll have to get on with those straight away if you're going to go to Canada as Mrs Luke Halliday!'

'But he hasn't even proposed to me yet,' Catt protested faintly, only to get the confident rejoinder:

'Oh, but he will lass! He will – just as soon as he knows what this is all about. This is the very push he's been needing – you'll see!'

8

'I shan't be going.' Luke was standing in Nell's kitchen, fists whitely clenched, pale but deadly firm. 'I'm sorry, Aunt Nell. I know most people would jump at a chance like this – and I don't deserve to have been offered it – but there it is.' His voice trembled. 'I'm grateful for being asked – more grateful than I can ever tell you. And I don't know what I'll do without you when you've gone.' He sighed ruefully. 'But all the land in Canada isn't worth a fraction of what High Moor means to me. It's my life and breath, and as long as it's there, I can't stray far from it. And you know I can't – you've always known.'

It took a lot more argument before Nell was finally forced to admit defeat. First, she tried logic. 'But Luke, you know very well that *you* are never going to get your hands on that wretched little farm! Yes' – and as Luke opened his mouth to object, she waved him silent – 'and it *is* a wretched little place, as you know very well in your heart of hearts! Oh, there was some hope for it when your father first got his hands on it and your mother still lived – but now he and your brother have well-nigh bankrupted themselves. And when your father's dead, it will all go to Will, what's left of it. Yes, we all know he's a drunkard, but he's tough all the same – he'll outlive your father, I'll be bound, and maybe you as well, for all the ale he sups! And anyway' – Nell's voice rose triuphantly – 'who's to say Will won't marry one of these days? We know he's a drinker and a bully – but, like all you Hallidays, he's not a bad looker, and there are some women who might even take a fancy to his bad points . . . not to mention the farm! And then

High Moor would pass to his children . . .'

But Luke held his ground stubbornly. 'I'd die if I were far away from that moor! I've got to be somewhere where I can get to and look at the farm – even if it can't ever be mine.'

He turned to Catt in desperation. While the argument raged she was standing, silent, half-hidden in the shadow near the range. How she longed to rush forward and hold him! She was appalled to see him so. In his dilemma she thought he resembled nothing so much as a helpless, hunted animal, with the usually kindly and placid Nell the ruthless pursuer.

In the stress of the moment, Luke's old stammer was rising to the surface again. 'C-Catt, y-you understand, d-don't you? Y-you s-see why I h-have to stay n-near? S-strange things c-can happen – s-suppose Father d-died and W-will c-couldn't k-keep up the rent, m-maybe I-I could still g-get the f-f-farm one day.'

Catt still said nothing. She was full of pity for Luke and for herself. The old ideas of setting up in business with Nell had been easy enough to abandon in the excitement of the letter from Canada and the even more prosperous future that promised – now, she saw all her dreams, all the plans she had been making for Luke and herself ever since reading it, fading before her eyes.

But, while she hesitated, hardly trusting herself to speak, Nell plunged in once again, with eyes blazing and an uncharacteristic stamp of her foot.

'Stuff and nonsense! You know it is nothing but pie in the sky, Luke! Just dreams left over since you were a little lad. But you should have got over them by this time, especially now you've got Catt, here. There's no future for you at High Moor and there never has been. And all this moping . . . why, the place has been nothing but misery for you from the very beginning. You've often said as much. Oh, I've no patience with you!'

Luke looked shaken, near to tears then, and Nell turned to cajoling. 'Come with me, lad! You know how fond we are of one another, and how well you and Tom have always got on

– not to mention Robert, your own brother. Why, it looks to me as though you might very well be a landowner, an *owner* mind you, not just a tenant, before you're forty, if you come to Canada. Doesn't Tom say there's land going begging in the west there – good, rich land, not just a scrag-end bit of heath! You could end up with a farm big enough to hold 20 High Moors! And in Canada life's freer, everyone says so. There are none of these differences you get here – differences between those who've been well-born and us ordinary folk. People are judged simply on what they are.'

Then Nell played what she was confident was her trump card.

'If you come with me, Luke, it means you can marry Catt straight away, before we sail – for there's a home in Canada ready and waiting for you both. There! How many lads in love get a chance like that, may I ask? Whereas here' – Nell shrugged contemptuously – 'you could be waiting for years before you can afford to wed – and Catt may not want to put up with that! Besides,' concluded Nell, sure that after this final sally Luke's resistance would be quite broken, 'if *you* won't come, the offer is still open for Catt to take it without you – and then where will you be?'

But Nell had not reckoned with Luke's determination – or daring. 'No, Aunt Nell. You're wrong. I don't have to decide to go to Canada before asking Catt to wed me.' He flung his arm round Catt's shoulder, his reserve quite vanished in the triumph of his decision. 'I'm asking her now – this very minute!'

He turned Catt to face him. Now she was held, almost mesmerised, by the intensity of his passion. His eyes were shining. 'Catt – dearest Catt! Will you marry me? And come with me to High Moor? I've enough money put by to pay my way with my father – and he'll surely give me a share of the farm when I go back with a wife. He always swore there'd be a welcome for me if I got wed. Oh, I know it won't be easy, but I think we could be happy . . . We'd be able to face any troubles together, and you're so strong, Catt, I know you'd help me.'

Luke's whole frame quivered with emotion. Never before had his aunt heard him talk so long and so coherently. 'Please, Catt! Darling Catt, please marry me!' His voice broke. 'Don't leave me and go away with Nell. My heart would break. I'd die without you. Truly, I love you so . . . but I can't go to Canada, and that's nothing, nothing at all, to do with loving you. You do understand, don't you?'

In the years that were to follow, Catt would often look back at this moment, and smile – thinking for the hundredth time that there could have been few more public proposals of marriage than that made by Luke there in Nell's kitchen.

At the moment it all happened, however, she simply nodded her head, blushing a little. 'Yes, Luke,' she said evenly. 'I'll marry you – and we'll go wherever you want.'

But, even as she spoke, a coldness was striking at her heart. And it persisted, was there all the while that Luke was holding her, gathered tightly in his arms. She seemed to hear a voice, deep down within her: *You would have been happy in Canada, Catt. Very happy. Happier than here . . . You know you would have been.*

However hard she tried, it was difficult to keep such misgivings from resurfacing. Catt knew that Luke had to come first – though if she could have persuaded him to go with his aunt, she would certainly have done so. She longed for Canada and the new start that it offered more than anything – except Luke. But she realised his mind was quite made up; there was no point in wishing for the impossible.

She had to be practical, face life as it was, take what she had been given and be thankful, not long for the unattainable. Luke and Canada would have been perfection. But the world – *her* world, at any rate – was far from perfect. And Luke's deep, unquestioning love for her was so precious that she simply dared not risk losing it by saying or doing anything that could somehow reveal her innermost thoughts – those thoughts of which she was so ashamed.

There were times when Catt had wondered if she were really capable of loving anyone properly since, so deep within her that she tried to deny its very existence, she still felt that infatuation for a man who was not only supposed to be a celibate priest but who was her own natural father. Never mind that, contrarily, she might feel she loathed him more than anyone else in the world – what if he had spoiled her capacity for real love for ever? Did she really love Luke, as she thought she did, or did she merely *like* him – a liking sprung, in the first instance, from gratitude? Was she simply in love with the idea of being loved – by anyone?

Luke loved *her,* of course – but was there really any future here for either of them? They were both the sort of people fated to work out their lives toiling for others.

Now Catt tried to reassure herself. Once I'm married, all these dreadful fantasies will disappear. Luke's love will smother them, and I'll be able to love him properly. Like a normal girl. There's nothing I won't do for him – I'll work every hour of the day and night, here in Yorkshire – to see we make a success of things. He and I will claw our way upwards, somehow –never mind the odds. And one day, we'll have a farm of our own without having to go all the way to Ontario for it . . . .

Aloud, she countered Nell's disappointed but increasingly muted protests. 'Don't fret, Nell. Luke and I will just have to make our fortune here. And we will! Then when you come back in your fine Canadian furs to visit us, you'll be able to stay with us in style in our very own farm.'

As she was speaking, she saw the look of gratitude and adoration in Luke's eyes. For the present, that was more than enough to blot out all the pain of knowing that she had just, quite deliberately, closed fast the door which could have opened the way forward to a new life in a new world.

9

In the years to come, Catt's regrets for what might have been were to be bitter indeed. For the present, however, far more pressing matters drove any such thoughts right out of her head. The next few weeks went by in an increasingly hectic whirl of activity, for there was a great deal to do, and not long in which to do it.

First, Luke returned to his cousin's farm, there to work out his hire-time till Michaelmas. As soon as that was complete, he would be walking the 30 miles across the moor to thrash things out with his father, and to persuade the old man to let him and Catt move in to High Moor, on a working basis, after their wedding.

'H'm!' Nell sniffed sardonically. 'If Luke can manage that, he can do anything!' She still found it hard to credit that her shy, timid nephew could summon up such courage and purpose to face his tyrannical father. At the same time, though she was sad that neither Luke nor Catt was coming to Canada with her, she was quite resigned to the fact, and harboured no resentment. Indeed, she confessed to Catt that she had felt instinctively, from the very beginning, that Luke would never agree to be parted from his beloved moors. It was only that, with Catt a part of the equation, she had dared, just briefly, to wonder if there might be the tiniest hope.

'All the Hallidays are stubborn as donkeys,' grumbled Nell. 'But at least, Catt, you got the best of the bunch. For Luke is his mother's son in everything except his pigheadedness, thank heaven! And I suppose, if I'd been in your shoes, with Luke my sweetheart, and he not prepared to budge, I'd probably

71

have done the same as you. What's all the land in Canada worth, after all, compared with the love of a really good man?'

Then Nell sighed, shaking her head. 'I wish you both all the happiness in the world, but all the same,' she went on hesitantly, not wishing to worry Catt with her forebodings, but feeling she had a duty to voice them, nonetheless, 'I do believe Canada could have been the making of the pair of you – and a much easier start to your life together than the one you're going to have here. Make no mistake, Catt – life at High Moor will be very, very hard. No matter what arrangements Luke thinks he has made with his father, mark my words – William Halliday is never going to change from the brute he is and always will be. He killed my sister with unkindness, he didn't need to poison her – ill-treatment and neglect were enough – and I'll neither forgive nor forget.'

Yes, yes, I know all this, Catt would think wearily, as Nell brought up the subject yet one more time. And I *am* afraid of what we're letting ourselves in for – I'm afraid for myself, as well as for Luke. But we'll survive. We've no choice; this is the only way forward for us. I'll work and work, she determined, until somehow I've made Luke a farmer in his own right, I swear it! Oh, maybe I haven't his burning passion – for there's something missing inside me that I can't do anything about – but, never mind, I'll show him how much I love him by the way I go about bettering him. By the time I've finished with him, he'll not be the despised, landless younger son any more, that's for sure!

She was to repeat these vows time and time again to herself, year upon year. She would succeed, she told herself, no matter what the cost was to herself. That there might also be a cost to Luke never entered her head until much, much later on.

Meanwhile, on Luke's next visit, he and Catt went to Whinborough Registry Office, to apply for a wedding licence. They fixed the date for the end of October – a few days before Nell was due to sail for Canada from Liverpool.

'Surely you could have made it in church?' cried Nell, when she heard where the wedding was to take place, shocked to the core by the thought of a registry office ceremony. Such things were newfangled in her eyes and best avoided. None of her family had ever been married this way. 'No one respectable goes to a registry office to wed,' she grumbled. 'It's mostly just lasses in the usual sort of trouble.' She gave Catt an unusually sharp glance. 'Why not go to your own church, Catt? Surely, for something like this? Something special?'

'No.' Catt was adamant. 'I'll not go near. I've done with all that, for good!' She was so firm that Nell knew there was no point in arguing further – but Catt, suddenly embarrassed by causing Nell yet another disappointment, felt bound to explain. 'If it can't be my old church – and it can't – it can't be any other, you see. It has to be the registry office. I was taught that way – and I couldn't do anything different, even now! And Luke doesn't mind. Besides' – Catt smiled – 'we both want it to be very quiet and simple. I shan't be needing a special dress or anything like that, and you and Jonah can be the witnesses. No one else will be there – I've no family and Luke's are miles away.'

And so Nell retreated, somewhat mollified.

Even so, it was not so easy to arrange even a registry office wedding in a hurry. In an effort to avoid all kinds of awkward questions, Catt lied without compunction, giving her age as twenty-one and therefore of age and independent. She hoped her severe hairstyle, worn specially for the occasion, would give the impression of a few extra years. When it came to naming her father, she gave 'Joshua Youngman, deceased,' without the slightest hesitation. That was how things had always been made to look, after all – and Josh was the one person from her past that Catt would dearly like to have had at her wedding. And when she went on to give Nell's house as her residence and her occupation as 'domestic servant', the official writing down all the particulars lost any interest he might have had in her family background and did not even give her a second glance.

As she and Luke emerged from the office, Catt sighed with relief. It would never have done if there had been any questions asked, if news of her intentions had got back to

Melchester or Leyton. All the same, from time to time teachings from the past gnawed at her: *All right. You're not marrying in some heretic church – you've saved yourself from that sin – but you know very well that a civil marriage is no marriage at all in the eyes of God* . . .

This was nonsense, Catt told herself. Surely, God – if God there was – accepted the fact that two people loved one another and were prepared to swear solemnly to stay together for the rest of their lives – it didn't need a priest to come between them, to murmur outworn ritual formulas . . . Yet the feeling of guilt persisted, and always would. In years to come, when tragedy struck, Catt would wonder increasingly: If only I'd been *properly* married – would things have turned out like this? Or am I being punished . . . ?

But for now there was so much to do that there was little time for soul-searching. Nell's lease was terminated and most of her furniture and belongings put up for sale, with a generous number of things held back to start Catt and Luke off on their married life together. 'For you'll not get a single pot nor pan from those Hallidays!' growled Nell. Luke refused point-blank to accept the money that had been sent for his passage to Canada, though Nell begged him to take it.

'Tom would have wanted you to. Since you're not staying here, you could use it to buy a few sheep – sheep of your very own,' she suggested, but even this failed to tempt Luke.

'It wouldn't be fair. Let Tom and Robert spend it – I'll find the money for sheep eventually. *They* had to make their own way – they shan't have to make mine, too!'

All the same, Luke was quite agreeable to Nell loading him and Catt with sheets and quilts and an iron bedstead and feather mattress, together with china and pewter and the family warming-pan – and a purse of sovereigns for Catt that represented part of the furniture sale. 'That's my proper present,' said Nell, 'and you must use some of it on a new dress, Catt. Even if you insist on marrying in that poky office, you ought to wear something new.'

Catt kissed Nell, but refused even this. 'No, there's no need

74

of a new dress – I'd like to keep every penny of this for our future. It can be the start of our savings towards our own farm. And as soon as we've got that,' she promised, 'I shall write to you, Nell, and you shall come back and see it – with *us* sending *you* the passage-money this time!'

If Nell had her doubts about this, she kept them well hidden. She was so happy herself, with so much to look forward to, she could not bring herself to say anything which might hurt Catt. Privately, she could see only the bleakest of futures for her nephew and his wife-to-be. Catt was strong, and determined, as Nell well knew – but how was even someone with Catt's steely resilience going to react when confronted with Luke's father and brother? Nell herself shivered with loathing at the very memory of them. How would Catt survive in that grim little farmhouse which had been a prison, then a death-trap for her own sweet sister – who had arrived there a smiling beauty and died, so it was said, looking more like a living skeleton, in misery and squalor?

The wedding morning dawned clear and bright. Catt and Luke's was the first ceremony of the day, held at the earliest permitted time. There would be few curious bystanders about then, Catt had decided – and they would have time to complete the journey to High Moor before nightfall.

After Catt's refusal to buy a wedding dress, Nell had insisted she have the dead Clarrie's best lavender gown and matching bonnet. As Catt descended the stairs, Nell clapped her hands. 'Why, you look really beautiful, Catt! You were quite right – it would have been foolish to buy new when we had this – and I know my Clarrie'd have been glad to see her best dress put to such good use. Luke will be proud of you.'

Luke had got to Whinborough the previous evening. Nell had insisted he must spend the night elsewhere to avoid the bad luck said to come to couples who spent the evening together in the same house before the wedding. So Luke put up for the night at Jonah the donkey-man's. He was in high spirits; his father, he told Catt and Nell, had proved remarkably amenable when told of the coming marriage.

'He's said we can live at High Moor – and share in the work there,' he told Nell. And, when she shook her head, half-disbelievingly, Luke grinned. 'Don't always be so suspicious, Aunt Nell! Why, Father's even said there'll be a surprise waiting for us!'

Nell grunted. Such talk did not tally at all with her ideas about Luke's father. There was bound to be a catch in it somewhere.

On the wedding day itself, Luke went out early and bought Catt a great bunch of red roses, which he handed her when he arrived at Nell's to take his aunt and his future wife to the Queen Street office. Now Catt felt like a real bride. All her life, red roses and Luke would be inextricably linked in her mind. She looked at Luke's tanned, smiling face, and the so blue eyes ablaze with love and anticipation. She longed – oh, how badly she longed! – to feel the same pitch of excitement and passion as she sensed he did. But even as she longed, even today of all days, she felt that cold hand clutching at her heart, trying to snuff out her emotions . . . the hand of Charles Leyton.

They drove to the registry office in Jonah's donkey-cart. The ceremony was very brief; they were in the drab little office no more than ten minutes, with not a flower in sight save Catt's red roses, and, as Nell later complained, a bored registrar who made it very clear that he disapproved of weddings so early in the day.

Still, nothing could mar the joy of the moment when Catt and Luke became man and wife. Now bride and groom and the two witnesses had to sign the register – Catt looked hard at Nell, willing her to keep silent at this point, while she purposely signed an 'X' against her name, like the other three present. Earlier, she had persuaded Nell, too, not to show off her new-found skill in signature-writing, either, for she had no wish to flaunt her own knowledge and show up her husband's illiteracy. Reading and writing were high on her list of priorities for 'getting Luke on', she had already decided. But there would be plenty of time for all that, later.

They returned, for the very last time, to Nell's house, for ham and eggs and fruit cake and a glass of home-made wine.

Luke went to Jonah's to get his father's borrowed horse and cart, which he had stabled there the night before, and then he and Jonah loaded everything onto it – clothes, bedding, pots and pans and furniture – and tied it all down with sacking against possible rain.

There were the final hugs and kisses, and promises from Nell that she would see that Tom wrote and told them just as soon as she reached Canada. And, of course, he would go on writing, and, well, maybe, one of these days, she might still be able to persuade them to join her! Everyone smiled and nodded, even though they all knew they were unlikely ever to see one another again.

Luke jumped up on the cart and helped Catt on after him, and they went off up the alley, towards the road that headed out from Whinborough down towards the market town of Pickerby. Catt turned to wave to Nell until they rounded a bend and she was lost to sight.

She gave a long, deep sigh. It was over. The happiest time of her life, she decided. At Whinborough she had found a real home, and in Nell a second mother – and one warmer and more generous-hearted than her real one had ever been. At Whinborough she had met the husband who was sitting beside her now. Catt remembered that first evening in the town, when she had crouched by the roadside in such misery – lost, penniless and friendless. Who could have believed then, that it would all end in such good fortune?

Back in Whinborough, Nell began her final preparations for the long journey to Canada. In a few days she would be off to Liverpool to board the boat. She was leaving with few regrets, save the sadness of knowing she would never see her daughter's grave again. Still, Catt had promised to come and tend it every year, and Nell knew Catt to be a girl of her word. She would keep that promise, to be sure – but, with all the will in the world, Nell could not imagine Catt being able to keep the other one – the promise that she would turn Luke into a prosperous farmer!

Oh, Catt would try her hardest, but eveything was against it. Nell's own life had convinced her that some people were born lucky – and that some were not. And, much though she loved them both and longed for their happiness, Nell felt, with chilling certainty, that Luke and Catt were destined to be among those who were unlucky.

10

A pale sun shone hesitantly down on the bridal couple as they
headed inland. As they travelled further away from the rocky
coast, passing through green, undulating country and a clutch
of villages, the weather grew more sultry. This landscape was
very far from the wild moorlands which Luke had described
so often and with such passion; indeed, it reminded Catt of
the Nottinghamshire fields of her childhood, and for a bitter-
sweet moment or two long-forgotten memories came
tumbling back . . . then vanished again, in her new-found
happiness.

There was a shorter way from Whinborough to Gelling,
Luke explained, cutting straight across the moor-top, but that
route was steep and would have taxed the horse, with its laden
cart, too much. And besides, he was anxious to call in at
Pickerby on the way, to introduce Catt to his sister
Susannah.

'She and I have always got on well. My father made her go
into service when she was not twelve years old – for all that my
mother was ill then, and badly needed another woman's
hands to tend her.' Luke's voice had an unusually bitter ring.
'That broke my mother's heart and I reckon it almost broke
Sue's, too. But things have turned out well for her, in the end –
her employers were good people and by and by Sue fell in love
with their game-keeper's son. Now she and John are married,
and they have their own smithy at the Gelling end of Pickerby,
and two grand little lads – you'll like them all, Catt, I'm sure
you will. And they'll certainly like you!'

It made Catt more than a little uneasy to see the contrast

between the affectionate way in which Luke always referred to his sister – and to the brother in Canada – and the attitude of virtual terror which came over him whenever he spoke of his father and eldest brother. She was certain that he was genuinely afraid of them, though he might not admit it, even to himself.

What were they going to say when she reached High Moor? Catt wondered. Oh, she knew all about Luke's going back there to tell them of his intended marriage. He was adamant that they had given this their blessing, and it was certainly true that they had lent him the horse and cart and even held out promise of a 'surprise' that would be awaiting the newly-weds. This last detail had made Catt particularly doubtful; and while Luke cherished hopes that it marked a fundamental shift in his father's attitude towards him, Catt, with her instinctive wariness of the unknown, was far less sanguine. Perhaps, she thought cynically, this new warmth sprang from the knowledge of the sovereigns she and Luke would be bringing with them, and which would be used to buy High Moor some extra stock. She guessed, too, that Luke would have praised her skills in cooking and cleaning – and these would undoubtedly hold great attraction for a household that sounded as though it had had little or no care lavished on it it since the day Luke's mother had taken to her bed for that last, agonising time.

Luke seemed to be able to boast a Halliday connection in almost every village through which they passed. In one, he told Catt, his grandfather – another Luke – who as another younger son, had been turned off the Farsyke farm on his twenty-first birthday, with a £20 inheritance and six silver spoons, had come to seek his fortune.

'Twenty pounds! That's a great deal of money now and worth more all those years back!' exclaimed Catt –'

'Maybe,' Luke shrugged. 'But it didn't come to much in the end. He had two wives, you see, and big families by each – my father's a younger son of the second one, and it's always rankled with him. My grandfather prospered for a while – my father was born in a farm he had beyond Gelling – but then his sheep came down with some disease and all perished. And there were other troubles – family quarrels and the like. We Hallidays are good at those! Anyway, old Luke lost his farm and the family scattered. He died at one of his children's homes, somewhere in Pickerby, before I was born – with not a penny to his name.'

'And the six silver spoons?' enquired Catt, intrigued.

Luke laughed. 'They went to settle a debt, I think. No one really knows. They were supposed to bring good luck – but I reckon that had run out by the time Luke got them. Our bit of the family seems fated to come to grief.'

Catt cuddled closer to her husband. 'Not any more,' she promised. 'Not now that you and I are together. I promise you, one day we'll have six silver spoons of our own – and more besides – and nothing will ever make us part with them. And that will be just the start. You and I are going to surprise the whole world!'

Luke glanced down at her eager, determined little face, radiant with its hopes. Passion overwhelmed him. He stopped the cart abruptly, leaned across and kissed her, long and hard, so that she had to push him away in the end, gasping for breath. Had they not been on such a well-travelled road, Luke would certainly have bundled Catt into the hedgerow and taken things a great deal further. He was in the grip of an emotion he barely understood. He only knew that his previous humdrum and lonely existence had been suddenly transformed beyond recognition by this tiny, vibrant woman, and he felt somehow reborn.

It was well into the afternoon when they reached Pickerby. John Carter's smithy lay at the far end of its long, broad main street. In recent years Pickerby had spread out and become a thriving market town. The busy shops, the neat rows of grey cottages, interspersed here and there with elegant red Georgian brick and the bustle of a coaching inn – all this radiated prosperity and security. Catt found it as attractive, in its own way, as Whinborough. Surely it was a good omen that she was to be living not too far from such a pleasant place!

At the smithy, their arrival was greeted with rapturous

excitement, the more so since it had been completely unexpected. There were hugs and kisses from Susannah for her new sister-in-law, and home-made wine and cakes for everyone. Susannah, fair and blue-eyed like her brother – they might almost have been twins, Catt concluded, they were so alike in both temperament and looks, though Susannah had a basic steeliness Luke so far lacked – was mockingly reproachful of their unannounced appearance.

'Why could you not have let us know you were getting married – and coming here?' she asked. 'We'd have been able to get you a proper wedding present.' Susannah rummaged in her linen-chest and finally produced a newly finished patchwork quilt, which she handed to Catt. 'Here – this will be something to be going on with,' and as Catt protested that the gift was more than enough in itself, 'I'll get you something machine-made for the next time you call – all this handwork is getting old-fashioned.'

The two toddlers were playing happily in the courtyard behind the smithy. The cottage walls blazed with creepers turning to autumnal red and yellow. In the cool little parlour, the copper glowed, the decorative ornaments shone, a clock ticked melodiously. It was all so tranquil. If only I were going to a house as happy and at peace with itself as this one! thought Catt wistfully.

Her expression must have given her thoughts away. For, as she and Luke were saying their farewells, Sue took Catt's arm and drew her to one side.

'I wish you all the happiness in the world, Catt, believe me! But I have to say it – I am afraid you are going to find that life at High Moor is very, very hard. Luke will have told you already, but even so, it's difficult for anyone who has never been there to imagine what it's like. Oh, I know there's Luke to take care of you – and he's a different person today, I've never seen him so sure of himself, you must have put a spell on him! But, where you're going to, it's hard to stay sure of anything . . . I could never go back there myself to live, not for anything.'

Susannah gave a shudder, then added earnestly: 'Please remember this, Catt; if ever you need help, any help at all

82

– shelter even, for you and yours – come here. Don't hesitate. Just come. Oh, I know you may be thinking, as we stand here now, that such things will never be – and let's hope you're right! But I mean what I say. Luke did his best – more than his best – for me when I was a child. If ever I can help him – and his family – I surely will!'

Catt was to remember Susannah's words all too thankfully, one day. But at present, she was determined to crush all her misgivings. This was not difficult to do, as they set off again, to start the long haul out of Pickerby, up onto Gelling moor.

Ahead of them were the high heather-covered hills, like some billowing purple ocean, willing her forward. The birds were singing. Catt was conscious of the warmth of Luke's body close to hers. There was nothing in the whole wide world that he and she together could not overcome . . .

It was a slow journey to the moor-top. The cart was heavy and the horse old and not too well-nourished. She and Luke jumped down and walked the last part, to lighten the load. They met scarcely another soul: another cart, going in the opposite direction, and a pedlar, most likely on his way back from Whitcar market.

The pedlar looked them over, assessed their situation, and smiled. 'What about a fairing, to bring you luck?' he wheedled hopefully.

Grinning bashfully, Luke selected a tiny white china sugar-bowl and presented it to his bride. It had on it a picture of a ruined church – Whitcar Abbey – and a gilt message: *A Present From Whitcar.*

Catt read the words aloud automatically as she turned the bowl in her hand admiringly. Then she caught Luke looking at her, and blushed. This was not the moment to tell him of her reading and writing skills!

But Luke assumed she had recognised the picture. 'I know you've never been there, but we'll go together, one of these days. And we had to buy something!' He watched the pedlar striding away in the distance, towards Pickerby. 'In these parts, you see, fairings are supposed to bring good luck to those just wed . . . Whitcar was my mother's home – that's why

I chose this for you. She and my father were married at a church just next to that ruin on the picture.'

Catt said nothing, simply nodded and put the little bowl carefully into her bag. It would be something to remember today by, long after her roses were gone – for the bridal bouquet lying on top of their possessions was already wilting, and Catt had left half of it in Pickerby as a gift for Susannah.

The sun was dropping rapidly from the sky and the heather turning to indigo as they branched off the Whitcar road just before Gelling village and made towards High Moor farm. The track here was deeply rutted and potholed, and the untended verges encroached onto the stones. It had the derelict, mournful look of a path little used. Catt shivered, and drew her shawl around her more tightly. The evening air was turning cold, and her earlier confidence was ebbing fast. Luke grabbed her hand reassuringly.

'Don't fret, Catt – we're almost there! You'll be able to rest and warm yourself then. After all, w-we're e-expected.' Catt noticed the sudden return of Luke's stammer, and recognised his underlying dread of what might be lying in store for them.

There it was, rearing up ahead of them against the setting sun, the moor falling away into a deep gorge behind it – a gaunt, grey house, with a few farm buildings tacked onto it across an arched entrance, and some run-down pens and coops alongside. In the fast-fading light it looked particularly sombre and sinister. Even the single beam of light shining from a downstairs window seemed to be mounting some kind of threat. Apart from the rattle of the horse and cart over the stones, there was not a sound to be heard. Even the birds had stopped singing.

* * *

The door flew open abruptly and Catt flinched and shrank back, half-blinded by the sudden shaft of light that hit them. An unkempt, stocky figure straddled the threshold, silhouetted against the brightness. There was a mug in his hand, and he was swaying slightly and clutching at the jamb to steady himself.

'Well, well! So here's the happy couple at last! We were beginning to think you'd turned tail at the last minute, Luke, and left the lady waiting!' Will Halliday peered sardonically at his new daughter-in-law. 'Welcome to High Moor, lass – we're having a double celebration today, and you and your man had best come in and join it, late though you may be.'

He belched loudly, took a further swig from the pewter mug and staggered inside. From within came the sound of ribald laughter, male voices mingled with a woman's high-pitched titter.

At the first sight of his father, Luke had seemed rooted to the spot. He had opened his mouth, but no words came from it. Now, however, galvanised into action, he sprang from the cart and handed Catt down. In the pool of light that spread out from the half-open door, she saw his face was deathly pale. 'It is going to be all right, really.' As Luke held her hand tightly and looked straight into her eyes, Catt sensed he was speaking to reassure himself as much as her. 'I promise – it will be all right. We'll see it's so, in the end. Only for now – try to say no more than you must . . . I think he has been drinking for hours past.'

'That was your father?' asked Catt, though knowing the answer even before she spoke. She was uneasily certain that the man who had just been bawling drunkenly at her had already predisposed himself to dislike her. Well, she was tougher than he might think, and, in spite of all that had happened, all she had been through, no one had been able to break her yet!

Catt gave a defiant toss of her head, took a deep breath and prepared to make the first steps into her new home.

She found herself in a stone-flagged kitchen, made dim and mysterious in the shadows thrown by the flickering oil-lamp. At first it was hard to pick out much detail through the tobacco-laden, harsh-smelling mist that lingered there – but Catt could see enough to take in the floor encrusted with dirt,

the flaking walls and raftered ceiling. At a long kitchen table –
also filthy with gobs of grease and remnants of meals long over
– sat the man who had just greeted them, Luke's father.
Slumped half across it, clearly even more drunk, was a
younger, dark-tousled man, and beside him, a slim, pert
woman little older than Catt herself.

Her cheeks were highly coloured; so much so that Catt
wondered if they were painted. But she was good-looking and
clearly well-aware of the fact, with rich auburn curls piled over
an ivory-white forehead. She was dressed in a gown of brilliant
blue silk which made Catt's muslin lavender look suddenly
dowdy and old-fashioned.

Will Halliday lurched unsteadily to his feet, holding onto
the table for support with one hand and giving his older son a
cuff about the ears with the other. 'Wake up, Will – you've got
the *other* newly-weds to meet before you go off to your
slumbering!' This was said with a purient snigger and a wink at
the two women. He gave Luke a grin that was at the same time
both malicious and triumphant. 'Oh yes, Luke, my lad! You
should have got home a bit sooner. Then we could have had a
double wedding. I told you there'd be a surprise awaiting you
here, did I not? And here you see it – for our Will and his Betsy
were married at Gelling church this very afternoon, by the
Bishop's special licence, if you please. None of your makeshift
government mumbo-jumbo for them, theirs was a *proper*
wedding. So now' – and the old man paused portentously –
'after having no housekeeper at all since your poor mother
died, we've got landed with two, both on the same day!' At
which he exploded into roars of laughter, young Will and
Betsy joining in with enthusiasm. 'It's Betsy Fox,' Luke
murmured in Catt's ear. 'Her father's the innkeeper at the
Horseshoe, in Gelling.' His face twisted in agony. 'Oh, Catt, I
swear I knew nothing at all about this – I never dreamt . . .' he
whispered.

But his father had caught the gist of what Luke was saying
and cut in. 'That's right, lass. He's telling the truth, he didn't
know. For it wasn't till he came rushing back here a month
ago, saying he wanted to bring home a wife, that I could coax

our Will into making an honest woman out of Betsy.' He smiled broadly displaying a mouth of blackened teeth. 'Will's my eldest, so *his* wife should be mistress of this house by rights and we don't really need another woman here. Still, I promised Luke you could come, and, as the Good Book says, we're obliged to be charitable! And I daresay Betsy can make good use of another pair of hands, at least for the present.'

Here the younger Will intervened, sounding surprisingly sober. 'But mind you understand this: my Betsy's the mistress here. Let's be quite clear about that from the start,' He stared at Catt, looking her up and down with studied insolence. 'Our Betsy's been brought up like a lady, I'll have you know. She's never had to dirty her nice white hands, and I don't want them dirtied now – so it's as well we've got you here to help her. There's a deal wants doing, too, as you can see . . .'

Here the older man must have noticed Catt first stiffen then tremble with shock and suppressed outrage, for he interposed almost placatingly: 'Well, what Will is trying to say is that we've been without a woman's touch around here for a long time now – too long, as Luke must have told you – and things have been let go a bit. Come now, the pair of you. Take a glass of port wine or some brandy and we'll all drink to you and the future.'

Catt glanced at Luke, waiting for him to reply. At first, he just stood there, ashen-faced and speechless. Then he began to stammer painfully. 'I-I-I . . .'

Betsy gave a coarse, cruel giggle. 'Still as tongue-tied as ever, Luke? Well, let's hope everything else is working, or you'll have a disappointed bride tonight – if bride she really is, after that ungodly wedding.'

A red rage swam before Catt's eyes. 'My wedding was just as lawful as yours! And at least my husband's not drunk on his wedding night!' she burst out. Then very coldly and deliberately, she went on: 'Our belongings are outside in the yard. It's dark and we're very tired. We've come a long way. We need to unload it all before we can get to bed. So there's no time tonight for wine for us. And I'll be up in good time tomorrow, I promise you, Betsy, so that you and I can make a start on the cleaning.'

She turned to old Will. 'Thank you for letting us come and live in your house. I promise you – Father – that I'll do my best to make this farmhouse the most spick and span in Gelling. Luke and I will do our fair share and more, never fear – that is, till we can get a place of our own – for I know your Will's the eldest, and now he's wed, too, he'll want the run of this place.'

'My, but you've got some spirit!' Her father-in-law looked at her with grudging admiration. Catt always looked at her most attractive when flushed and impassioned; even the rouged Betsy seemed faded by comparison. 'Who'd have thought our timid Luke would find a bold lass like you! Come then, I'll give you a hand with the cart. Will's past it tonight, I'm afraid. He and Betsy started celebrating before the wedding began and then there was a do at the inn afterwards, before they came back here . . .'

He patted Luke's shoulder with something amounting almost to affection. 'The best room's for Will and Betsy, of course, but you can have the one at the back. It's a fair size – you three lads used to share it between you once upon a time.' Turning to Catt, he explained, half-ashamedly: 'Don't judge us too harshly, lass. You'll soon get used to our wild ways. We may not have the Whinborough airs and graces but, all the same, it's not every woman who can boast of being married to a Halliday. For all we've had some bad luck lately, we're one of the oldest families in these parts – why, *we* owned most of Whinborough moor once, as Luke may have told you.'

Catt merely nodded, not trusting herself to say any more for the present. She supposed it was because she was so dreadfully, dreadfully tired – but everything around her seemed to have taken on a surreal, nightmarish quality. As if in a dream, she went through the motions of helping an equally silent Luke as he and his father emptied the cart. They manhandled Nell's brass bedstead and its feather mattress up the carpetless winding stairs and into a bare, bleak, chill room. Another prison, thought Catt. This is just another prison . . .

88

'It will all look quite different come morning,' Luke promised her, sensing her dismay. 'This room looks to the east – at sunrise you'll be able to look out, right over the moor, as far as the Bridestones and beyond.'

At last, Catt and Luke were alone together. If only, thought Catt, I could rid myself of this awful, deadening feeling of hopelessness. Forcing a smile, she said, as brightly as she could: 'Oh, we'll find a way of managing all this, Luke! Don't you worry, we'll make something of things here – until we can find a place of our own. As I told your father, we're not going to be here for ever, after all!'

But, even as she spoke, Catt saw that this was not the sort of reassurance Luke had been hoping for. 'This is my home!' Luke protested. 'I was born here – it's where I grew up – where my mother died. And there've been Hallidays here for a hundred years or more. Whatever happens I don't really want to leave.'

Catt pursed her lips. Then, speaking very gently and carefully, weighing every syllable, she said: 'But you're not wanted here, are you – not even with a wife? Your brother may be nothing better than a drunken layabout and good-for-nothing, but he know's he's the eldest son and heir, all the same – and all the advantages that gives him. And it's clear he won't be backward in pressing them. He's not going to give up anything to us, Luke. If we stay here long, we'll soon be no better than slaves. But,' she soothed, 'we can't decide anything tonight.' and she put out her hand gently stroking his cheek.

'No, not tonight,' echoed Luke. And then, all their fears, all their disappointments – everything – melted away as they touched and kissed over and over and over again. The candle flickered, spluttered and died. Luke tore off Catt's lilac dress and carried her over to the bare sheetless bed, and there they made love with such frenzied abandon that it blotted out all consciousness of the harsh drunken laughter still seeping up through the boards from the kitchen beneath.

And then, at last, they fell asleep, utterly spent and exhausted – in each other's arms. Two people, alone and lost till now, but alone and lost no longer. United, they had a strength that could surely conquer all the world's problems. Mercifully, on this occasion, Catt did not see the face of Charles Leyton come between them.

11

Catt awoke to find a pale golden dawn beckoning from the curtainless windows. As she slipped from the bed leaving Luke still asleep, and ran to look out, all she could see was mile upon mile of bare moor, not a building in sight.

Their room was at the back of the house, she remembered. Here the land fell away into a deep, wooded gully and then climbed up again to the moor beyond. Bare, purple, windswept moorland, hardly even a spindly bush there – only a line of massive dark boulders, some the size of cottages, and of every imaginable shape, straddled the horizon like a line of sentinels.

'Those are the Bridestones.' Luke had woken up and come to join her at the window. He pulled her to him, and Catt shuddered, part cold but part excited as she felt his heart beating through the rough woollen shirt. He kissed her. 'Years ago, my mother once told me, girls wanting to wed used to climb up there and touch the stones and expect to get a husband that way; and those that *were* wed went there to ask for healthy children.' He shrugged. 'But the custom's about dead now. They're just stones, nothing special about them. Sometimes professors and such come up on the train in the summer and measure them for this and that – they go back to the world's beginning, I've heard folk say.'

Catt was entranced with the story. She looked at the stones again, with new interest – they added to that fascination she had had for the moors ever since she first heard Annie talk of them, oh! so long ago it seemed now! She could not help thinking it must be a lucky omen that her first real view from

High Moor, on her first morning there as a new bride, had been of these luck-bearing landmarks.

'Maybe, later on, when we've got sorted out – and there's a spare hour of two – you and I can go there? I might try the spell!' Catt laughed. But she was surprised to see Luke stiffen slightly and turn away from her.

'They're further away than they look,' he mumbled discouragingly. 'And that old story – it's nothing but a pack of lies, really . . . how can it be otherwise? Poor Mother went and touched the Bridestones – like all the girls, in those days,' he went on, the bitterness only too apparent. 'Well, they may have brought her children – but they certainly brought her no happiness! I think it's best not to meddle with such things.'

Even as Luke was speaking, Catt felt she saw the line of the Bridestones quiver, seeming ready to begin to march towards her . . . and then? . . . Devour her . . . ? Oh, what nonsense! It was all a trick of the light, a stupid fancy!

All the same, she turned abruptly back into the bedroom. In the full light of day, its sordidness was only too obvious – the curtainless, filthy windows, the floorboards pitted with dirt. And there was their pathetic little heap of belongings piled anyhow in one corner, as they had left them last night – clothes and chairs and pans, and Nell's copper warming-pan topping the lot.

Catt crossed herself hurriedly, subconsciously seeking forgiveness for indulging in such foolish superstition. Now wholly back in the real world, she recalled her brave words of the evening before. She looked at Luke and gave a smile which she hoped concealed all the doubts that were crowding in on her.

'There's a power of cleaning to be done here – not to mention downstairs, I fancy. And I can't see that wife of your brother's being much help, since she can't soil her pretty hands . . . And *you'll* have plenty of work waiting for you outdoors, I'll be bound, for your father and your brother will have sore heads this morning, I shouldn't wonder. We'd best be up and doing.'

As she struggled into her working clothes, however, the thought persisted: All the same, I *would* like to touch the stones, whatever anyone says . . . It was as if she wanted to defy superstition, she told herself, to prove it could be treated light-heartedly – to show that even if no good came of the 'touching' no harm would either. Yes, before she left here, she *would* touch them; for this morning, Catt was even more determined than she had been last night that High Moor was going to be no more than a temporary lodging for Luke and herself. There was no possible future for them here, at the beck and call of his father and brother, that was for sure! Soon, come what may, she and Luke would have to move on again, on the next step towards acquiring a farm of their own, however humble it might be.

But it was hard to go on believing in this dream, in the hard days and weeks that followed. Sometimes Catt felt that for every step forward she and Luke took, they were thrust back at least two.

It was not for lack of trying. Oh, how they tried! On that very first morning, Catt cleaned and set their bedroom to rights even before the other occupants of the house were up; and before they went exhausted to bed that night, Luke had fixed the broken shutters and hung up Nell's warming-pan and Catt had set out the handful of ornaments they had brought from Whinborough. At least, for a few hours in each twenty four, she and Luke had somewhere to call their own. She could never be too grateful for that – without it, she was sure she would rapidly have been driven mad.

All her life she would remember what she had seen and smelt and felt when she went downstairs into the farmhouse kitchen that first morning.

It had looked squalid enough the night before, but in daylight it was far worse. There was the stench of stale tobacco and sweat and ale and brandy. The pewter mugs were still on the table. A pile of unwashed dishes stood in the stone sink. The kitchen range was rusting; it had clearly been left unleaded for years. Even the fire had burnt itself out. As Catt stepped forward to pick up the empty log-basket, she slipped on a puddle of beer and felt a frisson of pain as her knee hit the wooden table-leg. But this was far less sickening than the pain she felt in her heart – and not just pain, but fear, too. A choking pain, verging on panic. It was all so impossible! How could she and Luke ever make anything of this, however hard they tried? They would simply be overwhelmed . . .

Then she gritted her teeth, thought of Luke, already outside, milking his father's cows, and then, no doubt, going on to deal with his father's horse and his father's sheep – and even the poultry, she supposed, though she knew hens were generally considered women's work, and she would have to learn to cope with them in the future. And not a stick nor stone of this place was Luke's yet; he had no rights in it at all until he established some share by handing over the sovereigns he and she had so painfully accumulated.

While Catt and Luke laboured, Old Will and Young Will and blowsy Betsy slept on. As she worked, Catt could hear the heavy snoring above her head. It continued undiminished, even as she set to brushing and shifting furniture and clattering plates as she tried to put things to rights. She worked methodically, taking each task one by one. Gradually, as item after item was cleaned and put back in its proper place, some kind of order began to emerge. Life was looking a little brighter!

By the time Luke had finished the milking, Catt had lit the range, boiled kettles and pans, scrubbed the table clean of years of accumulated grease, even swilled the flagged floor. She was just starting the sorting of the pantry, throwing out half-empty jars of rotting food, scrubbing down the shelves, re-sorting what little was still fit to eat, when Luke came in, carrying a large pail of warm, fresh milk. He crept up behind her, silently. Then his arms were suddenly tight around her, and she was gasping with surprise and pleasure and reawakened physical desire as he covered the back of her neck with kisses. For a few short minutes the world around was forgotten.

'Why – this is a different place already!' exclaimed Luke, filled with admiration. 'This kitchen's not looked like this since – since Mother took to her bed.' His eyes clouded. 'Oh, Catt! If only she'd still been alive. Then you'd have had a real welcome – and what friends she and you would have been!'

He was so childishly pleased with what she had done that Catt had not the heart, now, to voice any of the misgivings which were building up inside her. She confined herself to remarking: 'There's a deal more needs doing, though, Luke. To begin with, all the flour's bad – I'll need fresh before I can even bake us a loaf – and that's only the start. The pantry's all but bare – everyone here seems to have been living on scraps and not much besides.' She paused. Really, it was not for her to criticise her husband's family, she knew. But, after her upbringing amid the order first of Leyton Hall, and then of Nell's well-run little household (not to mention the interlude at Miss Fredericks's, where the food had been adequate and everything clean and in its appointed place, whatever else was wrong) Catt was shocked to the core by what she had found here. How could people live so? And how could someone as uncouth as Old Will have fathered a son as gentle as her beloved Luke?

'They've been buying their food from the inn, mostly, since Mother died – and even before,' explained Luke. 'Betsy's mother's not bad-hearted. She started offering when Mother took ill – that was when all the drinking really began.' He gave a fleeting half-smile. 'But I'd never have dreamt that Will would find time between his pints to do some courting! And, somehow, Catt, I can't see Betsy ever putting her hand to much in the way of hard work. She was always full of airs and graces, even when she was a little girl. The prettiest lass in Gelling, folk used to say – and she knows it, though she's not a patch on you.'

Here Luke tried to take hold of his bride and continue with the interrupted kissing. But Catt shook him off. For the present, practical matters must come first. Lovemaking would have to be a strictly night-time luxury; there were more important things to do. Many years on, Catt would look back to this moment, and how bitter her regrets would be. How she

95

would wish, then, that she could turn back the clock and do things differently. But by then it was too late: the chance had passed.

'Not now, Luke! Hurry – go to the miller's and get us a sack of flour, and yeast from the inn, then at least we'll have a bit of bread to eat,' ordered Catt, returning to her shelf-cleaning. 'I'll have to come to some arrangement, later, with Betsy, for sharing out the housework,' she went on. 'Then it will all be much easier. We can get everything right and keep it so.'

She pooh-poohed Luke's only half-humorous shake of the head. 'Oh, yes, I'm going to do it, whatever you say – I'm not about to do the work of two women all on my own, that's for sure!'

But do it she did.

* * *

Betsy Halliday could be pleasant enough when things were going her way, but she was fundamentally lazy and self-centred. She reminded Catt of nothing so much as a handsome, inscrutable ginger cat, with her red curls and the green eyes that gave nothing away. It would usually be nearer midday than not, before Betsy sauntered downstairs, giving a feline stretch or two before summoning up the energy to brew herself a cup of tea and maybe eat a slice of Catt's new-baked bread before making off to her parents' inn on the Whitcar road. She liked company, so she told Catt, and the Horseshoe Inn attracted the passing carting traffic, so there was always something going on there – not like High Moor, which was set right off the beaten track and where visitors weren't encouraged, in any case.

Usually, Will would not be far behind his wife. He rarely had much to say to Catt, and most of his remarks had a spiteful edge. Occasionally, on days when his father awoke unusually clear-headed and lost patience with him, Will would give a grudging hand with the farm. Otherwise, he and Betsy would be gone most of the day, rarely reappearing before supper. It would be later still, should they happen to have taken the horse and cart and gone down to Pickerby, as they did quite often to get a new bit of finery for Betsy. By the time he got back to High Moor Will was invariably tipsy and often downright drunk; Betsy drank little, but spent much.

As for Old Will, though he might drink away the evenings, he worked hard on the farm during the day, and Luke worked with him. Before Luke's return, thought Catt, the old man's life must indeed have been a struggle. It was small wonder that he raged against the world as he did. Even so, it was all too clear that, despite all Luke did, despite all the hours he worked, it was never nearly enough to satisfy his father.

The older man seemed incapable of uttering a single word of thanks or praise for his son's labours; and he was quick to find fault with the most trivial detail. It was scarcely surprising, thought Catt wearily, that when she had first met him, Luke had been so shy and stuttering, so lacking in self-esteem; all the confidence had been drained from him by years of constant criticism and lovelessness.

One day, she came across a chipped daguerreotype likeness, wedged at the back of a cupboard she was tidying – and there was Luke, looking out at her through his mother's face, for this Susannah Halliday had the same defeated expression that Catt had so often seen on Luke's face after his father had been particularly cutting. Like her son, this woman must have been made to feel utterly worthless. As time went by, would she herself look the same? Catt wondered.

At present, it was true, Old Will was generally cautiously civil to her, even a little wary. He had actually thanked her for cleaning out the house at the beginning; and he would occasionally comment favourably on her smooth running of it, in a slightly bemused way. Catt would feel a stir of pity; after all, his life had been one long catalogue of frustration and disappointments. He was quite clearly a prisoner of his own bitterness. And she felt something near affection for him when, after a day at Pickerby market involving sheep-selling followed by celebratory drinking, Old Will had arrived home barely conscious, clutching a little tortoiseshell comb, which he pressed into Catt's hand.

'Here – you're not such a bad lass, for all you're a "foreigner",' he mumbled, before falling asleep over the kitchen table. Catt knew that anyone not born on High Moor was a 'foreigner' to her father-in-law.

But these feelings were quickly snuffed out by the resentment she felt when she heard Old Will mercifully castigating Luke, day in, day out; by her disgust at the violent drinking bouts with their attendant innuendoes and blatant blasphemies. As the weeks went by, Luke and Catt's efforts were increasingly taken for granted. Betsy grew more demanding and Old Will's initial gratitude all but evaporated. Sensing the change, Young Will's hostility towards both his brother and his brother's wife grew more open.

'You know, I think your brother is really quite afraid of you,' Catt whispered to Luke one night, in the blessed privacy of their bedroom. 'Indeed, I think he's afraid of both of us! Of me, because I've put the house straight and kept it so, and your father values that – and of you, because of the way you've helped make the farm pay its way again . . . He's afraid you're about to take his place.'

Guileless as ever, Luke shook his head. 'That's impossible, love. Will's prospects are safe enough – he's the eldest. The farm's his, come what may. But,' – he hesitated – 'that's not to say we won't get a share in things – if anything happened to father – in consideration of what we've put into it. That's understood . . .'

'Is it?' countered Catt; but she was not surprised when Luke made no reply. He is deluding himself, she thought uneasily. Yes, it was a fact that Luke had handed over some of the gold sovereigns which were a part justification for his being allowed back on the farm. These had enabled Old Will to replenish his sheep flock and even buy two new cows. But, in her own mind, Catt was sure that nothing had changed fundamentally. Above all, there was nothing set down in writing and she was certain there should have been.

'You should have made your father give us a receipt for our money,' she badgered Luke, in vain. 'A proper receipt – so that we had it all written down in black and white that we were entitled to a share of the farm and the takings. Without that, we've no proof of anything!'

Luke demurred. Why, his father could barely write his own name. How could he possibly have been expected to draw up a paper such as that? Besides, this was a family matter, everything was on trust.

Catt was outraged. 'We should have gone to a lawyer in Pickerby!' she cried. 'Even the best of families can fall out over land and money!' She became angrier still when Luke pointed out that his father would never, in a month of Sundays, dream of handing over good money in lawyers' fees. She was about to go on to say a great deal more, had not Luke at that moment taken her in his arms and stopped her mouth with kisses. Then everything was forgotten in the frenzy of their lovemaking, and the subject of their status at High Moor was dropped yet again. This is the way it always seemed to happen, thought Catt, ruefully, as, their passion at last totally exhausted, she snuggled close to Luke, who was already fast asleep.

Truth to tell, they were both working so hard and continuously that even their time and strength for lovemaking seemed limited – let alone the opportunity to brood over rights, real or imaginary, for very long. Catt often felt that she and Luke were running in a race where the finishing-post was set further back the more they ran.

There was no getting away from the fact that today's High Moor was a poor little farm. Its tiny strip of green pasture petered out fast into moorland scrub and heather. There was enough grass to keep a few cows, but sheep were the mainstay. The house was old and in poor repair, with none of the comforts Catt had known in Leyton, Melchester or even Nell's humble cottage in Whinborough. Water had to be drawn from an outside well and the sanitary arrangements were little better than those for the cattle. The few sticks of furniture had suffered from years of damp and neglect, and Luke implied that most of his mother's things had been sold after her death – to buy drink for the men and gowns for Betsy, no doubt, thought Catt cynically. There was not a picture in the place.

But that hardly mattered; whatever High Moor's failings, it stood in a landscape of such wild beauty that it was a painting in its own right.

The views were never the same two days running, varying with season and weather. At first, Catt never tired of staring at the changing skies and the expanse of moorland, and marvelling at their variations of mood – abandoned and carefree under the sun, solemnly brooding on grey days, mysterious in the moonlight . . . Whenever and wherever she looked, she was drawn back again and again to the Bridestones, towering above the gorge behind High Moor, and seeming to beckon . . . It was as if they possessed some secret she needed to learn, a spell she must break. Yet she was no nearer to going close to them than she had been on her first day at the farmhouse.

Now and then, spurred on by Catt, Luke would assert himself somewhat, and then Old Will would melt a little and let his younger son take Catt to market with him – in Pickerby, mostly. There Catt could go and call on Susannah, while Luke got on with farm business. For Catt, such occasions became increasingly precious. The moors continued to hold an attraction for the wilder side of her, but in the context of the farmhouse and all the ties and burdens it represented, they were fast ceasing to represent the freedom of heart and spirit she had once dreamed of. Now she began to hanker more and more for the civilisation of the little town at the moor's foot. It seemed the sun always shone there, and there were never any arguments or harsh words at Susannah's house.

As hopes that she and Luke might be able to move on to somewhere of their own seemed to be put further and further back, High Moor grew increasingly irksome. Catt became edgy, losing her temper even with Luke now and then, often over the most trivial things. Were the moors indeed becoming just another prison? Was High Moor on the way to breaking her, as it had broken Luke's mother before her? Catt was afraid, then, and sought desperately to control her nagging and complaining. She adored her husband and treasured her marriage, despite all the problems. Yet something seemed to be going wrong.

Luke had noticed the subtle change in Catt's mood; he realised she seemed more restless, less contented, whenever she returned from one of their Pickerby visits. He cursed himself for being so thoughtless; it was unfair to tantalise her with these brief glimpses of a way of life that was closed to them, at least for the present.

So next time Luke took Catt out with him, they went instead to Briddon, a village lying in a moorland hollow on the Whitcar side of Gelling – a pretty, peaceful little place, nestling beside a stream and a watermill, as charming in its way as Pickerby but with no Susannah and her laughing family to start Catt dreaming of the impossible.

Luke left Catt to wander through the village while he went off to arrange a sheep sale. But the day was very hot: she quickly tired of the main street and wandered down towards the river in search of some shade. She began to wish she was in Pickerby, and not here at all. She was sure the heat was making her giddy. When she saw the cool, inviting open door of what appeared to be some public hall, she hurried inside.

Then stood, transfixed. The smell of incense washed over her. In the gloom, she slowly made out the high altar, candles, a large gilt crucifix; on her left, was a statue of Our Lady. She had stumbled upon a Catholic church, here, in this little village – in the middle of nowhere!

It suddenly struck Catt that, wherever she went, her Church seemed to follow her; however much she denied it, it reached out . . . Instinctively, she lifted a hand to cross herself – then realised what she was doing and stumbled out, hurrying as if from some awful physical danger, into the arms of Luke, who was coming to look for her.

Why yes, he said, stroking her hair and wondering why she was so upset, Briddon was famous for being a Catholic village! There were a number like it on these moors. Had he not told her all this before? No? Well, Briddon was where the Hallidays had lived, hundreds of years back – in the days when they were said to have possessed both rich lands and the Catholic faith. It was something of a mystery why they had

101

moved away – but move they all had, in the end. Some of the family had gone over to the Protestant Church, like those at Farsyke; others had drifted to Gelling and kept the old religion for a time, while getting steadily poorer, like that cousin of his father's.

He looked at Catt's pale, strained face. 'I never thought you'd be upset like this. I asked Father to let me do the Briddon business, instead of going to Pickerby, because lately you always seem so sad on getting back from there. I wondered if all Sue's chatter was becoming a bit of a burden.'

'A burden?' Catt shook her head vigorously. 'Oh, no! Just the opposite! I always love going to Pickerby. It's – it's the coming back from somewhere so happy that hurts.' She shuddered ever so slightly; the giddiness seemed to be coming back. 'Don't bring me here again, Luke. Please! With this church . . . it makes me feel hunted, somehow.'

But how could she possibly expect Luke to understand? How could he know the welter of conflicting emotions aroused in her by the sight of the church which had once been so much a part of her? However hard she tried to distance herself from it, she could not rid herself of it – and it rekindled the image of her real father, who had once been for her the embodiment of all that church stood for. Only now, that image had changed to something monstrous, to something which was coming between her and Luke . . .

She struggled to appear calm and self-possessed, but her father's face swam before her. She felt his eyes boring deep into her very soul. She swayed, fought desperately for breath, then fainted dead away.

12

It was after this that Catt realised she must be pregnant.

Luke was quite beside himself with joy and excitement and wanted to tell the whole world the news straight away – which meant, in practice, his immediate family, since the Hallidays, as Catt had discovered, had few contacts, except essential business ones, with anyone else. But Catt begged him to keep things secret a little longer. She was determined that one particular thing had to be done first. It was something quite irrational, but something on which she had set her heart ever since that morning when she had looked out of the window at High Moor and seen them for the very first time.

'The Bridestones! Take me to the Bridestones first, Luke, please! I never had the chance to touch them and do my wishing before I got married, so I'd like to do it now – before the baby is born,' Catt smiled a little sheepishly. 'You know how they fascinate me. Every morning, on waking, they're the first thing I see – apart from you, of course! Sometimes I almost fancy they live and breathe, like we do . . . One day they seem to be so close, they're almost in our yard. Other times they're more distant. It's all on account of the weather, I suppose, but it makes them seem almost human. I get the feeling they're trying to say something to me.'

And, said Catt to herself, a visit to those heathen stones will teach that old faith that keeps chasing after me long after I've cast it off that it's finally lost its hold on me. However, she made no mention of this to Luke; she sensed how shocked such sentiments would make him. This, she knew, was a part of her which he could never really understand.

Luke's reaction was, as she had anticipated, highly sceptical. 'Are you sure, Catt? It's a rough walk up to the stones. The whole thing is nothing but old superstition. And best forgotten, I would think . . . I told you, my mother got no good from them at all! Oh! I know the stones don't mean anything – how can they? But I still think it's wrong to meddle with bygone things.'

But Catt had made up her mind. She had quite convinced herself that this act of defiance, as she saw it, would finally cut her free from all those inconvenient remnants of her old beliefs – and maybe also banish forever that shadowy figure who, with the passage of time, seemed to place himself more, and not less, between Luke and herself.

Oh, Luke, she thought sadly, how little you really know about me! For Luke had no inkling of that stranger present at the very heart of their lovemaking; he could not guess that when Catt cried out in the moment of passionate climax, she was crying not just to him but to the phantom lover who was ravishing his own daughter . . . How she hated herself for harbouring such fantasies! But they refused to go away. Perhaps the Bridestones, symbol of so much that was primitive and forbidden, could exorcise them where everything else had failed.

In the end, of course, Luke grudgingly agreed to Catt's idea. His underlying misgivings remained – but it did not do to cross a woman who was in Catt's 'condition', he believed.

So, one fine morning a few days later, Catt and Luke slipped quietly out of the sleeping house and set off across the moor, hand in hand. The way to the Bridestones from High Moor led first down a steep track into a narrow green valley. It reminded Catt of the old stories she had been told about Paradise – for down here, everything was serene, peaceful, unworldly. Only the beck's babble and the birdsong broke the dawn silence. The ground was shelterted from the breezes that buffeted the moors, and the grass green and lush, ablaze with poppies, daisies and buttercups. Once through the valley, they had to toil up the gorge again, crossing the beck to reach the moor on the far side. Flowers gave way to stones and heath, and the wind blew cold. For the first time, they realised how the dew had soaked them.

Suddenly there they were – the Bridestones, ahead and above them, strung out along a sheep-walk, towering, misshapen chunks of primeval black rock, like so many massive beads in a giant's necklace. Now she was so close to them, Catt felt their powerful magnetism more strongly than ever; she broke from Luke and raced through the heather to the nearest stone, laughing hysterically. Reaching it, arms outstretched, she flung herself against it. She could feel her heart beating wildly; some primitive force seemed to be gripping her fast, so that it was difficult to tear herself away and face Luke triumphantly.

'There! I've done it! I've done my wishing at the Bridestones! Now it's your turn.'

Luke hung back, reluctant, till an ecstatic Catt reached out and dragged him forward. Putting his hand on the stone, he did indeed then wish for the safe delivery of a healthy child – but, all the while, he worried that indulging in such doings here might, somehow, be courting bad luck, rather than good.

At that moment, like some sinister sign of troubles to come, the sun vanished behind a cloud. Others raced in across the sky, black and threatening, and by the time Catt and Luke had reached the shelter of High Moor once more, the storm had caught them up and they were soaked to the skin.

Old William was standing at the door, waiting for them. He was more concerned by the lack of breakfast on the table than by their sodden clothes.

Catt's excitement was quite undampened; the run through the storm had heightened her colour, made her almost pretty. She smiled at her father-in-law. 'Tell him, Luke! Tell him why we went to the stones! Or shall I?'

So Luke told his father their good news, somewhat bashfully, and somehow it seemed rather diminished and less world-shattering as the puddles dripped down from their clothes onto the cold stone floor of the kitchen, and Catt began to shiver and sneeze. But Old William was pleased enough in his phlegmatic way. Later that day he shambled up to Catt and held out his hand.

'This belonged to Luke's mother,' he explained gruffly. 'She came to me with nothing – and she left me with nothing, except this. She was a silly, weak thing, but I was fond of her, whatever you may have heard – and she was a good mother, too, till that last sickness . . . I promised this should go to the first daughter-in-law to make me a grandfather' – and more cheerfully – 'you'd best make sure it's a fine spanking lad, to help us on the farm, for my working days are nigh past!'

He had given her a little gilt locket, empty now. Maybe once it had held a lock of hair. Catt determined it should soon hold one of Luke's – or better still, a picture of him. There was a man in Pickerby who took photographs – they were all the fashion now, and not beyond the reach of ordinary people. Sometime, she would have to persuade Luke to go to his studio . . .

But this idea soon got pushed into the background under the mountain of work which now faced her.

News of the coming baby, while it had softened Old Will somewhat, merely served to infuriate Young Will and Betsy. They had no such announcement to make and none likely in the immediate future, so it seemed. In their disappointment and envy, they proceeded to make Catt and Luke's lives even harder than before.

Young Will had never made any secret, right from the beginning, that he disliked Catt and resented her presence at High Moor. But up to now Betsy, idle and feckless though she might be, had generally been fairly pleasant. Now her jealousy seemed to blight her whole nature.

She and her husband took to using the farm more and more simply as a convenient place in which to eat and sleep. Catt could have sworn that they deliberately dropped dishes, soiled floors and furniture, ate the larder bare. In addition, they seemed to have embarked on a policy of keeping Old Will permanently tipsy, in order to make it easier to poison his mind against her, she decided ruefully.

So Catt found herself working harder than before, at a time

when even a little easing of the burden would have been more than welcome. She was often hard put to it to balance the household budget, though balance it she always did, and with a little to spare – a very different state of affairs than that existing when she and Luke had arrived at High Moor. Then, they had been faced with constant debts, even if most of them were not large in themselves.

Those had all been paid off. But Luke was now running the farm virtually single-handed. There was no time to visit Susannah any more; no time even to think of getting Luke's photograph taken; neither time nor energy to continue the reading and writing lessons which Catt had started giving Luke in the evenings, with such enthusiasm, soon after their arrival. He could sign his name and read a few words now – further progress would have to wait. Nor was there time for any more abandoned dalliance with the Bridestones.

Now and then, Catt would catch sight of herself in the pewter-rimmed mirror that had once been Nell's and wonder that Luke could see anything in her any more – a plain, tired young woman in a shabby dress and broken boots, with a thickening waist and red chapped hands.

However, under Luke and Catt's care, the farm was prospering in a way it had not done for years. With the debts all settled, more gold sovereigns were able to join the little hoard which Catt kept hidden under the floorboards in their bedroom, alongside Josh's rosary beads. These represented their share of the farm profits – and there had been money over to buy some new farm tools and a few essentials for the kitchen, even though Catt felt that far too much of the new-found income was diverted to Betsy's new finery and prolonged sessions for the two Williams – accompanied, more often than not, by Betsy – at the Horseshoe Inn.

Luckily, Catt's pregnancy was an easy one. She went to bed dog-tired each night, but at least her exhaustion gave her less opportunity to brood, and the awful dreams in which her father invariably featured were fewer these days. Hard work had never frightened her, and she had to admit that, fundamentally, she had never felt healthier. One evening she sat up late, by the side of the bed, and wrote a long letter to Nell in Canada; most likely it would not get there until well after the baby was born, she knew, but she wanted Nell, more than anyone, to hear the good news. Oh, if only she had Nell to talk to, to confide in, now!

One day Susannah surprised her by coming all the way up from Pickerby. She had heard the news of the coming happy event from an acquaintance of Old Will's who had happened to stop at the forge for his horse to be shod. In her anxiety to share in Catt's pleasure, Susannah had broken the rule she had kept since her marriage – never to visit High Moor again except on matters of life and death – and she arrived on the doorstep with a bundle of outgrown baby clothes and all manner of good advice. She drew Luke to one side.

'This is no place for a birth. Send Catt to us a week or two before the baby's due. I can look after her properly.'

At first, Catt refused to contemplate such a thing. She did not want to leave Luke at the mercy of his family, tempted though she was by the tranquil friendliness and comfort of the forge. But Luke insisted she should do as Susannah suggested.

'You'll need a woman's helping hands, Catt – and you know Betsy's no use at all. I shan't be able to leave the farm much during the day.'

So it was all arranged. But, in the event, things were to turn out rather differently than planned.

*　*　*

A harsh and exceptionally cold winter was followed by an uncertain spring. During the worst of the snows, Luke was out alone on the top of the moor time after time in the dark and the blizzards, gathering in stray sheep. Catt had heard tales of shepherds in these parts perishing in the drifts alongside their flocks. She could never sleep easy when her husband was not by her side.

Nevertheless, despite all her work and worries, Catt bloomed and plumped through her pregnancy, her sharp little face becoming quite rounded and bonny. Luke, however, had grown thinner by the winter's end, and developed a persistent rasping cough which even the March sun could not seem to shift fully.

Then lambing began. That meant more all-night vigils on the moor for Luke. He shrugged them off. 'I like it, love – even though I wish I hadn't to leave you so often, especially now.'

Sometimes Catt found herself becoming quite jealous of Luke's sheep; he knew each animal individually, and grieved for any stillborn lamb or dead ewe as if for a human being. 'I only hope you'll be as fussy about *our* baby!' she would say to him, only half-seriously.

But in her heart Catt knew herself secure in Luke's love; even though she also knew that until she entered his life, Luke's sheep had been almost his only certain source of affection. No wonder his shepherding skills were known for miles around! With his limitless capacity for love, he would make a wonderful father – and that was just as well, she thought, for this child would badly need the display of affection she always found so difficult to show. Only in her lovemaking could Catt demonstrate to the full how much she adored her husband – and then, for her, all too often these precious moments were tainted by the recurring twisted images of Charles Leyton.

In Luke's skilled hands, the lambing went well. And the prospect of a new grandchiild had made Old Will a little mellower. However, Young Will and his wife continued to exploit Catt quite mercilessly – Betsy, in moments of particular spite, was even liable to set Catt extra tasks and stand gloating while she did them. But Catt was generally too wrapped up in herself, Luke and the coming baby to pay much attention. No longer did she talk to Luke of High Moor being just a temporary place of passage; until the baby was born there was no possibility of a move. So for the moment this potentially divisive topic lay dormant.

Then, one afternoon in early May, when the sky was a pale and cloudless blue and the air heavy with the scent of gorse and hawthorn blossom, a stranger arrived at High Moor. A stranger to Catt, at least.

She was surprised to hear the knock on the door. Visitors rarely came this way, for High Moor had a long-standing reputation as an unwelcoming place. Even pedlars avoided it. Who could this be?

When she saw a middle-aged, sober-suited man standing on the doorstep, she stiffened, and fought to control her rising panic. A priest! But what in the world was a priest doing here? Could her Church never let go? Yet no one here knew her secret besides Luke . . .

The stranger smiled and raised his hat. 'May I have a few words with you, Mrs Halliday? I'm James Newland, the Gelling parson. We've never met – but I married your brother and sister-in-law, so I do know something about your family.'

As Catt stayed silent, at a loss to know what to say, Mr Newland continued, half-apologetically: 'I'm afraid I have kept my distance because it's well-known that your father-in-law has little truck with the Church, save for weddings and suchlike. I believe he once even threatened to horsewhip my predecessor! But a parishioner told me of your – condition – and also that you were a stranger here, and I felt it my duty to call.'

The Protestant parson! Greatly relieved, Catt motioned him into her spotless kitchen. She wondered who had mentioned her to him. She herself rarely went into Gelling village, for the farm was reasonably self-sufficient. Luke or Will always picked up the flour from the miller's, but Catt went to the grocer's and the cobbler's now and then, and often looked longingly at the gowns on the dummies in the dressmaker's window opposite the parish church.

She had never been inside the church itself, of course. To do that would have been considered a sin, and although Catt considered herself now quite outside her own Church, she clung obstinately to many of the customs of her childhood. She was not really sure that she ought to be speaking to this heretical minister, pleasant though he undoubtedly was.

Her visitor's voice cut in on her thoughts. 'I really came to assure you that I shall be delighted to baptise your child when the time comes. You must send word, when the birth takes place.'

'No!' Catt was so appalled that the denial sprang spontaneously from her lips. Then, aware of the clergyman's puzzled surprise, she explained, more calmly, 'I beg your pardon . . . I know you mean to be kind. But I am not a member of your Church.'

Mr Newlands rose to his feet, smiling. 'Then it's I who should be apologising for interfering. I had no idea. Certainly I've no wish at all to poach. The Methodist minister and I are good friends, of course. Shall I ask him to call on you?'

'I'm not chapel, either!' Catt flushed, feeling increasingly trapped. There was nothing for it but to tell the truth, she decided reluctantly. 'I was born a Catholic, but I don't go to church any more. All the same, any child of mine could never have anything but a Catholic baptism.'

There it all seemed to end, quite amicably. The parson took his leave, assuring Catt of his good wishes for her future. She had found him pleasant and friendly; it was not often she had a chance to speak to anyone outside the family circle. It was a pity she had had to send him away with a refusal.

Catt was not to know that at the gate leading out from the farm onto the Whitcar road, Mr Newland had encountered Old William. The latter was on his way home from a drinking session at the Horseshoe, and feeling rather more anticlerical than usual as a result. 'What business have you been doing here?' he demanded aggressively.

'I came to offer your daughter-in-law my services at the christening, when it takes place. No one had told me she was a Roman Catholic, or I would not have intruded, of course.'

The remainder of the explanation was drowned by Old William's howl of almost demonic fury. Before he was fully aware of what was happening, the unfortunate clergyman found himself the victim of a punch which left him sprawling in the dust.

'Get off my land! Get off it this instant, you lying bastard!

And don't come near here again if you value your health and strength! There are no papists in my family now, as you well know – and though she's a foreigner to these parts, our Catt's not a bad lass. I'll not have her name blackened by such foul slander.' Old William had paused to draw breath and then added, as an afterthought, 'We'll do all we need to do at the chapel, in future!'

With that, he lurched straight on to the farm, leaving a discomforted Mr Newland to struggle to his feet and make his way ruefully back to his vicarage, nursing a bleeding nose.

Catt was at her range when her father-in-law came storming in, half-angry, half-triumphant. 'I've just had a pretty pack of lies from the parson,' he announced. 'I always knew the fellow was a poor thing from the city but I didn't know he told fairy tales, too! Would you credit it, Catt – he tried to make out to me you were a papist.'

Catt sensed disaster looming. She swallowed hard. 'What did you say to that, Father?'

'What did I say? Well, not a lot, but I hit him fair and square.' Old Will grinned at the memory. He had forgotten he could still carry such a punch. 'And I told him to keep away from now on. My grandson can be christened at the chapel.'

Now there was no escaping the truth! Catt was, even nowadays, far more terrified of what she saw as mortal sin than of her father-in-law. 'But – Father – he was only telling the truth.' She paused nervously, watching Old Will's expression change slowly from incredulity to anger. 'At least – almost. It's true I was born a Catholic, so I suppose I'll always be one in a way. But I don't go to Mass any longer, I never shall again. Still, I couldn't have any baby of mine baptised in a Protestant chapel.'

Now it was Catt's turn to bear the full brunt of Old Will's rage. Blinded by his fury, he struck out at her, catching her off balance. She fell to the stone floor, her head striking the wooden table. As she clung to it, trying to pull herself back onto her feet, the old man hit her, again and again. Then he kicked her, and he might have gone on and kicked her into

112

oblivion, had not Young Will and Betsy happened to come in at that moment. Between them, they managed to drag him away from her.

While Old Will's drinking had made him doubly aggressive, his son seemed, by contrast, more affable than usual. 'Now then, Father, surely she's not that bad.'

'Isn't she then? She's a bloody papist, if you want to know – a bloody papist, who's bewitched our Luke and wants to do the same for my grandson.' But Old Will was fast losing his fire and becoming more and more comatose. Betsy, showing a degree of sympathy, for once, and consumed with curiosity into the bargain, was able to help Catt upstairs to the bedroom, while Will steered his father to his usual chair by the kitchen range. There the old man fell asleep almost at once, snoring stentoriously.

Catt lay on her bed, barely conscious, cocooned by pain. She heard Betsy and Young Will talking to her, but their voices were faint, seeming to come from far away. 'You'll feel better in a while . . . He didn't mean to hurt you, you know – it's just that dreadful temper of his . . . Are you really a Catholic? My, you'd have done better to keep quiet on that one, he's like a madman on the subject . . . He's old, and the worse for drink. You have to make allowances . . .'

Catt could not answer. Something very strange was happening to her body; all these terrible pains could not simply be the result of Will's kicks and cuffs. She tried to raise herself on one elbow, but slumped back, gasping, as another wave of pain hit her. 'Betsy, I think it's the baby – I think the baby's coming, go and get the doctor . . .'

But Betsy and Young Will could not understand. 'No, Catt, it's just the drubbing he gave you! It's much too early for the baby yet.'

Betsy tried to make light of the matter. It would never do, she thought, for the doctor to see Catt's bruises. 'You rest a bit. I'll get some tea. And, with unusual energy, she disappeared downstairs, Will stumbling after her.

The room was very quiet. Catt could hear her own uneven breathing, and the sound of a fly monotonously hitting the window-pane in its frantic efforts to escape. A prisoner, just like me, she thought, and managed to stagger to the window, open the catch and let the sufferer out. For a moment the pain eased; perhaps Betsy had been right and it was simply shock and bruising. But no – back it came, worse than ever. Catt bit her lip till the blood ran, trying to stop herself from crying out, curling up her body in an attempt to deaden it. Her brow was wet with sweat, yet her feet felt deathly cold.

If only Luke were here! But she knew he was far away in the pasture below the Bridestones and not expected back till dusk. For Luke would understand what was happening, he would know exactly what to do . . . he would soothe her, get help.

When Betsy brought up the tea, Catt pleaded: 'Can you not get Will to fetch Luke? Please?'

All in vain. Betsy's short-lived sympathy had evaporated. 'Get this down you and stop whining! You're not the first woman Old Will's struck, you know – his wife got a hiding more days than not, so I've heard. You were mad to upset him so – you know what a temper he has – and he'll never forgive you!'

And I shan't be forgiving him, either, thought Catt. They had left her alone again. The room seemed to be getting ever hotter; she felt close to suffocating. The pain returned, sharper and more frequent. She heard someone moaning, then realised with a shock that she was listening to her own voice. She tried shouting, but the sound died in her throat. Surely, soon, someone would come and help her?

But no one did. Old Will snored on, and Betsy and Will opened the bottle of port they had brought back from the Horseshoe.

It was fortunate indeed that Luke happened to get back a little earlier than usual, to be told that Catt had had 'a sort of fall'. When he rushed upstairs he found his wife far gone in labour – and it was only now that Young Will, finally convinced of the seriousness of the situation, saddled the horse and set off to get the doctor.

He came just in time to deliver the two tiny babies – the one

114

living and the one dead. Or so the doctor said. For Catt, exhausted as she was, still clung tenaciously to the little waxen creature wrapped in the strip of torn sheeting and refused to let go.

'Get me some water, Luke. A bowl of water,' she begged him – and to humour her, he did so.

Catt dipped her fingers in the bowl. She made the sign of the cross on the baby's tiny cold forehead – just as she had seen Charles Leyton do at countless baptisms in Leyton chapel, long ago – and said shakily, 'I baptise thee, Luke, in the name of the Father, the Son and the Holy Spirit. . .'

Then she held the baby out to her husband. 'Now you can take him away,' she murmured. 'He is baptised now, and can go straight to the angels.'

Catt seemed scarcely concerned to glance at the living baby. This was a little girl, small but healthy, and already showing a hint of her Leyton grandfather's imperious features. Instead, she sank back on the pillows with a sigh, and, clutching fast to Luke's hand, fell into a mercifully dreamless sleep.

13

Catt's sleep was short-lived. Soon little Kate was awake and grizzling, and needing feeding. But Luke was there now, beside his wife, ready to talk and care and comfort. He gazed spellbound at his little daughter, scarcely able to drag his eyes away from her.

'My, but she's bonny, Catt! Just like her mother.' All too aware of Catt's blank, stricken face, he put his arm around her and pressed his cheek close to hers, murmuring soothingly: 'I know – it was heart-breaking to lose the little lad. I'm as sad as you. But, after all, we're both young, there'll surely be other babies, more sons . . .' So many babies never lived beyond their first day, Luke comforted himself – then clumsily tried to raise Catt's spirits by trying to lighten things a little. 'In any case, we hadn't bargained on having two at once, had we? I'd only made the one cradle.'

Catt remained quite unconsolable. She shook her head. 'No one – no other child – will ever be able to take that first baby's place for me,' she declared. 'I'd so badly wanted our first child to be a boy – a boy like you, Luke – and so he was, until . . .'

By now she was feeling a little less drained, and as her strength returned, so did her anger. 'Our son ought to have lived! And he would have done, I'm quite sure of it, if only things had gone right. If only I'd been in Pickerby for the month's end, as I should have been. If only your father hadn't struck me as he did. If only Betsy had called the doctor when I asked her . . . Don't you see, Luke?' Catt's voice rose almost to screaming in a crescendo of grief. 'Our baby was strangled by

116

his very own birth-cord. He never had a chance! And' – as the grief gave way before that new, implacable hatred – 'it was your father who saw to that. After all you – and I – had done for him and his precious farm, he murdered his own grandson!'

'No, no.' At first, Luke tried to protest. Surely, he thought, these wild accusations were little more than the wanderings of a woman exhausted after the labours of childbirth and temporarily unbalanced by sadness at a baby's death. The rest of his family had taken care not to tell either him or the doctor of the fearful happenings which had precipitated the events of the previous evening. He had noticed, of course, how they had all kept well clear of Catt's room since his own return, but had thought little of it. After all, his father and brother would never have dreamt of intruding on a woman in childbirth – and as for Betsy, who might normally have been expected to help, well, she was notoriously impractical and idle where domestic matters were concerned.

Very slowly and deliberately, Catt began to tell the whole sorry story. She started dispassionately enough, but by the time she had reached the wretched end of it, her emotions had got the better of her again, and she was almost hysterical.

'I can't stay here any longer!' she cried. 'You must see that, Luke, surely? Not after what has happened. You have got to take me away – at once. I've done my best, my very best – but it is no good . . . Your father won't want me here, anyway, after yesterday. If you don't act first, he will turn me out himself. For I do believe he thinks me bewitched – and bad, through and through. Oh, I know there's no reason in it – but there it is. I saw how he looked at me yesterday. I was terrified then . . . and just the memory of it terrifies me now. He hates me, me and everything to do with me – and he always will!'

Luke longed to believe otherwise – but in his heart, he admitted sadly, he knew that Catt was right. His father could be totally irrational, especially on religious matters. The fact that the dead baby was a boy could only make matters worse. Old Will had been expecting a live grandson, and he would blame Catt, and not himself, for the disappointment. A boy was our best hope for our future here, he thought, and now that's gone . . .

Still, whatever had to be decided for the future, Catt was in no condition to be moved straight away. For the present, she would have to stay here, surely.

'I'll take the cart and go into Pickerby as soon as it's light,' Luke promised. 'Will and Father will have to manage alone until I get back – as they did before you and I came here. I'll ask Susannah if she can come back with me for a few days. She'll look after you until you're back on your feet again. I'm sure she won't refuse me, when she knows how bad things are – for Betsy is worse than useless, even if she weren't so jealous.'

'No!' Catt's explosion of fear and fury gave her an almost demented look. 'No! I can't stay – not even with Susannah here! Not another day! I'm too scared. Oh, Luke,' she cried, grabbing his hands, refusing to let go, 'let's leave *now*. Now – while they're all still asleep. The two – no, the three of us.' Almost as an afterthought, she glanced down at her little daughter sleeping so peacefully in the crib beside her bed.

As Luke still remained silent, Catt persisted.

'Please, Luke! For it's the only answer. Things will never be right while I stay here. And I'm perfectly well able to travel. Besides, think how much better I'd be looked after once I got to the forge – there's a doctor living just near, and Susannah to see to things. And she did tell me, that very first day I met her, that I was to come to her if I ever needed to – and I need to now.'

Within the hour, Luke was carrying Catt in his arms, handling her carefully into the cart. He'd made her as comfortable a place to sit there as he could. Catt held little Kate close to her breast, and Susannah's patchwork quilt was wrapped tightly round the pair of them to keep out the night cold. Catt had taken her own and the baby's clothes with her, and the baby's cradle, and a few little odds and ends and trinkets, including Nell's warming-pan – Catt's favourite reminder of her happy days at Whinborough.

'You'll need everything else here, Luke, till you can find us a new place.' Catt spoke with confidence. Once the decision that she should leave High Moor at once had been agreed, she seemed to have acquired new energy and strength. Luke looked at her hard and long. The pallid woman lying back on the pillows had been transformed into someone almost radiant, her face flushed with excitement and anticipation. – Well, he hoped devoutly it *was* excitement, and not the first signs of that dreadful fever that carried away so many new mothers.

The horse's hoofs rang out in the stillness of the night's end. The moor enclosed them, dark and shadowy and, to the overwrought Catt, more than faintly threatening. As they crossed the yard, the Bridestones stood out against the lightening sky.

Catt caught her breath sharply. The new-found colour drained from her face. 'If only I hadn't gone there! I should never have made you take me to those stones, Luke. You were right, it *was* a foolish superstition – but a wicked one.' She gave a half-sob. 'I was so happy that day, so very happy – and I thought I was so clever, too, laughing at God like that. But now I've paid for it, haven't I – and so has our little lad.' Her voice broke. 'The Bridestones wanted a human sacrifice, didn't they? And we gave it them – or rather, I did, for you never wanted to go there at all. It was all my doing.'

Luke could find no words to answer immediately. He urged the horse faster, anxious to get the Bridestones behind them and out of sight. Only then did he speak, trying to reassure. 'It's nothing but an old tale, Catt – for how could lifeless stones possibly harm a baby? There's no power in them – only what some silly folks imagine.' He attempted to steer the conversation onto safer ground. 'We'll be having to knock Susannah up, I don't doubt. We're a bit early in the day, even for a smithy. You know I'll not be able to visit you much – not with the farm so busy, and you know what Father's like.'

Only now did it strike Catt that while she would be safe in the warmth and security of Pickerby Forge, Luke would have to return to the life at High Moor, with all the explanations and excuses that this would involve – and the curses and recriminations that would invariably follow. And these, she knew, would go on and on and on. She was horrified by her own thoughtlessness. How could she even think of leaving Luke alone like this?

But she managed to overcome her misgivings. After all, she told herself, it would all be for the best in the end, for Luke, as well as for her. High Moor had never held any real future for him, she was sure of that now. The problem went deeper than Old Will's resentment of her and all she stood for. No, her leaving now, like this, could be the means of her and Luke making a new start with real prospects.

She spoke her thought aloud. 'You'll start looking for another place – whenever you've time to spare – straight away, won't you? That's the most important thing – more important than your trying to come and see me, and Kate, that often. We can manage – so long as I know you're looking.'

'I'm bound to Father till Michaelmas,' Luke reminded her. 'And farm jobs aren't easy to come by at present, round here. And it's especially hard for a man with a wife and child – for there has to be a cottage with the job, you see. Besides' – he frowned, and sighed ruefully – 'I think it's quite likely Father will turn me out as soon as I get back to the farm this morning – after all that's happened. Times are going to be very hard, Catt. Harder than ever. That's for sure.'

Catt did not respond. Now that she had begun, once again, to plan their future, this time with High Moor no longer any part of it, she really wanted Luke away from there for good as soon as was humanly possible, whatever the consequences. Why should he be bound to his father for even a day longer, after what had happened?

But she knew this was unrealistic. Luke was right; farm jobs, especially shepherding, at which Luke excelled, were becoming scarcer during the present agricultural slump. He would do well to stay at High Moor till Michaelmass if he could, unpleasant though it might be. Their own savings, too, were still pitifully small – and it was only at this point in her thinking that Catt remembered that she had left High Moor in such haste and distress that she had quite forgotten to bring with her the little pile of sovereigns which, along with Josh's beads, were hidden beneath their bedroom boards! Oh, well, surely they were safe enough. No one else knew they were there – and in any case, family did not steal from family. All the same . . .

'Best bring our sovereigns to Pickerby, love, when you do next come to see me,' she said, trying to sound calm and unruffled. 'They shouldn't stay where they are, not with me away and you out of the farmhouse all day.'

When Luke got back to his father's farm, later that morning, however, he found the money already gone. His father and brother, roused by the sound of the cart leaving the yard, had crept upstairs, seen the empty room and spied the loose floorboard. As well as pocketing the sovereigns, Old Will had torn Josh's little rosary apart in a fresh outpouring of frenzied anger. Luke found the wooden beads spilled irreparably all over the floor; there was nothing to be done but to throw them away and hope against hope that Catt would have forgotten they had ever existed.

*   *   *

It was several weeks before Luke could bring himself to tell Catt about this, and even then it was circumstances which forced the revelation out of him.

Meanwhile, Catt, happily oblivious of the loss of their nest egg, remained at the forge. She and baby Kate bloomed. Life at Susannah's flowed along serenely and smoothly. Here there were no drunken tantrums, no bitter jibes and innuendoes, no feeling, whenever you ventured out, that folk were looking down at you as someone from a place that was not all it should be. John and Susannah Carter were a kind, steady couple, open and uncomplicated. They had a wide circle of friends and acquaintances, so that there was a constant stream of visitors through the smithy's little front parlour to admire the new baby. Catt was showered with little gifts for Kate from people she had never even met before.

121

If only Luke could have been here, her happiness would have been complete! It was not just his company she was missing – his love and affection – it was the gnawing worry she had that, in abandoning him for the safety of Pickerby, she had left him more vulnerable than ever to the unkindnesses and injustices of his family at High Moor.

But there's no point in worrying, she told herself fiercely, in a vain attempt to quash her own guilt feelings. Had she not taken the initiative and fled the farm, Old Will would undoubtedly have turned her out himself, once he had sobered up – and Luke too, like as not. As things stood at present, Luke still had some kind of living, and time to look for somewhere else where she could join him.

But she couldn't shake off her misgivings. Luke could get to Pickerby only rarely, and whenever he came, he seemed listless and downcast; even little Kate could scarcely make him smile. He mentioned High Moor hardly at all, but Catt could guess that it would have quickly reverted to the pigsty she had found on her arrival. It was clear enough, however, that only his sheep and his moors made life bearable for Luke these days. Catt sensed her name was no longer mentioned at the farm, though once Luke had let fall that Old Will occasionally asked after the granddaughter he had never seen, and had even gone so far to suggest, 'Maybe there'll be a lad, next time.'

The parson had read the Anglican burial service over the baby boy in Gelling churchyard, with only himself and Luke present. There was no stone to mark the tiny grave close to the north wall. It was a kindness for the parson to have done all this, said Luke, in view of the baby having been stillborn. Catt did not reply.

'I'll take you up to Gelling, when you're stronger – and show you where he is. I've been keeping wild flowers fresh there for him,' added Luke.

Still Catt did not respond. She could not imagine ever visiting Gelling again, and not even the prospect of seeing little Luke's grave could tempt her. His actual burial place did not concern her, for he had had a Catholic baptism, had he not, and all that mattered was that he must now be in Heaven, since he had not lived long enough to sin . . .

She thought a lot about her dead child; she had convinced herself that he had been made in the mirror image of Luke. By contrast she could see nothing at all of Luke in Kate, who had her own sharp features and hair as dark as she remembered Charles Leyton's. Perhaps it was this Leyton resemblance, real or imagined, which made Catt quite unable to feel any real empathy with her living baby. Kate's material needs were meticulously taken care of by her mother; but it was her Aunt Susannah who did the cuddling and the kissing, putting Catt's lack of demonstrative affection down to the circumstances surrounding Kate's birth, and telling herself that, given time, Catt's feelings would surely change. But they never did.

Then, on his next visit, Luke had a letter with him – a letter from Canada.

'It'll be the answer to mine,' exclaimed Catt, as she tore open the envelope. 'I wrote to Nell when I first knew about – about Kate – months and months ago, now. I never really thought my letter would ever get there, posted from that little box in Gelling.'

But it had – and what an answer this was! The letter, as usual, had been written by Nell's son Tom. It told how the farm which he and Luke's brother Robert worked was going from strength to strength. They had had a bumper harvest. Now they were planning to expand further – and so Tom was writing to ask Catt and Luke to think again about coming out to Canada to join them. For it all made so much good sense – especially as Luke was probably having an extra mouth to feed by now.

'It's the answer to everything! Our worries are over!' Catt was ecstatic. She clapped her hands and ran to hug her husband. 'Oh, I knew our luck was bound to change in the end! Those savings we've got will pay our fares – and, of course, Susannah shall have anything we can't take. We could set off after Michaelmas – just as soon as we could get a passage.' She was dizzy and breathless with the excitement of it all. 'Just think, love, we'll be a part – a real part – of a big family farm, a business, really. It'll mean a fresh start for you and me and a perfect beginning for Kate here – and any brothers and sisters of hers that come along. And we'll see Nell again.'

It was only now that Luke admitted the loss of their sovereigns. 'Gone,' he said. 'Stolen,' so far as Catt was concerned.

When she first heard what had happened she could hardly believe it – could even Old Will and Young Will have stooped so low? Had they really been so greedy? And hated her so much? 'How could they?' she kept repeating. 'Why? Why?'

'Catt, they were still drunk from the night before when they crept into our room and found us gone. My father's rages can last for days, you know that. One of these days I'm sure they'll be the death of him.' Luke was searching for excuses, any excuse, to wipe that dreadful look from Catt's face. 'It was rage as much as greed that made them do what they did – for they broke your little beads, too – smashed them to smithereens.'

Catt gave a cry of anguish. She shook Luke's hand away roughly as he stumbled on, desperate to calm, to explain. 'I asked them what they meant by it all. Father said he was only taking what we'd owed them, that we'd been living off them well, with bed and board – and they needed money for the quarter rent.'

'They needed money to pay the bills from the Horseshoe and the Gelling dressmaker's, more like!' interrupted Catt. 'And as for talk of us living well, it was *us* keeping *them*, as well you know! You, Luke, working all God's hours and more on the farm – as you still are, I shouldn't wonder – and me left to do everything in the house . . . I'd like to see your father and your brother safe behind bars – and Betsy too! And *we* can put them there, you know!'

But, even as she spoke, she knew this was quite out of the question. Whatever the wrong done, family was family. One could not prosecute one's own flesh and blood. Besides, as Luke pointed out, Old William, as master of the house, could claim ownership of everything in it.

'So, you see, love, there isn't any way we can go to Canada. All our savings are gone. We shall just have to begin all over again. Still' – Luke brightened a little, forcing a half-smile – 'you and I wouldn't really have wanted to go, would we? I've said it all before – what's the joy in a farm that's all corn, just mile after mile of flat cornland, with not a sheep to be found there, let alone a moor. Why, we'd never stand it!'

Ah, thought Catt, suddenly so sad that all the spirit went out of her. Anger gave way to despair, then resignation. Oh, Luke, you say you couldn't have stood it in Canada, she thought, but *I* could! Oh, how I could! After what has happened, these last few months, your moors terrify me, they've no appeal any more – I'd like to bid them goodbye for ever and go right away, put oceans between me and them – and all the bad memories that began in Leyton and have carried on here since . . . And now we can't. We're trapped, for ever.

She sensed this might be the last escape-route they would ever be offered. And this combined with an even more ominous knowledge – that Luke did not accept that they needed an escape-route at all, that he was quite content, willing even, to go on here, just as they had been doing . . . And there was no way that Catt could see of changing him.

Pointless to try to put these thoughts into words, Catt knew, so she merely said: 'But it's so unfair! Everything we do – however hard we plan and work and save – it always ends in failure. There's no sense in it, no justice. Why is it *you and I* who always have to suffer so?'

Luke tried to make light of things. 'Oh, never fear, we'll pick ourselves up. And' – he grinned reassuringly – 'all's not lost, anyway. We've all been so busy talking about Canada I've not had time to tell you my own good news. And nothing can set this wrong!' He smiled. 'There's a shepherding job going up at Allercliffe. I'm off to see the land agent when I leave you now – and there's a cottage with it, too. If I get it, we could soon have our own place again.'

Maybe, mused Catt, trying to show an enthusiasm she was very far from feeling at the present. All the same, it's going to take us years even to get back where we were. Meanwhile, Luke, you get thinner and more worn, and our youth is fast being left behind us – if we ever had one!

Where was Allercliffe anyway? The 'up' sounded ominous. Could it be back on the moors, somewhere? That was the last thing she wanted! But she had not the heart to probe further at present; she could not risk shattering his obvious pleasure. Particularly after her own earlier outburst.

Later, however, Susannah confirmed Catt's worst suspicions. Allercliffe was, indeed, on the moors – on the far side of that narrow valley which separated the Halliday farm from the Bridestones. Allercliffe House itself was off the moor's top – maybe a mile or so below the stones.

'It's a fine big house,' said Susannah, with enthusiasm. 'The farmer's a gentleman – not a working farmer who has to soil his own hands.' She thought for a moment, then volunteered: 'There used to be a shepherd's cottage on the moor, though – not all that far from the Bridestones . . . It wasn't very big, if I remember rightly – one up and one down, a bit of a squeeze for a family,' she went on doubtfully. 'It could be on the cold side – for it faces north, straight into the wind and towards the sea.'

And towards the Bridestones, too, thought Catt. She looked away, so that Susannah should not see the fear and disappointment in her face. She tried her best to sound cheerful. 'I daresay we'll manage – and it may not be for long, after all. Something better may turn up, in a while – and with just one baby, two rooms should be enough for the present.'

Susannah had gauged the real sentiments behind Catt's smile. Now she patted her arm reassuringly. 'There – I can guess what you're feeling. I can't abide those moors myself – not after what I went through on them when I was a child! They don't magic me like they do Luke. There's all that empty space. And yet, in spite of that, I don't feel free at all when I'm up there.' She leaned over, adding earnestly: 'Whatever happens, you know you're still always welcome to come here, Catt. Always! And when the next baby's on the way, make sure you get here a bit earlier than the last time.'

Nonetheless, Catt felt it a dreadful wrench to leave the placid warmth of Pickerby and its smithy and return to a life on the moor. And this was a moor which, as Susannah had warned, struck even chillier than the side on which the Halliday's farmhouse stood. As Susannah had predicted, their cottage was tiny and two-roomed, and when Luke had laboriously moved his few belongings across from High Moor singlehanded – his father and brother declined to help at all – it looked crowded out. Upstairs, there was little space for more than the bed and the cradle. When Kate is bigger, she'll have to share with me, thought Catt, and Luke will have to sleep on a mattress on the kitchen floor.

Still, it seemed that Roland Sowerby, Luke's new employer, was a pleasant, fair-minded man; and when Catt arrived at her new home she found a basket of eggs, a jug of cream and a side of bacon waiting for her – a gift from Mrs Sowerby. And Luke's wages here were above the average.

'So they should be!' cried Catt. 'For you're above the average! Susannah swears you're known for miles around as the best shepherd there is.'

Luke was less sanguine. 'Farming's going through a bad patch. Jobs are hard to find and it's getting harder all the time. I was very lucky, for they didn't really want a married man – they said the cottage wasn't big enough. I had to persuade them we could manage. And I'm not my own master any more.'

'You were hardly that at High Moor!' Catt retorted tartly. 'But you *will* be, Luke, before we've done! I'm going to make quite sure of that.'

It was going to be hard, she knew it was. Not only was there the obstacle of Luke's temperament – his fundamental placidity, shyness and tendency to expect the best of anyone, coupled with that stubbornness which had twice led to him declining the chance of a real future in Canada. There was much more. Their savings were gone, and they were now all alone on the moor, a mile from their nearest neighbour.

Across the gully stood the mocking outline of High Moor.

And on this side and much closer, the Bridestones; an ever-present reminder to Catt of how she had once dared to mock God to His face – and paid for it, so she believed, with a baby's life . . .

No, it was far from being the most auspicious of fresh starts. But, because she knew that she had been the cause of Luke's having to leave his family home – and because she knew, too, that a part of him continued to find the rift with his father almost unbearable – Catt was even more determined to make it succeed.

14

It really did seem that their luck had changed, despite all the odds.

Catt dated the improvement of their fortunes from the morning, not long after their arrival, when she and Kate were gathering up the eggs from the paddock beyond the cottage. She heard the thud of horses' hoofs, looked up and saw a pretty young woman riding towards her across the moor.

'I wanted to see just what the person was like who was willing to live in this wilderness!' She laughed – and Catt laughed with her, feeling an instictive empathy with Adelaide Sowerby, her landlord's wife.

Despite their differences of circumstance, class and upbringing, the two women had a lot in common. They were both independent and ambitious; both frustrated by the conventions of the period which laid down strict parameters for what women – even the well-to-do – could and could not do.

In Catt, Adelaide quickly recognised a kindred spirit desperately trying to press ahead. Here was someone not too shy or proud to invite her into her home, humble though it might be. As she sat drinking Catt's newly-brewed tea, Adelaide's eyes alighted on the elaborate piece of smocking lying on the sewing bag by the fireplace. Catt's childhood training in church embroidery expressed itself these days in a riot of decoration of even Kate's most everyday clothes. She recognised that here was a way of helping Catt along without appearing patronising.

So, the next week, Adelaide was back again, this time

bringing a pile of silk bodices which she begged Catt to smock for her own two small daughters. At the same time, she diffidently produced a parcel of the Sowerby children's cast-offs, hardly worn at all, to Catt's way of thinking.

'Ah, but the girls have outgrown them,' Adelaide interjected hastily. 'And I thought it was such a pity to let them go to waste with so much wear left in them.'

'Why, that gown's grand enough for a christening!' exclaimed Luke, when Catt laid everything out to show him, later that day. And he added, a little wistfully, 'Could we not get Kate properly christened, Catt, now we're living out here? If you don't want to go near Gelling, there's the church at Pickerby – or even the one next to Allercliffe House – and Kate would look such a picture! I'd be so proud of her – and of you.'

But Catt refused to listen. 'Kate's christened already, and properly christened, too,' she replied shortly. 'Just as properly christened as little Luke was.'

Luke knew there was no moving her. At some time in the past Catt would have taken a bowl of water, he guessed, and sprinkled some drops on Kate's forehead and said those same words, over the living child, that he had heard her utter over their dead son.

He sighed. His passionate love for Catt had grown even deeper as time passed. He was certain he knew her far better than anyone else had ever done or ever could. Yet there was a part of her that remained totally separate from him, a barrier between them which he could never overcome.

He let the subject of a christening drop. Why ruffle the waters? Life at present seemed almost perfect, thought Luke. Even Catt seemed content, her underlying ambitions channelled, for the time being, into limited practicalities.

In the evenings, Catt would sit and sew under the oil-lamp; or carry on with her efforts at teaching Luke to read and write. But progress was slow. Luke would come home, more often than not, too tired to do much more than eat his supper and fall into bed. Even when she could get him to sit down with paper and books, Luke's mind rapidly wandered.

'I'll never make a scholar, love,' admitted Luke one evening. 'Best take my word for it and give up trying. Then you can get back to your own reading. You've taught me enough to get along with – more than I thought I'd ever be able to learn. And it might be a help one of these days. But the fancy reading and writing's best left to you.'

In the end, Catt had to accept this, and the lessons stopped. But she had at least taught her husband to write his name and read and understand a simple letter. And she had found him naturally agile with figures, so it had been relatively easy to show him how to set down on paper the calculations he had previously had to carry around in his head.

'Well, we've got this far, at any rate,' she said. 'And whatever you think, Luke, what I've taught you will come in handy when we get our own place.' After all, thought Catt, she herself would always be by his side if anything really complicated had to be written or deciphered.

Luke nodded, secretly relieved to be rid of the burden of his evening classes. Catt could talk on of their mythical future as much as she liked, if it kept her happy. For the present, he was more than satisfied to be so settled here at Allercliffe, among his beloved sheep and even more beloved family.

Barely a year after she had come to Allercliffe, Catt was back at Susannah's. The birth of this second child was as uneventful as that of the first had been fraught. Within a fortnight she returned to the cottage with her new daughter, named Susan after Susannah and Luke's mother – and looking the picture of her father, with the same fair curls and blue eyes.

So different from Kate! Every time Catt studied Kate's serious little face, her black hair and deep-set eyes, she was forcibly reminded of her own real father. Was this why she found it impossible to treat the elder daughter with the affection she felt for the younger?

Luke saw no difference between the two. He adored and loved each equally – and he had plenty of love to spare, too, for the next daughter, Nellie, who was born a couple of years after Susan. He had suggested this child be named after Catt's mother, but Catt would have none of it. She could never think

131

of Mary Jane without thinking of Charles Leyton as well. And though her 'bad dreams' were fewer, these days, they still came back to haunt from time to time; it would never do to have Mary Jane's name as a permanent reminder of a past she was still so desperately trying to forget.

The Sowerbys were model employers. Luke was allowed to build another room onto the cottage, to make room for his growing family. Adelaide Sowerby continued to send over her daughters' outworn clothes and plied Catt with sewing orders for herself and her friends; these kept Catt so busy that she had scarcely time now to sew for her own children.

Though Luke was often kept away overnight, sometimes for days on end, especially during lambing, there were other times when he was asked to do carrying jobs and leave the sheep-caring to one of the lesser shepherds. Then he could pack his whole little family into the cart, along with the packages he was delivering to Whitcar or Pickerby, or even Whinborough and the villages between.

Catt loved these outings, just as she cherished her stays in Pickerby, even though these were limited to confinements. In Pickerby she felt so very safe. She had quite lost her earlier fascination for the moors, though while life remained on such an even keel, as at present, she could mostly ignore their underlying threat. But it never really quite left her.

If only I had not gone to the Bridestones that day. Every time she looked out of her window Catt was reminded of that fateful, foolish 'touching' of long ago. From it had sprung tragedy, she was convinced of it – the death of her little son. It was one thing to abandon one's faith – and at least, thought Catt, all the children have been baptised into it, for there had been her own secret baptisms of Susan and Nellie, as well as Kate. But it was quite another matter to indulge in pagan practices. That was to defy God – and Catt would remember Charles Leyton's homilies and his descriptions of the pains of Purgatory and the flames of Hell.

On the moors, of course, superstition lurked everywhere. Even stolid Luke was not immune. He had been relieved to see their cottage had a witchpost, as High Moor had done – a certain protection against evil spirits, so it was said. When he talked of Hob, the goblin who could turn from well-intentioned helper during lambing to a demon luring travellers into fatal moorland bogs on dark nights, she sensed he half-believed the stories, even while making fun of them.

And of Whinny Moor, Luke made no fun at all. This was the thorny barren wilderness which, so moorland folk whispered, the unredeemed dead had to travel before they could reach Heaven. These days, folk might make more light of witches and hobgoblins – but even now, few mentioned Whinny Moor without a shudder. Luke certainly regarded it as all too real.

This was confirmed for her on the day that Young Will Halliday turned up at the cottage.

Catt had not set eyes on him since the day of Kate's birth. She had never been back to High Moor, even though she was reminded of it every time she looked across the gorge, and though she knew Luke visited it now and then, to see his father. Only last time, she now recalled, he had mentioned that his father was looking like a sick man – and that Betsy had miscarried yet again. She had not been able to bring herself to feel a shred of pity for either.

Now she greeted Will, stony-faced. 'If you've come to worry Luke, you'll be disappointed. He's away on the moor with the sheep – we keep early hours here, unlike some folk I could mention.'

She had braced herself for some surly response, at best. But this was a different Will from the other one she had known – uncharacteristically sober, and strangely solemn and civil.

'It's Father. He's had a fit. The doctor says he's dying. Luke had best come at once.'

But by the time Luke could be found, and got to the sickbed, Old William Halliday was dead.

*　*　*

Despite all Luke's pleading, Catt flatly refused to attend her father-in-law's funeral.

'I know how he hurt you, Catt, but he hurt me too. And, God knows, he made my mother's life a living hell. But maybe some of the pain he caused sprang from his own neglect as a child – and then being so disappointed in his expectations later on.' As Catt stayed stubbornly silent, Luke stumbled on desperately. 'Anyway, when all's said and done, he was still my father . . . and now he's dead, you must forgive him, love. We all must.'

Catt's mouth was set in a thin, hard line. 'Why?' she asked relentlessly.

In his anxiety, Luke's old stutter crept back. 'B-because – b-because the B-Bible s-says s-so! And we're Chr-Christians, surely to goodness! Aren't w-we s-supposed to forgive our enemies, even? Besides' – he reddened and looked away from her in confusion – 'I-I c-can't b-bear the th-thought of my own f-father, wandering on Wh-Whinny Moor for ever – whatever h-he's done in the p-past. No one deserves that!'

'It's nothing but a fairy tale,' cried Catt – but felt abashed, all the same, by Luke's stricken face, and reflected the tale might be truer than it seemed. It sounded, when she came to think about it seriously, not too unlike the Catholic Purgatory where sinners could be helped by the prayers of those still living.

She pressed her arm around Luke's shoulder, and felt ashamed of her outburst. All that mattered was that Luke should be reassured; she had no business to make such a luxury of her own bitterness and unbelief.

'I'll pray for your father's soul, love, I promise,' she said. 'I'll pray that he rests in peace – even though he gave us little enough of it in his lifetime. But' – and here Catt's voice rose determinedly. She had to speak her mind here, whatever the cost; she couldn't help herself – 'I can't go to his funeral. I won't go inside that house again, not after all that has happened there. In any case, what would be the point?' She shrugged dismissively. 'I can't set foot inside that church of yours, as you know very well.'

Luke knew he was defeated when he heard Catt's final

sentence. However, he could not resist a rejoinder, only half-joking, which Catt would remember with pain many years later. 'Well, so be it, love. All the same, I hope this conscience of yours won't stop you from coming to *my* funeral. For I tell you now, whether I ever get back to High Moor or not, I want to be buried from Gelling church and in Gelling churchyard, come what may – alongside that little lad of ours – whenever and wherever I happen to die.' Then he stopped, halted by Catt's suddenly agonised expression.

Whenever I happen to die, Luke had said. Thank God that's years off, thought Catt in panic. Such a thing did not bear thinking of! A cold finger of fear seemed to reach to her very heart. Any thought of a life without Luke was utterly beyond belief.

She tried to hide her fears, attempted to laugh the subject away. 'Oh, love, you know very well I'd sell my soul for you a thousand times and more!' Then she added, 'But going to that church – well, going there *now* – that's different.'

So Luke set off alone for High Moor on the evening preceding the funeral. Catt stood in the yard and watched him, awkward in his one and only suit, a hand-me-down from Nell's long-dead husband, and the one he had worn on their wedding day. Past the Bridestones he went, then down the steep slope and out of sight into the valley. By and by she saw him clamber up the far side of the gully, and on towards the farmhouse. He turned and waved, and Catt waved back, blowing kisses on the wind. Then she went slowly back into the cottage, lips grimly pursed, her mind a whirl of confused thoughts.

She tried to picture the scene now at High Moor, seeing in her mind's eye the filthy kitchen – for she was sure it *would* be filthy, even though Betsy would no doubt have tried to give it some sort of a clean for this special occasion – and the open coffin. There'd be Will and Betsy and Luke and Betsy's parents and their cronies from the Horseshoe gathered around it. Would Susannah and John be there? Reluctantly, Catt decided they would, from a sense of duty – and she was glad of that, for they would surely look after Luke. Then her

135

conscience pricked her again, for it should have been *her* task to be there to support her own husband. But she managed to banish this thought by reflecting further that Susannah and John would help Luke add respectability to what she knew would be an occasion for very hard drinking, lasting well into the small hours, as these funeral wakes invariably did.

She supposed there'd be the customary pair of new boots by the coffin, and some coins for the church poor box, which Luke had explained represented the charity a dead person had failed to provide during their lifetime, and which was supplied at death to try to guard against a perpetual wandering on that dreaded Whinny Moor. Catt shivered, and for the first time in years crossed herself against dwelling any further on such unhealthy superstitions.

As she went back to her regular tasks of cleaning the house and caring for the three little girls, not to mention the hens and her sewing, and even the milking, tonight and tomorrow, Catt's thoughts kept returning to the subject of Old William's will. It might be wrong to be thinking about this with the funeral not yet over, but she could not help wondering what it would hold in it for Luke. At the last, would the old man have shown any remorse for the treatment he had meted out to his youngest son – any regrets at the memory of those precious sovereigns he had stolen? Surely, there had to be some kind of recompense for all this!

Of course, Catt knew all too well that the farm itself was not worth much, and was, in any case, only a tenancy. That would naturally pass to Will, as the eldest son, however unsuitable he might be. And the stock and furnishings would mostly be bound to go to Will and Betsy, too. How long that pair would manage to go on paying the rent was anyone's guess! Still, providing Old Will had left Luke a substantial enough sum of money, he might be able to bid for the lease when it next fell vacant – which could be sooner than one might think, given Will and Betsy . . .

And that was the last thing Catt wanted! For her, High Moor represented nothing but misery and disillusion. Yet she knew how passionately Luke still loved it, despite all that had happened. Was it not in his blood? But she, Catt – she must never let him return there. It could do him nothing but harm, whatever he might think. It was a wasteland, a place of lost hopes, poor and barren . . . Luke deserved something far better, more gentle and fertile – in Pickerby, maybe, where he could still see his moors but not be exploited by them any more.

So if there should be a worthwhile legacy, Catt decided, that was the direction in which she would have to lead her husband. Already she was imagining a cottage like Susannah's, framed in the roses that were too delicate to stand the cold air of High Moor and Allercliffe. Then Nellie's cries roused her from her day-dreaming, and for the rest of the day she tried hard but not wholly successfully to keep her dreams at bay.

Only for them to be rudely shattered when Luke at last returned home, tired and dispirited. Almost too dispirited to respond to Catt's welcoming embrace and the children's whoops of excitement. Catt had never seen him so shaken. She steered him gently to the chair by the range. It was like leading a blind man.

'You'll have been up most of the night, I daresay,' she murmured. 'I knew what an ordeal it would be. Don't fret, love – you're worn out with it all. I know you felt for your father, in spite of everything.'

Suddenly roused from his torpor, Luke sprang to his feet, seizing Catt by the shoulders so violently that she almost lost her balance. He looked straight into her eyes. She felt him shaking with fury, his face scarlet with rage, the blue eyes blazing as if with a fever.

'Oh, yes! I felt for him – once! But all I feel now is,' and his voice broke into a near sob. 'Wh-what I-I f-feel now is n-nothing! Worse than n-nothing!' He seemed to be fighting for breath and at the same time trying to control his old stammer, but failing miserably, because his anger was so overpowering. 'N-nothing but *h-h-hate!*'

Bit by bit, Catt managed to push him back into the chair,

soothing him as she would a baby. Bit by bit, Luke's story came out.

Now it was Catt who had to struggle to keep calm. Old Will had remained true to character right to the last. The furniture and farm stock, as they had already known they would, went to Will, together with £30. For Robert in Canada there was £30 too. For Susannah £20. And for Luke . . . £2.

'It's my fault!' moaned Catt, rocking to and fro in despair. 'It's all my fault! He's done this because of me – because of what happened the day Kate – and little Luke – were born. Oh, Luke! You should never have married me. I've done you nothing but harm – and now I'm the cause of you losing your inheritance!'

Catt's anguish brought Luke back to his feet – and his senses. His usual calm reasserted itself: taking his wife in his arms, he covered her mouth with kisses. 'Lass! Lass! Don't take on so! You know very well you're worth a king's ransom. I didn't know what life was about till I met you.'

Gradually, Catt's misery subsided, and Luke's own anger diminished. 'It was nothing to do with you, love,' he explained patiently. 'Father's will was drawn up years ago – just after Mother died. It was most likely on account of what I said to him then that he left me this – this pittance. He'd never liked me, you know, no matter how hard I tried to please him. I was always the odd one out with him – it went right back to when I was a little lad.' Luke paused, remembering childhood slights, then his anger welled up again and he burst out: 'It's the cruelty of it! For now the whole world will know what he thought of me, and that he's done this to slight me and to make me look a fool. I'd far rather he'd left me nothing at all!'

'We don't have to take the £2,' said Catt. 'And this can go back to High Moor, too.' She put her hand to her throat and brought out the locket from under her blouse – the locket given her by Old Will on a day that now seemed another age ago. 'This can join the rest of Betsy's baubles.'

'No!' Luke spoke with such authority that Catt was quite startled. 'We'll keep the locket. It was Mother's, after all. It's

138

the only thing of hers we've got. One day it shall go to Kate. And next time I'm in Whitcar, I'll buy Susan and Nellie a brooch of Whitcar jet each with the money, so they'll each have something. But the locket stays with us!'

And so it did. But Catt never wore it again. It lay, first, in the back of one of her drawers, and then, for years after her death, at the back of one of Kate's – for Kate did not care for such things. Years later, a great-grandchild was to come across it, still empty, and still waiting for the photo of Luke that was never taken.

15

It was not long after the funeral that things began to change for Luke and Catt. And, once again, the changes were not for the better. As their troubles deepened and their hopes faded, Catt would glance over at the Bridestones more and more, muttering a shamefaced Act of Contrition, even as she told herself this was nothing but a meaningless form of words. There must be some way in which their seemingly constant run of ill fortune could be halted.

If only she had not played fast and loose with the Devil, on that mad May morning, so distant now that it seemed another world away. If only she had heeded Luke's warnings. At the time it had seemed just harmless fun, running through the early dew, then, hot and breathless, pressing her body against the stone as if it were a lover, kissing it like a holy relic.

How could I have ever have thought it could bring good luck? she asked herself over and over again. No matter that she was no longer a believer – she had still committed blasphemy . . . and that was bound to invite some kind of punishment.

If she had not done what she did – who knows? Might baby Luke have lived? Might that wicked will have been changed, and the insult to Luke struck from it? Might they still have their precious savings? Might Luke even have been persuaded, despite all the odds, to abandon his moors and take his family to a new life in Canada?

During the relatively good years they had had, thoughts of the Canadian opportunity which Luke had turned down had scarcely troubled Catt at all; but now she remembered it with bitterness. It was unfair as well as foolish of Luke to have rejected a future which offered so much – and on account of such a foolish obsession, too.

Yet her own obsessions were no better. The Bridestones were becoming omnipresent, these days. Now and then, as she looked at them, she almost fancied they were growing larger and taking on a life of their own, edging closer and closer . . . so that one day, they might crush the cottage and everyone inside it.

And at the same time, those dreadful, shameful visions of her father which, in the early days of her marriage, had so often flooded in on her at the moments of her lovemaking with Luke, and which had been mercifully absent for years now, started to haunt her once more. She was filled with a terrible guilt and self-loathing.

At Allercliffe House, Adelaide Sowerby died in childbirth. Soon afterwards, her distraught husband left the district and the estate was sold. The new owner was a harsher employer –a self-made Halifax weaver. He had bought Allercliffe for commercial reasons alone and had no personal interest in it or its workers. New work-schedules were enforced; now Luke was constantly on the move with his sheep. He was away more and more, often for days and nights at a time, and this at the point when Catt had most need of his presence, as she slipped deeper and deeper into depression.

Luke's carrying jobs to the surrounding villages, on which Catt and the children had often joined him, came to a stop. Most packages were being sent by rail now, as the trains became more and more reliable. So, at the same time as Luke was away longer and more often, Catt and her daughters were increasingly confined to the immediate surroundings of their isolated cottage. It became almost as much a prison for Catt as Miss Fredericks's Melchester House had been; there seemed no escape from it.

Catt's sewing work, the source of much-valued extra income, also ended abruptly with Adelaide Sowerby's death. As did the toys and hand-me-downs for Kate, Susan and Nellie. These were bitter blows – but not a fraction so bitter as the personal loss Catt felt she had suffered.

She had only seen Mrs Sowerby two or three times a year, and then on formal terms, but she had regarded her as a real friend – one of the very few she had ever had. Oh, how I miss her! she mourned, time and time again. It seemed she had only to love something for it to be snatched from her – and such thinking would reawaken her irrational fears for Luke and make her still more wretched.

She risked perdition by going one day to Allercliffe church, to see the marble plaque put there in Adelaide's memory. The girls went with her. It was the first time any of them had ever been inside a church, and Kate, usually so silent and reserved, seemed particularly fascinated by it.

Catt looked at her curiously. However hard she tried, she could never manage to feel close to her eldest daughter – the one whose features were a constant reminder of Charles Leyton and whose stolid temperament was so different from her own mercurial one. Kate would surely go through life without a single day-dream – or nightmare! Could it be, thought Catt, that Kate possessed some of her own suppressed religious fervour – or was it yet another inheritance from her Leyton grandfather?

To Catt's horror, the very act of thinking of Charles Leyton set one of those shameful images dancing before her eyes. She felt irrationally resentful of Kate for reminding her once again of the past she was determined to forget.

'We've no time to stay here longer,' she cried, bustling the children out, with a particularly sharp tug at the lagging Kate.

The isolation and poverty were all the harder to bear when faced with the knowledge that Will and Betsy were now firmly established as master and mistress at High Moor. True, they were still childless, and seemed likely to be so permanently, and no doubt, despite their inheritance, their debts were mounting.

If only Luke and I had had that windfall! sorrowed Catt. We could have done so much with it . . . But not at High Moor, she added. Never there. It would have had to be spent somewhere

142

else. There is a curse on us while we stay up here.

Then Catt found she was pregnant again. Apart from the tragedy of little Luke's actual birth, all her earlier pregnancies had been easy; she had bloomed and felt full of new energy as well as new life. But this time, she felt chronically sick and permanently exhausted. All the children – and not just Kate – seemed constantly under her feet, demanding, irritating.

She was horrified to find herself finding fault with them so often, shouting at them, even slapping them far more than she should have done – so that even placid Luke, who so rarely interfered in her running of the family, was forced to intervene. 'They're not much more than babies, love. Don't treat them so hard.'

Mortified beyond belief, Catt flung herself into his arms. 'Luke, Luke! I'm sorry – I'm so very sorry,' she cried hysterically. 'I know as I do it that I'm doing wrong, poor little mites – none of this is their fault. It's as if I can't help myself. But I'll try – I promise you I'll try!' She clung to him tightly, as if drowning. 'Oh, Luke! I love you so much! Don't ever leave me, whatever happens, whatever I do, will you? For I'd die without you. Truly I would! You're all I've got.'

When Luke, in his efforts to calm her, mildly and half-laughingly observed that she had the children, too, Catt shook her head vehemently. 'No, Luke. For me, there's no one but you! Only you! For I *chose* you. I didn't choose the children – they just came along, love them as I do – but you I *chose*. And without you, nothing would have any meaning.'

* * *

One evening Luke got back to the cottage even more drawn and exhausted than usual.

'The new master's cutting back still further,' he announced heavily. 'He wants a shepherd here who's a single man – one freer to walk the moors than I am.'

'You mean, one he can pay less!' broke in Catt, in a rare flash of pre-pregnancy spirit. But her gloom returned, and deepened, when Luke went on:

'That's to say, I shan't be wanted beyond Michaelmas. We've got to be out of here straight after that.'

'Michaelmas! Why, that only gives us just over two months!' cried Catt, aghast. Two months for Luke to find a job and somewhere else for them to live – and the baby due at the end of October! 'What in the world are we going to do?'

Luke tried to remain outwardly more optimistic than he felt. There was no need to worry yet, he assured her. 'Something's bound to turn up. If the worse comes to the worst, I'm sure I can get Will to take us in for a while.' It was well known that High Moor was in a terrible state of neglect – no doubt, thought Luke aloud, his brother would welcome some temporary extra help.

'Never!' Catt's voice touched screaming point. 'Never in this world!' She stamped her foot. 'Why, I'd sooner sleep out on the open moor in a blizzard, and give birth there, too, than do any such thing! How could you even think of it, Luke, after how we've been treated? I'd sooner die . . . It would be like a kind of living death on your famous Whinny Moor,' she added sarcastically – and then, seeing the flash of hurt in Luke's eyes, 'Oh, love! I don't mean to sound too bitter – I know they're still your kin, when all's said and done. But *I* could never go back there, however bad things might be – and I won't let the children go either. You understand that, don't you?'

Luke nodded sadly. For a brief, fleeting moment he had been tempted to try to seize the chance of getting back to High Moor, even for a little while, even if it meant going on bended knee to his brother. Yes, even if it meant enduring all the old humiliations! But in his heart he knew it had always been fantasy.

However, despite Luke's initial show of confidence, the days ticked by remorselessly without his hearing of any other job that offered a family house with it. No matter that he was known all round the district as an excellent shepherd, hill farming was in the doldrums at present. Flocks were being cut back, and at times like this no one wanted to take on a married man with a young family.

144

As their worries increased, Catt looked ever more wan. Increasingly, her general lethargy was interspersed with bouts of near-hysteria. The three little girls, seeming to sense their parents' troubles, grew querulous, too, and fell to catching every cough and cold about, even though it was high summer.

Luke came to a decision. 'I'm taking you to Susannah's – this very night,' he announced one evening, after Catt had greeted him even more listlessly than usual. 'After all, she's always promised us a home if we ever needed one.' He brushed aside Catt's feeble protests. 'I know the baby's not due for two months yet, but Susannah knows how awkward things are for us at present. You were promised to go there for the confinement, anyhow. If nothing's fixed by Michaelmas, I can ask John if I can store our bits and bobs at the forge – then, if the worst happens, I can always take a single man's job, until something comes along that will take care of all of us.'

Catt was too worn out, too ill to protest. In her heart, though, she was full of misgivings. Luke was in his mid-thirties now. If he once gave up the cottage and went back to a single man's work and conditions, would he ever be able to get a home of his own again? Would they be condemned to a permanent separation?

She had heard of this kind of situation – and then of husbands acquiring a taste for their new-found freedom and vanishing into thin air, leaving wives and children to end up in the workhouse. Of course, Catt told herself, there was not the slightest chance of Luke doing anything like that – his devotion to her and the children was beyond question. But still, the thought of physical separation was hard to bear. If she was honest with herself, Catt knew she was the more passionate partner. Luke worshipped the ground she walked on, of course, she was well aware of that; but it was she who possessed the most fire – usually she who made the first advances in their lovemaking, leading Luke forward with her, even though he might not realise it.

Naturally, Catt said nothing of this to Luke. They were not matters normally spoken of, not even between man and wife.

Now she simply gathered up the family belongings, and the clothes and cradle that would be needed for the new baby. That done, the sad little family drove down to Pickerby. Luke left his wife and daughters at the blacksmith's and then returned home, arriving back at Allercliffe in the small hours.

Susannah and John were as welcoming as they had always been; Kate, Susan and Nellie revelled in the company of their little cousins. Every day, the sun shone down – but then it always seemed to do that whenever Catt came to Pickerby! She ought to have been happy. She had the chance now, to rest; her pregnancy sickness suddenly disappeared and she began to regain a little of her bloom.

But she kept on fretting. All in vain, Susannah assured her that she and the children could stay as long as was necessary – she felt over-indebted to her in-laws already. Her life had been a constant succession of flits to the forge, she thought. If only she could see a light at the end of the dark tunnel which seemed to make up her family's present existence. She worried about Luke continually. How could he manage his little holding on his own – and his employer's sheep – and still find time to look for a new position? They were caught in a vicious circle.

News trickled down to Pickerby of Will and Betsy's eviction from High Moor. Their landlord had grown tired of rents unpaid and a property and land falling into rack and ruin, and had finally sent them packing. With Betsy's parents now dead, there was no one to take them in. They had eventually found a tumbledown cottage in Gelling village itself. Will was now day-labouring and Betsy taking in washing and mending, so Luke reported, on one of his all too rare visits to the forge.

'I know how you dislike them, Catt,' he added. 'Still, it's sad to see one's own flesh and blood fallen so low.'

Catt could not trust herself to reply. She knew she should be feeling pity. Betsy had not only lost her home. Her good looks had faded, people said, and she had no children of her own to comfort her. But the memory of the past, of all the inflicted pain, made it impossible for Catt to feel anything at all. She

146

suspected that in recent months Luke had often given his brother the price of some food – and drink, no doubt! – out of his own meagre earnings, and would probably do so again in the future.

'I even went up to High Moor,' went on Luke, 'and called at the Home Farm to see if they'd pass the tenancy on to us. But I should have thought better than try to benefit from someone else's troubles – especially my own brother's.' His voice broke. 'But I was so sure this might be a real chance for us! It was no use – it turns out that High Moor's not being offered for lease any more. The landlord says he's sick of being troubled by tenants . . . and maybe my name being Halliday didn't help me.' Here, Luke even managed a faint smile, before adding bitterly, 'Why, we could have set the place to rights, you and I, Catt, in the end – and made it pay, I'm sure. But for now that's out of the question . . . High Moor's been put up for sale – and if there are no quick takers, it's all to be amalgamated with the Home Farm. The asking price is far beyond anything we could raise – so High Moor's lost to us for ever.'

Luke put his head in his hands to hide his misery. Catt leaned over, to comfort and caress. For a few moments, they were closer than they had been for weeks past. And when Luke finally raised his head and looked at Catt, he saw her eyes were shining. At once, all his troubles and disappointments seemed quite unimportant.

'Oh, Catt, love,' he murmured. 'I shouldn't be worrying you with all this – not now, especially – after all, we have each other . . . and nothing else matters, does it?' He buried his lips in her hair.

Catt nodded. But she felt a deep, inner shame. For the light in her eyes had been that of triumphant relief, and not of love at all. Would Luke be talking of trust if he realised that her reaction to the news that High Moor could never now be theirs was one of overwhelming joy?

For once, she thanked God for their continuing poverty. Now there could no longer be even the slightest threat of her having to go back to the place she had come to hate so. And,

Catt promised herself, as soon as the opportunity arose – and surely, one of these days, it must! – she would the more easily be able to persuade Luke to make a fresh start well out of sight of Gelling, of the farmstead at High Moor, and of those accursed Bridestones!

16

Their own future was once again thrown into the melting-pot. Yet, though Catt fretted over this and grieved that Luke was suffering such inner agonies at the collapse of his own most precious dream, the conclusive end to any threat that she would ever have to go back to High Moor, lifted her spirits and gave her a new burst of energy.

Now, at the smithy, she threw herself into helping Susannah with such enthusiasm that her sister-in-law had often to beg her to slow down, for the coming baby's sake. She took up her sewing again. She played more often and more intimately with her three daughters and took to walking them into the town, among the shops and through the water-meadows alongside the river.

But she never even attempted to walk where the moor started. Until, one day, half in a dream, she took the children beyond the last houses of Pickerby's long, straggling main street. This way led in the direction of Allercliffe. On a sudden impulse, Catt raised her eyes towards the moor. What was Luke doing now, she wondered; It seemed so long since he had had time to come and see her. She sighed, desperately, wanting the reassurance of his presence close to her. . .

It was then that she saw it. At the entrance to a small farmstead. A board, announcing that the freehold property and its 15 acres and stock were being auctioned in two weeks' time – unless it could be sold before that by private treaty.

Catt stood, momentarily transfixed. Here it was, the house of her dreams! Suddenly all her visions of a splendid, secure future for herself and her children sprang back to life.

She gazed at the neat grey house with its white-painted windows and doors and – as in all her happiest dreams – the garlands of roses cascading down the front – and even ventured a little way down the side-path to see the leanto sheds at the back. There were chickens in the backyard and, beyond, some fruit trees and a field of cows. No sheep – the love of Luke's life, after her – but still, sheep could only serve as reminders of all the things Catt was now trying so hard to forget: the harshness of High Moor, the slights and insults she had endured there, the death of her son, the ever-present threat of the Bridestones.

If only it were to rent, she thought – with such passion, she might have been speaking aloud. If only she and Luke had some significant savings put by! Why, this could have been the means to a wonderful new beginning, with untold prospects for the future. Then Nellie began pulling impatiently at her arm and she fancied there was a tweak at one of the farm's lace curtains. Catt seized the children and fled the scene precipitately.

On the way back to the forge, however, she seized her courage in her hands and called at the auctioneer's office. 'I wonder if the owner would be prepared to consider a tenancy,' she enquired tentatively.

She was to be disappointed, yet again. It was the matter of an inheritance, Catt was told. The farmer owning the property had died suddenly and his widow was anxious to move in with her only child, a married daughter living in Melchester, and cut her ties with Pickerby as soon as possible. Of course, if she was interested in buying, the price was very modest. And so it was. But, nevertheless, far beyond the means of people like Luke and herself.

And there, rationally, Catt's dream should have dissolved and died in the light of cold reality. But it stubbornly refused to do so.

Back at the smithy, Catt was quite unable to contain her excitement and her longings. She waxed lyrical as she described what she had seen of the smallholding. 'And the house nearly as pretty as yours, Susannah, with the roses . . .'

She thrilled at Susannah's gasps of admiration when she described how she had actually dared to step into the man's world of the auctioneer's office and discuss such traditional male subjects as terms and prices.

'Just think,' she cried, 'if Luke and I could only get a place like that! It would mean he'd never need to be away, except, maybe, on some of the market-days – and there'd be a nice school close by for the children, and you and John near us, as well. And I'm sure I could make a good business from the chickens, here in the town, and probably there'd be a demand for fine smocking and such, too.'

'Yes, Catt,' Susannah broke in. 'That's all very well – and I agree, it *does* sound wonderful – but you know it's too good to be true. You can't possibly afford the place. Townend may be cheap at the price – but it's still more than is being asked for High Moor. And, you've just yourself said, there's no chance of a tenancy.' Acutely aware of Catt's downcast expression, and anxious not to upset her, particularly in her present condition, Susannah went on, more gently. 'Well, never mind! After all, it's no doubt for the best – for you know that Luke would be quite miserable without his moors and his sheep. They were his whole life until you came along – and even now, I can't see him settling down as a dairy farmer. Best you forget all about it, Catt,' she said with determination – Susannah knew how stubborn Catt could be – 'Townend is not for you. But something suitable is bound to come along soon, I'm sure. Try to be patient a bit longer.'

Of course, Susannah was right. Townend was and would always be no more than a dream. Something more within their grasp must surely turn up one of these days. And Susannah had made another valid point. Sheep, were, indeed, an integral part of Luke's life and he had always said he could not live without his moors . . . After all, had he not given up the chance of a life in Canada on their account?

But it's really all nonsense, this fixation of his, thought Catt. And the more she thought about it, the more cross it made her. It was an idea which had become rooted in Luke's head simply because he had never in his life been very far away from his birthplace, had never had a chance to see the world beyond it. His life before he met her had not been happy and the moors and the sheep had come to be his only solace – his retreat from the miseries and frustrations which were all the outside world seemed to hold for him.

As for Luke's turning down the chance of Canada, well, he had been younger then, and the knocks fewer – and Canada was a terrifyingly long way away, one had to admit, and the life there sounded so different. It had put off more people than just Luke. But a simple change within the county from moorland shepherd to vale dairy farmer – surely that was not very much out of the ordinary! Especially when it promised so many advantages.

After all, Catt reasoned, *I* was in love with the moors once, too – all that wild openness seemed to promise such freedom, until I found out that the moors could be as cruel and confining as any prison. Now that Luke has me and the children, surely they can't mean as much to him as they once did. Oh, if only Townend were theirs – his life, and her life would be transformed and they could at last hope to build something of worth for their children and themselves!

But, of course, Townend could *not* be theirs. They simply had not the means to buy it. So there was no point in bothering to ask oneself whether or not Luke could be made to be happy there – the possibility did not exist.

We are trapped – by our own poverty, thought Catt bitterly. And, for the thousandth time, she wondered why life had to be so unfair.

For a long time she had scarcely given more than a passing thought to Leyton Hall and her life there – or to the scandal of her parentage and the disasters which had followed. Now, the unattainable image of Townend was bringing it all back. And with it, something which had never before crossed Catt's mind – the realisation that, had things been a little different, had Mary Jane not been an illiterate servant-girl, she and Charles Leyton might have married, and then she would have been Catherine Leyton of Leyton Hall, and no doubt Townend would have seemed very unimportant by comparison!

She gave a long, tremulous sigh. It was dangerous and pointless to dwell on such things – it could do no good, and only add to her frustration. She must stop it and return to the real world.

Catt was able to carry out her resolution so far as forcing herself to say no more about Townend to Susannah. But she could not prevent herself from inwardly dreaming on . . .

*　　*　　*

A few days after Catt's discovery of Townend, there was an unusual bustle and commotion at the forge. A large coach rattled in; one of the horses had cast a shoe. This was not the kind of custom John Carter usually attracted, for his was mostly farm and local business.

The ever-curious Susannah pressed her nose against the lace curtains. 'Why,' she reported, 'to think of it! All the passengers look to be clergymen. There must be something going on Melchester way – something to do with the cathedral and the bishop there, maybe – for they're certainly not local people . . . I can't recognise a soul among them.'

Catt did not bother to raise her head from her sewing. She was quite uninterested; clergymen were no concern of hers and she had not even spoken to one since the disastrous day of Kate's birth.

'You'll not see much through all that net,' she commented, half-amused, half-irritated by yet another example of Susannah's avid taste for anything smacking of gossip. 'And I want to finish this seam before I start putting the girls to bed.' She sewed steadily on.

The new shoe fitted, the coach rolled out of the yard. John poked his head around the door, red-faced after the heat of the forge, and grinned knowingly at his wife's expectant face.

'I knew you'd be wanting to hear all about it, Susie! No,' he teased, 'it wasn't our bishop . . . but you're very warm! It was one of those *Roman* bishops – well, he was more than a bishop, I think, what they call a cardinal. He's come to open that new

153

church they've been building for the Catholics, up on Potterhill – the day after tomorrow. One of his chaplains said his name was Leyton.'

Leyton . . . Catt felt the world turning upside down and wondered if she was about to faint. A wave of conflicting emotions engulfed her, sucking her down into a bottomless whirlpool – a mixture of shock, disbelief, perhaps even a little pride.

Leyton? A Catholic cardinal called Leyton? Was it possible that her father – her natural father – was here, here in Pickerby, and that only a few minutes ago he had been but a few feet away from her?

No, she told herself. I'm dreaming. Leyton is not that uncommon a name, it's not possible . . . In any case, Catt found it hard to visualise Charles Leyton rising so high. He had been little more than the family chaplain at Leyton Hall, after all, clever though he undoubtedly was – and almost as fond of his fox-hunting as of his chapel, it often seemed. She had never thought of him aiming higher.

Nevertheless, it was hard to keep the tremor out of her voice when she was so desperate to learn more, and equally desperate not to appear unusually interested.

'Did you speak to – this – this cardinal, John? What was he like – was he a very old man?' For if he was, that would settle the problem, thought Catt – I could forget all about Charles Leyton again.

John shook his head. 'He never left the coach, but I spoke to him as he did the paying – and he paid handsomely, too, way above what I asked for, and insisted I took it all. He wasn't so old – in his fifties, maybe – very distinguished-looking. A real gentleman! The man I spoke to most, one of his household, told me the cardinal's famous in the big new cities. He's done a lot for the poor there. But I'd never heard of him till today. Of course, the Catholics in Pickerby will know all about him – but then they aren't folk we mix with, much.'

He's done a lot for the poor . . . That did not sound much like the Charles Leyton Catt remembered! All the same, the more she thought about it, the more convinced Catt became that the

154

man in the coach could indeed have been her father. The age, the distinguished appearance – they all seemed right – and, after all, as he grew older, Charles Leyton's character could have changed a great deal; had not her own?

That night, as she tossed restlessly in her bed, with little Kate – the Kate who had Charles Leyton's nose and eyes, and sometimes, she could have sworn, his very expression – lying sleeping beside her, and the new baby kicking within her, Catt's jumble of thoughts swelled into an idea so audacious that it quite terrified her. Yet she could not let it go, fantastic though it was. She lay awake into the small hours, planning its carrying out, and imagining the wonderful consequences that its fulfilment might bring. When she eventually fell asleep her dreams were all of Townend.

Next day, she could hardly wait for the afternoon to arrive. Only then did she feel able to leave her children with Susannah, with the excuse that she had some 'woman's shopping' to do, where they were better left behind. Surely, Susannah must notice her unusual excitement, and wonder. . .

Catt did not feel at peace until the forge door was shut behind her and she was walking slowly and a little shakily up Potterhill, towards the priest's house where John had said the 'Romans' had been holding their services up to now, and where he had heard the cardinal was going to be staying. Apparently he had declined the hospitality of Pickerby's one modest hotel, leaving that to his staff alone – yet another gesture which sounded out of character with the Charles Leyton of Catt's younger days.

She walked as if in a kind of trance. The tall grey priest's house seemed to bend and wave in the full heat of the August sun. The brash new redbrick edifice alongside it, soon to be Pickerby's first Catholic church for over 350 years, seemed equally ethereal.

This is sheer madness, she thought. I'm drunk on my dreams! I ought to turn around now and go back to the forge – before something dreadful happens. But she pressed forward. However crazy it might seem, this was something she *had* to do for Luke and for the children – fragile though her idea

155

might be, she had convinced herself that it was the only hope for their future.

After all, thought Catt, he can easily refuse me – he can even refuse to see me – and then I will go away and no one need ever know I have been here . . . But at least I will have tried.

She reached the black front door and rattled the heavy brass knocker with a boldness she was very far from feeling.

For a very long time indeed, it seemed to Catt, no one answered. Everything around was still; just the bees, buzzing in the clematis on the wall above her. Finally the door opened a little to reveal a gaunt, black-gowned woman, hair scraped severely back from a lined but not unkind face.

She looked Catt up and down. 'Do you want to see Father Buxton?'

This must be the parish priest, Catt decided. She struggled to form the words she wanted. 'No – it's his visitor . . .'

'Not the cardinal. Not His Eminence!' The housekeeper looked shocked. 'That's quite impossible – not without a special appointment.' She started to close the door.

Catt's desperation brought the words pouring out. She pushed herself forward, putting one foot firmly across the threshold. Pink spots of emotion stood on her cheeks.

'Please wait! I can explain! I think he might see me – you see, I think I was one of his – congregation – years ago . . . That is, if he is who I think he is. I once worked for his mother, the Lady Anne at Leyton Hall in Nottinghamshire. I wasn't much more than a child, then.'

The housekeeper's expression softened a little, but the door remained half-shut. 'You must be a visitor here, for otherwise you'd know that you'll be able to see His Eminence when he dedicates the new church tomorrow.'

'No, I can't come then – and I would so like just a few words, ma'am. He'll surely remember me, he knew my parents well – my name was Catherine Youngman.' Catt's new-found confidence began to falter. 'Could you not at least give him my name and see what he says? Please.'

'Well . . .' For the first time the other woman seemed to take in Catt's distracted air and advanced state of pregnancy. She held back the door. 'It's very unusual. But you'd best come in and I'll ask.'

There followed what seemed like another age of agonised waiting in a grey, sunless room filled with books and holy pictures such as Catt had not seen since the days she had helped her mother clean Charles Leyton's study, all those years ago. She shuddered and suddenly longed to rush out of the door. What in the world had possessed her to come here like this? A dream, a mad, mad dream – and a dangerous dream, too, she was starting to think. She felt a rising tide of nausea at her own boldness.

Just at that moment, a door behind her opened. Someone took her by the hand.

'Catherine!'

17

Catt's fast-dwindling courage came surging back. It was her future, and not only hers, but Luke's and the children's, that was held here in her hand – her clasped hand. Their whole lives depended on what she could achieve in the next few minutes . . .

With a supreme effort of will-power, she forced herself to look up, straight into her father's face. I must begin slowly, formally, she thought. It all has to be done correctly.

'I – I am so very grateful to you, Your Eminence, for seeing me like this – without notice – I beg to apologise for troubling you . . .'

'There's no need to keep up appearances any more, Catherine,' the cardinal interrupted briskly. 'Let us drop the formalities, shall we? We shall both feel more at ease then.' He smiled, and for a fleeting moment Catt caught a glimpse of that radiance which had so captivated her as a child. Then his mood changed. 'I know now that you were told the whole story – our whole story – at the same time as myself,' he went on gravely. 'But I didn't know that was so until much later on, not until after your – disappearance – from Melchester.' He sighed. 'I tried so hard to find you, then – I wanted to explain, to ask your forgiveness, to offer any help you might be needing. But all to no avail. You had vanished completely. It was as if you had disappeared from the face of the earth!'

Catt stared at him, totally mesmerised.

Charles Leyton had aged considerably in the ten years that had elapsed since her expulsion from Leyton Hall. His long, thin face was heavily lined now, and the dark hair turned to iron-grey. But the deep-set eyes – her eyes, and Kate's too – were as luminous and penetrating as ever.

He's changed, thought Catt, and it isn't just that he's grown older . . . there's something quite different about him. He had become more human, she decided, and yet, at the same time, more impressive.

Later on, reflecting on the events of this memorable afternoon, she realised that she had been able to sense a kind of goodness, a feeling of serenity which had in some way communicated itself to her. The handsome, glamorous man whom she had idolised in her childhood, and, before she had been aware of his true relationship with her, had loved romantically, had become a prince of the Church who yet understood and empathised with the burdens of the poor and the weak.

How had this transformation come about? Was it triggered, in the first instance, by the burdens Charles Leyton himself had had to bear? By his guilt – guilt on account of her, the daughter who had been victimised simply for having been his daughter?

Now she heard her own voice, echoing as from a distance: 'They sent me away – right away – and said I could never come back,' she was saying dully. 'They sent me away in disgrace – and yet I had done nothing wrong.'

'Oh, Catherine! Do you think I don't know that – now? You were most dreadfully treated – most grievously sinned against. There are not words strong enough to describe it . . . One could say it was quite unforgivable – except that I do, in all sincerity, believe that God in His mercy can forgive all those who truly repent.' The briefest of smiles flickered across the cardinal's ravaged face. 'And, believe me, Catherine, I *have* repented – for the hurt I did your mother and yourself, and for all the subsequent damage that ignoring and trying to conceal those wrongs did to my mother's soul.'

He faltered – then continued purposefully: 'When you were first sent away, my mother absolutely refused to tell me where you had gone. She had made your mother and your – foster-father – promise to keep the secret, too, and they were so

159

mistakenly loyal, they carried it to their grave. My mother thought she was protecting me, you see – she knew no other way, God forgive her! Her love for me quite blinded her to the fact that *I* had responsibilities, too. It was not until you had run away from Melchester that I was told where you had been sent . . . and by then it was too late – no one could find any trace of you! I tried so hard to discover where you'd gone. I came to Melchester and walked the streets, looking for you. I asked scores of people if they had seen you. I even posted a notice in the Melchester newspaper – but it was no use. Nothing but silence . . . It was not long after that that my mother died – and then I set enquiries going all over again, but still there was no response. I really believed, then, that you must have perished, that your death was yet another burden of sin to be laid upon my family. For years now, I have been praying for your soul's repose, Catherine. Now, thank God, I can pray for my living daughter!'

Suddenly, Catt felt as if a great weight had been lifted from her and the words poured from her lips. How it had all begun – her adolescent's mistake in thinking, ridiculous though it now seemed, that Charles had been trying to seduce her, that fateful day in the chapel. 'I was so very innocent, in those days, as well as foolish,' she said bitterly. And then how Mary Jane had given away the fact that he was Catt's natural father . . . from which the rest had followed – the decision arrived at jointly by his mother and hers, Lady Anne and Mary Jane, to send her away for ever.

'Yes, you are right – it *was* a joint decision. They both decided it was for the best,' interjected the cardinal. 'Despite the fact that it was their own daughter and granddaughter they were abandoning.'

'That house in Melchester – you have no idea what they were condemning me to! It was a dreadful place – a place without any love in it at all, for all it reeked of religion,' cried Catt, made angry again by the memories. Then, more calmly, she described how she had made up her mind to bear it all for Josh and Mary Jane's sakes. Their death had changed all that – it was following that that she had decided to run away – and as soon as the chance arose, had done so. And then her expression changed from resentment to love, as she described how she had met Luke, and eventually married him . . .

'Your guardian angel must have been protecting you,' exclaimed Charles, 'as I prayed so often that he might!'

Catt shook her head, stony-faced once more. 'My faith died in Melchester,' she declared flatly. 'Maybe before that, even. It was the actions of your family – and my own – that started the killing of it. Melchester was probably just the final blow.' She shrugged defiantly. 'I even got married in a regristry office, though' – and her voice softened, and her words were spoken less certainly – 'my children – my three little girls, not to mention the boy who died – I did baptise myself, the Catholic way, the way I saw you doing it, all those years ago.' She tried to smile. 'So *they* have a chance of reaching Heaven, even if I have lost mine.'

Charles Leyton shook his head. Catt was aware of the sadness and compassion in him. 'You're a baptised Christian, Catt – Heaven will always be waiting for you! But you have to accept its presence first.'

When she did not respond, he continued. 'I have prayed for you since the day you ran from me in the chapel – and I shall go on doing so until the day I die, and beyond. I understand your anger and your bitterness – you were abominably treated, and nothing can excuse it. My mother, God rest her soul, was blinded by the pursuit of what she believed were my best interests. In her devotion for me, she lost all sense of justice, and all love for the rest of humanity. She saw you –you, a helpless, young, innocent child – and her only grandchild – as nothing more than a terrible danger, an evidence of sin, that had to be scotched, eradicated, forgotten . . .' Wistfully, he concluded, 'In so many ways, she was very like a saint – but where I was concerned, I can see now that she was quite ruthless.'

Catt looked at the red sash, the scarlet cap, the jewelled pectoral cross. She could not control her resentment. 'Her ruthlessness seems to have succeeded, does it not?' she remarked acidly. 'For you have risen very high.'

Charles shrugged. 'That happened later – and *you* must take much of the credit for it.' As she shook her head, he persisted, raising his voice emphatically. 'Yes, *you,* Catherine! For I do believe it was following the treatment I had seen meted out to you that I set to asking God what He really wanted from me – how I could atone – and He answered.'

He went on to describe to Catt what had happened in Leyton after her abrupt departure from it. On learning the truth, that Catt was his own daughter, Charles Leyton had, he confessed, experienced a very personal crisis of faith. The tragic deaths of Mary Jane and Josh, and the death of his own mother not long afterwards, had exacerbated this. He had felt himself utterly unworthy, had seriously considered leaving the Church altogether. Instead, he had chosen in the end to leave Leyton Hall to work among the poor, Catholic and non-Catholic, in one of the big northern cities. There he had preached much and written much – and done much, too, though of this he made no mention to Catt. It was only a year ago that he had been made a cardinal – some people said, on account of the number of converts he had made, he said, deprecatingly.

'And Leyton Hall?' asked Catt. 'Do you still go back there?'

'No, my brother, who would have inherited, died in India a few years ago. He had never married. So I – and you, Catherine – are the last of the family. The estate is sold – there are no Leytons there any more – a Nottingham lace-manufacturer is the squire now. I believe he has pulled the chapel down . . .'

Had I been your legitimate daughter, I would have inherited all that, thought Catt, remembering, with sudden nostalgia, the house and the gardens and the chapel, all the sights and sounds of her childhood, lost and gone for ever. It was almost as if her father could read her mind, for he said, somewhat distractedly:

'It does seem doubly unjust. If circumstances had been different, it would have been yours. All yours. Oh, Catherine! It's too late – and that can never be – but now that I have found you, now that you are here, I can surely do something to make up for what you have lost.'

His obvious discomfiture gave Catt renewed courage. 'I swear to you – Father' – it was the first time she had dared use the word to him in its literal sense – 'I did not come here to try to take advantage of your position,' she said steadily. 'Nor to blackmail you.' As her father shook his head, she went on, 'No – I'm sure you must be thinking that that is why I'm here. After all, a cardinal with a daughter – what a scandal that would cause! But I promise you I have no such intention. I never have had, and I never will have. But . . . I *have* come to seek your help.' She took a deep breath. 'If you refuse me, that will be an end to it. I will go at once, and for ever. No one knows that I am here. Not even my husband knows that you are my real father – it is the only secret I have kept from him, but . . .'

With that, Catt plunged into her story. Of how her Luke – good, gentle Luke – had been so sorely dealt with, how he had been slighted by his own father, and was now about to lose his present situation. How she and the children were living on a relation's charity. And then she went on to tell how she had seen Townend up for sale, but at a price which, though a bargain, was still beyond her means and Luke's. If she could but borrow the money for it, her whole family's lives would be transformed.

'Believe me, it was terribly hard for me to come here. Had he known my plan, my husband would have forbidden me, absolutely. He may be poor, but he's proud, and has never asked for anything. But when I heard you were in Pickerby, and had become a great man – I dared think you might help me, for my mother's sake, if not for mine.' Catt stumbled on, breathlessly. 'It's a loan I'm asking for – just a loan, for a few years. We would pay you back each month, with interest – Luke and I are hard workers and honest, anyone will tell you this. And I will never bother you on any account ever again, I promise you.'

Charles Leyton looked at her quizzically. 'And you'd swear that on the Testament – despite all you've said about the Church?'

'If that's what you want, of course I would,' Catt retorted earnestly. 'But, please believe me, my word is as good without – I would not want to take advantage of God, now that I've parted company with Him.'

Her father reached out, took hold of her hand again, 'God never parts company with anyone, Catherine . . . But of course I will help you. Most surely! It has been my dearest wish to do so – ever since I heard whose daughter you were. As for blackmail, why, I have known you since you were a child. I know your character, even if I was too blind to recognise my own flesh and blood until that last day in the chapel. But we must be practical. You can safely leave everything in my hands. Be patient; there will have to be formal arrangements made, and those take time.'

Catt could hardly believe what she was hearing. She had succeeded! The money for Townend was going to be lent. Townend was hers, and Luke's. Luke's . . . the thought of her husband brought her swiftly down to earth again and she interposed swiftly: 'There's one last favour I want to ask. I've promised you I'll never trouble you again – and the lawyers will see to our repayments – but please, *you* must not get in touch with *me,* either. We have always lived in different worlds,' she tried to explain, 'and we still do . . . Perhaps even more so, these days, than before, for since I broke with the Church, we have not even that in common. But, believe me, I will be giving you thanks till my dying day, from the bottom of my heart.'

And, despite all her father could say, Catt remained adamant. Even when Charles Leyton asserted that her husband, at least, would now have to be told the whole story.

'No, Josh Youngman is down as my father – my dead father – on my marriage lines. Luke will understand' – and here Catt was unconsciously speaking to bolster a confidence she was increasingly finding it hard to sustain – 'that this is simply a loan made for the sake of the past, on account of the ties between my family and yours. Which, indeed it is.' She smiled, a little wanly.

For a few more minutes they talked on, like any father and daughter who have been apart for a long time. They talked of things that had happened long ago, small things, but ones that still evoked vivid memories in both of them. As they talked, Catt grew less strained, more relaxed, allowing herself to mention her own children, even remarking that she had often thought that Kate looked a little like her Leyton grand-father.

'And the next child? A boy, perhaps? To make some amends for the little one who died,' her father interrupted gently.

Catt looked at him sharply. And it was now that, altered though he was, mellowed by age and the great changes in his way of life and thinking, that she was hit by that same overwhelming emotion that she had felt in Leyton chapel on that fateful day. It was then that Charles Leyton had put his arm around her in the shock of his sudden recognition that she was his daughter. But her response to him had been the white-hot passion of a lover, and it was a response which had haunted her for years afterwards. All too often it had come between Luke and herself in their most intimate moments of lovemaking, and left her filled with an indescribable guilt and self-loathing. Gradually, the passion had faded. She had believed it dead – but now, after all this time, it had returned to engulf her yet again. She longed – oh, how she longed – to throw herself into Charles Leyton's arms . . .

Sick with disgust, Catt felt suddenly faint. She rose unsteadily to her feet. Her cheeks were burning.

'I am sorry, I – I have to leave. Now. I have stayed far too long as it is – my sister-in-law will be wondering where I have gone.' She brushed aside Charles's protests. 'No – no – I have taken up too much of your time already.'

He tried to hold her back. 'At least, Catherine, let me give you a blessing. Surely you will allow me to do that!'

But Catt broke from him and made for the door. 'You have given me blessings enough in promising what you have! I will never forget what you have done for me today, never. And – Father' – her voice shook and she felt ridiculously near to

165

crying – 'please believe me, the past is forgiven. All forgiven – everything concerning you, and Lady Anne – everything!'

18

Outside in the safety of the open street, Catt leant heavily against a tree and took in great gulps of breath, struggling to recover from the emotional turmoil from which she had just extricated herself. She felt physically sick as well as emotionally shattered. But gradually the blinding intensity of the late afternoon sunlight brought her back to reality. She stirred uneasily. Acutely conscious, now, that some passer-by might notice her distress or that she might still be visible from the house she had left so precipitately, she started to retrace her steps down the hill. She picked her way carefully, fearful lest she stumbled; the forge seemed an unattainable hundred miles away!

Pickerby's parish-church stood at the foot of the hill – tall, graceful, grey-spired – dwarfing completely the ugly redbrick building which her father was to dedicate next day. Its door was ajar. Exhausted by all that had happened, Catt forgot her fears of damnation and staggered inside, sinking thankfully into a back pew.

Her spinning head began to clear. It was cool inside the church, and so silent she could hear her own heartbeat. Here she was quite alone – a luxury she rarely had these days. She stared around her curiously.

There were marvels all around her – for a feast of paintings covered every wall of the nave, all immediately recognisable to Catt from her own religious upbringing. The Nativity, the Crucifixion, the Assumption – and a huge St Christopher facing the door through which she had entered. A tiny Child Jesus was perched on his shoulder, and happy grinning fish swam in the swirling waters at his feet.

But it was the painting of St Catherine which struck her most forcibly – Catherine, after whom she had been named, wearing her martyr's crown and saint's halo, and carrying the wheel upon which she had been broken until she died.

Catt looked hurriedly away. Her new-found calm evaporated. As a child, the story of St Catherine had always upset her; the saint's smiling, perfect face and body in all the paintings seemed obscene in view of the appalling death she had suffered – and which the pictures never showed . . . Now she felt herself undergoing a mental torture comparable in its way to the physical one endured by her patron saint.

What in the world had possessed her to approach her father as she had done – and actually dare ask him to lend her money? Was anything – even the apparently imminent realisation of a dream – really worth the revival of the past, with all its remembered miseries, injustices and illict passions? How could she have been so rash?

And what was Luke going to say about all this? How would he take the news that she had gone to beg for money – even if it were only a loan – and been promised it? At this point Catt even began to wonder whether her father might yet go back on a bargain struck between him and herself alone, and without witnesses – especially when she had fled from him so abruptly at the end. There was nothing written down. Despite all his protestations of affection and remorse, might the cardinal not now regret having acknowledged his daughter, and resolve to take the matter of the loan no further?

But the next minute, Catt was reproaching herself for her lack of faith and trust. However poorly Charles Leyton might have conducted himself in the past, she recognised that this afternoon she had been in the presence of an exceptional human being. A humble man, notwithstanding his exalted position, and a good man. Such a man would never break his word.

'Wherever have you been all this time?' cried Susannah, on Catt's return. 'And not a shopping bag in sight!'

'I just walked . . . It was too hot for shopping, I decided.'

Catt disregarded Susannah's doubtful expression and plunged into a fresh discussion about Townend. Susannah probably thought she had been there yet again, and this was no bad thing . . . and after this afternoon's events, the farmhouse was back at the forefront of her thinking. Why, it did her good just to talk about it!

'It would suit Luke and me perfectly – and think how near we would be to you,' she concluded.

Susannah nodded placidly. She had by now come to regard Catt's obsession with Townend as no more than the extravagant fancies of the sort that women often acquired during pregnancy – like a sudden passion for eating strawberries – and which vanished as soon as the birth had taken place. Aloud, she remarked soothingly that she only wished she and John could help – but then Catt already knew that the kind of money needed was quite beyond their means.

We are on dangerous ground here, thought Catt, in view of the present circumstances – and she hurried to steer the conversation into safer channels and determined to let her favourite topic drop.

But without this outlet, the next few days seemed to drag interminably. Catt felt herself suspended in a limbo of anticipation. Would she hear further from her father – or his solicitors? And what were Luke's reactions going to be, should her dream come true?

It would be best, she decided, if everything could be signed and sealed before Luke next visited. Then, whatever he said, whatever pride he felt was at stake, there would be nothing he could say of do to destroy the dream she was trying to turn into reality for him and her family, even more than for herself.

So she was relieved when another Sunday came and went without Luke being able to visit.

The opening of the Catholic church took place without Catt being present to see it; when the ever-inquisitive Susannah pressed her to go with her, she pleaded her condition as an excuse for refusing. She would dearly have liked one more glimpse of her father, but was terrified her emotions might give something away. Susannah returned, with vivid descriptions of the vestments and banners and the handsome cardinal, but reported that the new church itself was not a patch on St Peter's at the bottom of the hill.

The cardinal and his entourage had been back in London for some time, and Catt was almost beginning to wonder if the meeting with her father had ever really happened at all, when there was a knock at the smithy door. It was a messenger-boy, with a letter for Catt.

She could scarcely open it, her fingers were shaking so. When she finally did so, she saw it was from Martin, the Pickerby solicitors. It simply asked if she, Mrs Catherine Halliday, would confirm if it was convenient for her to call at the office in three days' time when she could be able to sign the transfer of the property called Townend and the land that went with it into her sole possession.

Catt tried to assemble her thoughts rationally. She frowned, puzzled. She had asked her father for a loan; but this letter sounded as though it was referring to an actual sale. Ah, well, she thought, I'm not used to legal jargon. It's probably all a form of words . . . She was suddenly aware of Susannah peering curiously over her shoulder. Instinctively, she folded the letter over, even though she knew Susannah could not read.

Letters to the forge were virtually unknown. Catt herself had never received one there before, either; for, despite all her tuition, Luke had never reached the stage of being able to write one. She hesitated. Susannah must be finding the whole business very strange – some kind of explanation was called for urgently. Something approaching the truth seemed the easiest thing to say. 'It's just a lawyer's note,' she told Susannah, and then to the messenger-boy, 'Please tell Mr Martin I shall attend at the time he suggests.'

Closing the door on him, she turned to Susannah again, smiling. 'You see, Sue, I've been enquiring a bit further about Townend – and Martin's have now given me an appointment so that I can go and talk about if, see if there is any way we can get our hands on it – but,' she concluded smoothly, 'I don't imagine for a moment that anything will come of it.' At this stage it was best not to tell Susannah more than was absolutely necessary.

'But Catt! What in heaven's name do you think you're doing?' Susannah was aghast. Catt's pregnancy fantasies were beginning to take over from reality, she thought, and that was dangerous – people like the Hallidays and the Carters never had dealings with lawyers except for the odd will-making. It didn't do to waste people's time like this – and it was bound to cost something, too. Catt had to be stopped. 'What is Luke going to say to this? You can't go behind his back and see a lawyer without him being there too. And what's the point of it, anyway? For you know you haven't the money for Townend – and even supposing you had, Luke would surely want it all spent on getting hold of High Moor.'

It was then that Catt remembered, for the first time in weeks, that High Moor was also on the market at present – High Moor, Luke's abiding passion. For a moment she felt like a traitor – a traitor to Luke – but she rapidly pushed any such thoughts right out of her mind. It was obvious she herself could never be expected to go back there; after all that had happened, Luke knew and accepted this. In any case, she told herself, Townend was so much better for Luke and the children – a real family home, here in the sheltered valley, far, far healthier than damp, dank High Moor. Faced with the choice of smooth, fertile acres or a stretch of half-barren moorland that could support nothing but a few skinny sheep – well, there was no comparison!

Aloud, with a calm confidence she was very far from feeling, Catt said: 'Of course, Luke is going to have to know about this – and agree anything that needs agreeing. But all in good time. He's not here, at the moment, and in any case, I'm only making enquiries . . . Nothing is certain, absolutely nothing. If things did happen to go further, maybe the solicitor would be able to find us some way of raising the money, with a loan we could pay back, bit by bit, over the years. It's not unknown . . .'

Susannah was unconvinced, but she confined herself to

muttering something to the effect that, within her own admittedly very limited experience, this did not seem likely.

At this point Catt managed to switch the conversation to something safer and resolutely avoided the whole subject of Townend over the next few days, declining absolutely to go into it with her brother-in-law when, spurred on by his wife, he attempted to broach the subject. Once or twice she caught Susannah and John whispering together. They would stop when they saw her, and step guiltily apart. Catt guessed they were mulling over once again the problem of her 'odd' behaviour.

Not for the first time, she was heartily grateful that Luke was too busy to come down to Pickerby at the moment. She hoped she would not have to see him until, please God, something had been decided, until she could present him with the Townend affair all signed and sealed. And she thought lovingly how, if this dream of hers really did become reality, it would be her supreme way of thanking him for all he had done for her.

Since Susannah's mention of High Moor, Catt had been plagued by the nagging fear that Luke might not want her offering, however splendid. At the same time, she determinedly avoided thinking through the problems of how she would be able to explain the cardinal's conduct without disclosing her relationship to him. It was Josh who was down on her wedding certificate as her father, and she had never even hinted to Luke that this was anything but the truth. It would be difficult to backtrack now.

※　※　※

Catt made sure she allowed herself plenty of time for the walk into Pickerby centre to keep her appointment. As she walked, she tried to rehearse in her mind exactly what she was going to say. But it was difficult. This was partly because she was distracted by the vision of Susannah and John back at the forge, undoubtedly discussing her at this very moment, possibly with one or two of their friends – but also because she had not yet puzzled out to her own complete satisfaction the full meaning of the solicitor's letter.

She was anxious lest she should appear ignorant and silly, and painfully aware that unaccompanied women did not often visit lawyers' offices – let alone women of her social class. So she found it a real effort of will to ring the bell and maintain an outward calm as she was ushered in through the brass-plated door.

But her worries had been unnecessary: she was received with considerable courtesy and swept straight into the senior partner's room. Henry Martin, white-haired and Gladstonian, rose to welcome her and see her to her seat, facing him across his desk. Catt perched on the edge of an enormous velveteen chair, rigidly tense and feeling uncomfortably tiny and insignificant despite her eight-month pregnancy.

'Well – Mrs Halliday – I should like to think that this meeting is the beginning of a long professional association – unless of course, you already employ the services of another solicitor?'

Catt shook her head, determined not to let these formal surroundings intimidate her. 'Oh, no – we've not had cause before.'

'Splendid!' Henry Martin smiled. 'I am sure we're going to get on famously.' He opened the folder on the desk in front of him and looked at Catt meaningfully. 'And so to business! I have here an agreement for you to purchase Townend Farm and its 15 acres and all its stock – the house and land to be your freehold, of course.'

Henry Martin caught Catt's look of bewildered astonishment. He smiled reassuringly. 'If you are concerned about the cost, dear lady, you have absolutely no need at all to worry. It's true, the completion formalities will take a little time – it may be a few weeks yet before you and your family can have possession – but I can assure you that the money for the entire purchase has already been gifted to you absolutely, down to the very last halfpenny of the legal costs, by a benefactor who wishes to remain anonymous.' The solicitor gave a discreet cough. 'I believe you know who he is – and I understand from his solicitors that you too wish all the circumstances of the transaction to remain private.'

'Yes, but . . .' Catt leaned forward, blushing. 'Please forgive my confusion. But surely there must be some mistake? For I had only asked to borrow the money, with my solemn undertaking to pay it all back over a period of time . . . yet you are talking of the property being "gifted"?'

'I have been told the nature of your original request, Mrs Halliday. But your – benefactor – was quite insistent. The farm and its land is to be yours, as a gift. There is no question of any repayment at any time. And this is a final offer; there is no scope for any modification, not' – and Henry Martin smiled again – 'that you would be advised to ask for any! This is a wonderful opportunity for you, Mrs Halliday – the offer is one such as I have never had to deal with in the whole of my career. I strongly advise you to put your hand to it without delay.'

'My husband . . . I shall have to tell my husband,' muttered Catt faintly, as the full import of what she was being presented with began to sink in at last.

The solicitor nodded reassuringly. Her nervousness and initial lack of comprehension had come as no surprise; the matter was, as he had said, unique in his experience as well as hers. But a solicitor's office was the repository of many strange secrets; and absolute discretion and tact were second nature to him.

'Naturally you will be discussing all this with your husband. However, the legal arrangements have been specifically tailored to make the land and property over to you, absolutely – and to no one else. The donor was quite definite on this point. This is a gift to *you;* it makes *you* the sole owner of Townend. It is to be *your* property, not your husband's. Of course, what you choose to do with it later on is entirely your own affair, but I gather' – and here the solicitor turned to another document on his desk – 'I gather the donor's intention is that you should, in the fulness of time, pass it on to any son you may have.'

Catt swallowed hard. Was it her imagination – or did she feel the baby within her stirring a little? She recalled how her father had mentioned that perhaps this child would be the living healthy boy that she and Luke had been longing for. Now she was acutely aware that this baby would also be the cardinal's grandson.

Everything was coming right at last! Catt felt a sudden wild abandon – she wanted to dance and shout, she was so happy. It was a real effort to sound reasonably decorous. 'Of course I accept this gift – and please tell the – donor – that I shall never cease thanking him, from the bottom of my heart, to my dying day . . . And now,' she said, in what she hoped was a suitably businesslike voice, 'can you show me where I must sign my name?'

The clerk was sent for to witness Catt's signature. She gave it with a special, triumphant flourish. Henry Martin stepped out from behind his desk and shook her warmly by the hand.

'Allow me to give you my very warmest congratulations and best wishes,' he said, 'on becoming a landowner in your own right!'

19

Catt walked back to Susannah's in a daze of delight. For the first time in years – not since the heady days of her first meeting with Luke, in fact – she felt the whole world spread at her feet, ripe for the taking. What a triumph she had had! It was all quite, quite unbelievable.

She longed to give Luke the good news. Had she still had faith in miracles, she would have considered what happened this afternoon a miracle indeed! At last – at long last – after so much waiting, after so many disappointments and so much pain, she and Luke had the prospect of real advancement. For the very first time, *they* had become the privileged ones. And how marvellous that felt!

Nevertheless, it was a shock to reach the smithy and find Luke waiting impatiently for her in the yard. He looked worried; and Catt's new-found confidence collapsed abruptly. She remembered what she had quite forgotten during her recent burst of euphoria – that she had not yet worked out how best to break her good news to her husbans.

The enormity of the whole undertaking now hit Catt with crippling clarity. Luke, after all, knew absolutely nothing about Townend; she had gone ahead with it quite alone, from start to finish. No matter she might say to herself that there had been no chance to tell him anything – that things had moved ahead far too quickly – she knew quite well in her heart of hearts that even *had* there been she would still have tried to act without him, for fear he would have forced her to draw back . . . Let alone the question of her deliberately choosing the acquisition of Townend at the very same time as Luke's beloved High Moor was also on the market.

She had done it all for Luke, of course. Even to the deliberate choice of Townend in preference to that dreadful, luckless place on the top of Gelling Moor – but would Luke see things in that light?

Too late, Catt was having to face the fact that there was one secret from her past that she had never revealed to Luke – that Charles Leyton and not Joshua Youngman was her real father. Looking at the subject realistically, she knew it was going to be hard, if not impossible, to stick to the story she had originally thought of telling – that the cardinal, in making this generous gesture, was merely acting out of kindness to the child of one of his family's old servants. Such a tale might have seemed faintly plausible if she had been the recipient of a simple loan, but now that Townend had been given to her outright, it seemed, she had to admit, quite beyond the bounds of reasonable belief.

Suddenly Catt was struck by the awful – if slightly inconsequential – thought that maybe the lie on her wedding certificate might mean that hers was no valid marriage at all, that her children were as illegitimate as she herself was. No – surely not . . . And then she comforted herself that Luke had never yet failed to understand and sympathise with everything she had told him of her life before she met him.

But this was something rather different. Catt wished devoutly, now, that she had told Luke the whole story from the start, leaving out absolutely nothing, not even the fact that her father had been the son of the house – and a Catholic priest . . . In those early days, she had been too ashamed, as well as terrified that such a revelation might frighten Luke away and wreck her chance of happiness and security for good.

Now, with the benefit of hindsight, she could see that the whole unvarnished truth might in fact have been easier, not harder, for Luke to tolerate when their relationship was new and fresh. But now? After all these years of deception? And any plea of shame could be said to sit badly with the fact that she had just happily – oh, how happily – accepted a substantial gift from the very person she held responsible for that shame.

Luke had just completed one of his rare carting jobs. He had been to the fashionable spa town of Harrowby, and brought back a tiny china ornament for everyone – tiny Goss cups for the children and German sugar-bowls with *A Present From Harrowby* inscribed on them in gilt lettering for Susannah and Catt. These were newer than Goss and considered superior, being more expensive and all the rage. Susannah marvelled at the price Luke must have had to pay and could not resist a dig at his extravagance. 'My – and you with no place of your own, Luke, and no job either, soon!'

Catt's cheeks burned. Little did Susannah know that very shortly Luke would not only have a roof of his own over his head but a job in which, for the first time, he would be his very own master – thanks to her, and her father. There would be money for even bigger and better presents, too, once they were settled in. Why, with a milking herd and a thriving market garden, they could be quite comfortably off in no time! And without sheep to care for, there'd no longer be need for Luke to be out all hours and even away overnight, living that hard, lonely life upon the moor – so there would be all that extra time for holding and loving.

She felt a surge of physical longing and she looked at her husband and wished she could take him upstairs with her this very minute, strip off his clothes, pull him onto her, make him take her – no doubt unnatural, even wicked thoughts for any woman, let alone one who was more than eight months pregnant. But she could not help herself. And perhaps the lovemaking would blot out all those old, unnatural images of her father that had been returning to plague her.

Aloud, she simply said: 'I expect they've already told you there's something I have to say – something very important.'

Luke exchanged a meaningful glance with Susannah, and Catt knew with chilling foreboding that her sister-in-law must already have had time to mention Townend and the solicitor's

178

appointment, before her own arrival back at the smithy.

She was right. 'If it's about Townend, love, that's quite out of the question,' Luke began gently. He was speaking very carefully and slowly, Catt noticed, as if she were a child in need of humouring, and she felt a stab of resentment. 'Why, even if we could raise the money somewhere – which we couldn't – we'd be mortgaged for life. We'd end up in the workhouse, without a doubt! And in any case, Townend's not a sheep farm – it's nothing but cows and apple-trees and cabbages and such –'

'Please, Luke, let me explain! It's not as you think – not at all!' Catt turned to her sister-in-law. 'Sue – could you see to the children just a few minutes longer and I'll take Luke upstairs and tell him what happened this afternoon.' The two youngest girls were dragging at her skirts, seeking attention, while Kate, silent and inscrutable as ever, had her face buried against Luke. Catt saw Susannah's hurt, inquisitive face and winced. 'Please don't fret, Sue! You'll hear all about it, just as soon as I've explained it all to Luke – I promise.'

As she reached the stairhead, Catt was obliged to steady herself against the banister. Her head was throbbing; anticipation was making her feel sick and queasy.

Luke bounded up behind her, to support her. 'Whatever's the matter, Catt? What's come over you? Is it the baby. . . ?'

Roughly, Catt pulled herself from him and faced him across the bed. 'No!' she almost shouted. 'No! It's not – but it's going to help the baby, and the rest of us! Oh, Luke!' She clapped her hands in triumph. 'Townend's to be ours! Really ours! No – not on lease – we're to *own* it! It will be a week or two before all the details are sorted, before we can actually move in, but the agreement's signed, the money's already paid – it's ours!'

Luke stared at her, dumbfounded. For a few seconds, which seemed like an eternity to Catt, he was absolutely silent. Then, even more hesitantly, he said, 'Catt, love, it's your condition – it's the way you're feeling . . . you're not seeing things quite straight at the moment. This is all a fantasy. Whatever have

179

you been telling this solicitor Susannah's been talking about? For it's nothing but a load of nonsense – you're imagining things and it's not good for you.'

'No! No!' Catt smiled ecstatically. 'It's all as I've said! I'm sorry it's come as such a shock. Yes, I thought of a loan at first, and I can see that would have been hard to manage, though we'd have paid it back in time, somehow, I'm sure. But then, quite suddenly, the farm was *given* to me – yes, *given*. I couldn't believe it myself when I first heard it – but it's true! At last our luck has changed!'

While Luke continued to look as bewildered and incredulous as ever, Catt started to blurt out the details. 'I was out walking and I saw Townend being offered for sale – it was all quite by chance – and I knew it was exactly what we wanted. Oh, it's not on the moor, of course, and there are no sheep, but it's a farm, for all that! And it's here in Pickerby, near to your Susannah, and there's a school for the children and shops to hand and the weather so much kinder than at Gelling or Allercliffe. And with cows instead of sheep, you'll not keep having to be away from us, like now, and I can help with everything –'

'But –'

'I knew we'd hardly any money. I thought there was no hope for us, much as I loved Townend – from the first moment I set eyes on it I knew it was right for us. Just right for a family, quite apart from the land . . . But then a sort of miracle happened. My father came to Pickerby! I went to see him – I was only asking for a loan to let us pay for Townend – I gave him my word we'd pay back every penny! But the next thing I knew was that he'd arranged to have the farm *bought* for me –yes, for *me* – but of course,' added Catt rapturously, 'it will belong to *both* of us, whatever the lawyers' papers say.'

Luke's eyes were dark with anxiety. 'Catt, you're not yourself – all this is just one of your dreams! But you're taking things too far. Didn't you tell me yourself that your father had been a lodge-keeper, and that he and your mother were burnt to death in a fire, years ago, before you and I had even met?' He moved round the bed to his wife and tried to put his arms around her, but she shook him off. 'Calm yourself,' Luke persisted. 'Please, Catt! It's so bad for you, carrying on like this – and bad for the baby, too.'

Catt stamped her foot, emboldened by frustration and rage to say what she had previously lacked the courage to say. 'No, you're wrong! It will be *good* for the baby. And for the rest of us, as well. Josh Youngman was my *foster-father!* I didn't know it until I was more than sixteen. I loved him as I would a father, and I always will . . . But my real father, my natural father, was Charles Leyton. He was the son of the house where my mother worked as a maid. He became a Catholic priest, and now he's the English cardinal – even higher than a bishop! Not much more than a week back I found out – not just what a great man he had become, but that he was actually here in Pickerby, to bless the new Catholic church. I screwed up my courage and went to see him . . . and that's how all this came about.'

As Luke continued to stand, stock-still, silent, white-faced, apparently unable even now to take in what he was hearing, Catt poured out the rest of her story. She told how she had learned 'by chance' whose daughter she really was – 'and he didn't realise he was my father, either, till then' – and how 'the family' with her own mother's connivance and approval, had then sent her away to Melchester 'just for being someone's daughter I should not have been'. The rest, of course, Luke knew already.

Two secrets Catt still withheld from her husband. These she would carry with her to her grave – her own guilty passion, which had precipitated her fateful flight from Leyton Hall and from which everything else had followed – and the fact, which she scarcely admitted even to herself, that Charles Leyton could still arouse feelings and emotions in her which were not those normally felt by a daughter for a father. Catt recalled the powerful wave of physical desire that had swept over her at the very moment when Charles had taken her hand in the prim Pickerby presbytery, and felt a hot flush of guilt.

When Luke at last managed to speak, it was not to comment on the gift Catt had just set before him but to cry: 'Oh, Catt!

Why didn't you tell me all this long ago, at the beginning? I had always thought there were no secrets between us.'

'I was too ashamed.'

'But why?' Luke shook his head ruefully. 'None of it was your fault. None of it! I would have understood. . .I had told you all about *myself*, had I not – and some of that was hard enough to say.'

Catt covered her face in her hands. 'You don't understand. . .' She was painfully aware that the hurt of her deception had, for the moment at any rate, snuffed out any interest Luke might have begun to feel for all she had accomplished, and her own pride and excitement in it were ebbing away. Desperately, she cried: 'I am so sorry, love! So very, very sorry! God knows, I never meant to hurt you. I only thought – I was afraid – that if you knew the truth – that I was a priest's – bastard – daughter – you'd think me some kind of a monster, something unnatural . . . and leave me. And I couldn't bear the thought of losing you! Please believe me!'

Now it was Luke's turn to show remorse. 'Oh, Catt – you know I would go to the end of the earth and into Hell itself for you, a thousand times over.' He cradled her in his arms, buried his face in her hair, covered her face with kisses. For a few moments there was silence – the only sounds, their own gentle breathing, and the solemn tick of the grandfather clock in the hall below.

Eventually, more prosaically, Luke said: 'I know you only acted as you did for my sake, Catt – and for the children – and I know what an effort it must have been for you. All the same, we can't possibly accept this offer. You know we can't. Even if it had been for High Moor itself' – and Catt winced as she heard what she had hoped Luke would never mention – 'we couldn't. Above all, not someone like you, with all your pride in yourself. For, can you not see – it's charity, pure and simple charity, that we're being offered here. And payment, no doubt, for keeping quiet about a past your father'd like to think safely buried. Is it not? However poor we may be – and I know our future's uncertain – at least we have each other and our self-respect.'

182

This last sent Catt into a sudden passion of blind fury. She tore herself from Luke, turned, and hit him flat across the face.

'How dare you speak to me like this! It's not charity I've been asking for, it's not charity I've been offered, and it's not charity I've taken!' she screamed, not caring that her words might be echoing clearly in the room beneath. 'It's my *rights! And your rights, too!* If there was any true justice in this world, I'd have stood to inherit a whole estate. Surely a dairy farm and 15 acres are modest enough compensation for being barred from that. Think what you and the children would have had if I'd been the legitimate daughter of the heir to Leyton Hall! You've no right to suggest I should have rejected this offer! Granted, it was more than I wanted, let alone expected – but now I've got it I can see how right and just it is! And as far as your High Moor goes' – she continued sarcastically – 'you were turned down for that, were you not? And in any case, could you really expect me to consider going back to live in the place where my – our – son was virtually murdered by your own family? And what are 25 acres of barren heathland and a few score sheep, and the cold and loneliness and poverty of it all, in comparison with Townend and what it can give us?'

Catt paused for breath, appalled, despite her rage, to see the red stain of her slap on her husband's face, mortified by his continuing refusal to respond. If only he would *do* something ' whether it be rebuke her or even chastise her . . . As he continued to stand there, silent, looking so sadly at her, her anger redoubled and her voice rose even higher.

'Anyway, you can do nothing about it now! The solicitor told me so. The agreement is signed. Townend is all mine – mine absolutely – and neither you nor anyone else can take it away from me!'

As she spoke, an agonising pain seemed to rip her whole body apart. Gasping for breath, Catt slumped forward onto the bed. The excitement, the violence of the argument, had precipitated her into another premature labour.

20

A blood-red mist swirled all around her, rose and fell, and from it, a host of images and faces from the past appeared, gestured, vanished . . . Charles Leyton; Mary Jane and Josh; Miss Fredericks; Nell; Old William . . . there were even some Catt had known only by name and had never seen – a sad, pallid woman whom she knew to be Luke's mother and who pointed an accusing finger. Why? What had she done? Then Luke himself was there, very gaunt and deathly pale; she thought he must be dying . . . But it was she herself who was dying, surely?

In her frantic terror, Catt summoned the energy for one despairing, piercing scream. She wanted to run away from all this, but something was holding her down – invisible, searing chains, it seemed. As her scream echoed and re-echoed, she made one final supreme effort to break her bonds. She had to get free, even if she died in the attempt! Then, in the far distance, she fancied she heard a baby's thin, trembling wail. 'A boy,' someone said. 'Why, he's a real bonny little lad, even though he's such a tiny one!'

Then the mist closed in again, the voices faded away and the succession of distorted, half-demented faces of those she had always loved the most – Josh, Nell and Luke – were as menacing as the rest . . . and she felt cold, too. So very, very cold.

The nightmare seemed endless. Later, Catt was to find out it all happened within the space of a few hours, when she had indeed seemed for a time to be hovering between life and death. Then, at last, came the slow awakening. She opened her

184

eyes to find herself between the lavender-scented sheets of Susannah's front bedroom. Standing there, looking down at her, were Luke, and Susannah and John, and the doctor.

Then Catt knew it was all over, and she felt a stab of panic as she remembered the last time she had gone into a too-early labour and that much-wanted little son had died . . .

'The baby! Where's my baby?'

And here was Luke, smiling his old, familiar, loving smile once more. But there was a new pride in his face. 'Why, Catt, our little lad's here, in the crib beside you – and he's healthy and bonny, for all he's so small!'

The world rushed back in on Catt in a sunburst of happiness. The pain and quarrelling of her previous consciousness were quite forgotten and, for the time being, Charles Leyton and Townend were forgotten also, as Susannah gently lifted up the tiny, beshawled bundle so that Catt could put her new little son to her breast.

She gazed at him, overcome by wonder and delight. She stroked the pale blond down on his head, and believed he was not simply the image of his father but the exact likeness of that little dead son who lay buried in the corner of Gelling churchyard . . .

Such perfect bliss could not last for ever, of course. Catt's recovery was unusually prolonged. The birth had involved a difficult forceps delivery, and a few days after little Luke's birth, Catt began bleeding heavily. Postnatal haemorrhaging was a common killer; once again, Catt's life held by a thread. But she held on, and when at last she started to show a real improvement, she emerged from her coma to find little Luke being bottle-fed by Susannah and already putting on weight, and a sheaf of papers from Henry Martin regarding Townend awaiting her attention.

Once again, the question of the future had to be faced – the question which had caused such anguish and argument earlier on, and had led to little Luke's arrival in the world rather sooner than expected. And this time, faced logically and calmly.

It was now that Catt started to realise that since she had first broken the news of her real parentage – and of her new property – to her husband, Luke had undergone a profound change of attitude. While she lay ill, he had had ample time to think matters over more coolly and to talk to his brother-in-law, the blacksmith. He kept to himself – as he always would – the secret of Catt's parentage. He merely explained that a childhood acquaintance had suddenly and totally unexpectedly left his wife the means to purchase Townend. How did John Carter think he should respond?

Even as he spoke, Luke was well aware that the story seemed a far-fetched one. But there was the evidence of the solicitor's papers to back it up. Whatever John really thought of the facts as given him by Luke, he did not query them. He and Susannah had long found Catt difficult to fathom, much as they liked her, and they supposed some family mystery – even a scandal, maybe – was behind all this. But John was too discreet to probe further, and restrained Susannah from doing so. This was Catt and Luke's business, and no one else's.

So John Carter confined himself to urging Luke in the strongest terms he knew to take advantage of the situation and seize the opportunities it offered.

'Surely, Luke, it's more than time you had a bit of good luck – and this is good luck with a vengeance!' he declared. 'Just think of the shabby way your own father treated you – and look what a pretty state you'd be in now, but for this inheritance! Why, you'd still be a man with a wife and four children to feed, and no home of your own and no steady job . . . The fact that Townend's no sheep farm isn't all the world – shepherding's not what it used to be, as you yourself have said time and time again.'

Luke held his bluff, honest brother-in-law in the deepest respect and the logic of John's argument was inescapable. So, despite all he had said earlier, and despite the fact that he was giving up for ever the dream of his life – the eventual possession of High Moor – he determined to adapt to the way of life that Townend offered him. It made every sort of sense, as he well knew – and it fulfilled Catt's dream, if not his own.

He felt a deep sense of gratitude towards his exalted father-in-law, even while not being able to conquer entirely his underlying resentment that Catt had not told him the full story of her life much earlier. It was fortunate, indeed, that he was never to know the real reason behind Catt's ambivalent attitude towards Charles Leyton . . .

For all his acceptance, however, the whole affair was to leave Luke permanently scarred. In his heart, for all the years that remained to him, he would go on hankering for his moors and his sheep, wandering up from Pickerby whenever he had a few hours free from his labours at Townend – alone, or with one or more of the children. If children were with him, he would delight in pointing out to them High Moor, walking them to the Bridestones, and showing them the places in Gelling churchyard where his parents and their little brother lay buried. To the end of his life he unconsciously regarded Townend as a kind of cage – a fine and gilded cage, indeed, but a cage, nevertheless – in which he was irrevocably trapped.

Affectionate and tender as he remained towards Catt – who never went with him on these moorland pilgrimages – she sensed a subtle difference in him, which occasionally frightened her. *She* had always had, and always would have *her* secret self, which no one, not even Luke, could penetrate. Now, for the first time, there was a part of *him* which had become remote from *her*. Try as she might, she could not reach it – and though Luke remained outwardly as placid and pliant as ever, there was a vein of toughness in him now which had not been there before.

✻   ✻   ✻

This new Luke first manifested himself when Catt began showing real signs of recovery. Only then did the couple return to the subject of Townend. At the start, both approached the topic very carefully and somewhat gingerly.

Catt had been fearful that Luke would be as opposed to it as ever. But she was quite wrong. For her husband now declared his total acceptance of the situation.

'I've had time to think about it a great deal – and I've discussed it with John, without naming too many names, of course – and I agree with you, love. It's a wonderful offer, and it's one we can't possibly refuse,' said Luke soberly. He took Catt's hand and looked deep into her eyes. 'When you first told me, it was all such a shock, so unexpected, I couldn't take it in – and I couldn't really believe it, either. But now . . . I promise you, love, I'll not say anything more against it, ever again. Nor mention how you came by it – and from whom.'

Catt tried to speak, but Luke hushed her and went on: 'And there's another thing, Catt – how could I possibly blame you for whose daughter you are? What fault is it of yours, how your parents acted all that time ago? You've been paying dearly for what they did for years, have you not – it's only right you should get some return in the end. I'm so, so happy for you – and for us all – so very, very happy! Only, I wish you had told me the whole tale sooner . . . that's what upset me the most – that you'd kept anything from me.'

Then Luke's tone changed, acquired an unfamiliar edge. 'But there's one condition I'm setting to all this. I want the little lad to be baptised in Gelling church, just as I was – and the three girls can be baptised along with him there, for all they're no babies any longer.' And, as Catt began raising objections, Luke plodded stolidly on. 'Oh, I know you think my Church of England can't do a proper baptism – but if it's not a proper one, how can it matter to you, one way or the other? Anyway,' – he shrugged dismissively – 'my mind's quite made up, Catt. I've already been to see the parson and everything's ready and arranged. And,' added Luke, 'there's one more thing that must be done. The lad has to be named after your father as well as me. And you should tell the lawyer about this, so that he can pass the news on. You owe your father this, at least, after what he's just done for you, whatever the hurts of the past – and don't ever forget, love, that it's your father's gift that will pass to our son, his grandson, one day.'

Catt was left with no choice but to nod her agreement. The

naming would, she thought, mean that her father's memory could never now let her be; it would be reawakened each time she looked at or talked to little Luke Charles. It would be a keeping green of certain things she would far rather try to forget – but she could not expect Luke to understand this unless she disclosed the one secret that she could never tell him . . .

The matter of the christening itself would nag at Catt's conscience for the rest of her life – quite irrationally, as she often told herself, for she had taken care to give Luke Charles a 'Catholic' baptism of her own, as she had the girls before him. She absolutely declined to attend the ceremony up at Gelling herself, pleading that she still felt too weak to cope with it after her difficult confinement. Luke was forced to accept this, and in fact Catt's non-attendance raised few eyebrows. It was common knowledge that she had been so ill during and after the baby's birth that she had been lucky to survive. She would be able to have no more children in the future.

So Catt remained at the forge, alone, with only John's apprentice for company, while Luke and his children and the Carter family set off in John's cart one early autumn afternoon and headed up the moor to Gelling village.

There, Luke Charles and his three sisters were all baptised in the Norman font, where generations of Hallidays had been christened before them. The little girls were dressed in their Sunday best. The Halliday christening gown remained unused in Will and Betsy's keeping for Catt had flatly refused to consider asking to borrow that, so the baby wore the Carters' one, with a touch of extra smocking added by Catt, at Susannah's insistence, 'for good luck'. The church rafters echoed with Luke Charles's indignant howls as the water splashed on his head – another good omen, asserted Susannah, since it meant the Devil had quite gone out of him!

All in all, despite Catt's absence, it was something of a party. On the way back to Pickerby, they all stopped awhile, got down from the cart and wandered in the heather, not far from High Moor, and Luke managed to find a sprig of white heather among all the purple and tucked it into his son's christening shawl.

'Now he's a real Halliday, and no mistake!; cried Susannah delightedly. 'He's all properly christened, even if we've never had a Charles in the family before. And he's got a bit of white heather from the old family moor for good measure. Oh, it's clear everything's changing for the better for you now, Luke. For all of you.' She flung her arms around her brother's neck. 'And we're all so happy for you! Who could have deserved it more?'

Luke looked from her to his little family and then smiled back. Yes, he thought, thanks to Catt – and her father, the father whom he had never met and never would and to whom he would never be able to express his own thanks – there was a future ahead which, only a few weeks back, he would have believed beyond the bounds of all possibility.

Nevertheless, as they breasted the top of the long hill leading down to the vale and back into Pickerby, he looked back, with an aching longing at the heather-laden slopes stretching away to the distant grey smudge that was High Moor farm. Just then, a cloud raced across the sun. The heather turned suddenly dark, like a greedy, menacing sea that threatened to swallow everything in its path – and on the horizon he fancied he saw the Bridestones starting to march towards him . . . He felt a stab of quite irrational foreboding. Surely, their good fortune could not last . . . ?

This feeling passed soon enough. But Luke's gnawing yearning for his moors was never to leave him.

At the moment, however, there was so much work to do, connected with Townend, that the days seemed scarcely long enough. Catt and Luke became familiar figures in Henry Martin's office. Catt sometimes felt she had almost taken up residence there, with so much signing to do. But she was glad to be kept so occupied. For, in her few odd idle moments, there was too much opportunity to feel apprehensive, even a little fearful.

Had she really been right to start all this? It was so complicated, – was it fair to have dragged Luke –

straightforward, simplistic Luke – into this legal jungle? Might it not have been better, in the long run, to have let him stick to shepherding, to have accepted that they would always be poor, with a future always uncertain – to have gone along as before, simply looking for another place back there on the moors, however humble?

But she determined to put any such misgivings right behind her. Not long ago, she and Luke and the children had had no future at all, to speak of; winter was on the way, Luke's hiring nearly done, with no prospect of work beyond, and they were living on a relative's charity . . . but for that, they could have been in the workhouse long before this!

Catt shuddered at the nightmare that haunted all working people – and, at the same time, gave silent and heartfelt thanks to her father for providing them with such a glorious chance to go forward into a future that promised endless possibilities.

But oh, if only she could think of Charles Leyton only in terms of pure, unadulterated filial love! Surely, she ought to be able to do that. Why was it that thoughts of him still had the power to awaken in her shameful, dreadful passions from her past? Could it be that she was being punished? For her Bridestones dalliance long ago? For her loss of faith? For allowing her children those heretic christenings? No . . . this was just ridiculous superstition.

I've got to stop being so emotional, Catt resolved. I've got to stick to thinking about the future – forget everything else.

And what a future it was! There was nothing they might not do now. Their lives had been transformed at the stroke of a pen. Luke would soon be able to add to their initial 15 acres, Catt had no doubt at all of that, so that by the time Luke Charles was old enough to help, their holding would already have been increased. The girls could go to the new government school here in Pickerby, that was only minutes away from Townend . . . Townend, where she would be creating a real home for them all – a proper home, in the house she had fallen in love with the moment she set eyes on it. It was a house that shouted security and safety, nestling as it did in the heart of the sheltered vale, surrounded by green, rich pastures. Here they would be shielded from the gales and blizzards of the moors she had so come to hate. Here they would be far happier than they had ever been before. Here, please God, they would be free from all those malign spirits and misfortunes which had seemed to dog their past.

21

Catt and Luke were able to move into Townend well before the onset of winter. And with them went the furniture and belongings that had been stored for the past several weeks in the forge outbuildings.

As she stood still for a moment and looked around her on her first evening in her new home, Catt realised for the first time how pitifully meagre their possessions were. The three little girls were exploring the house excitedly, and their shouts and footfalls echoed around the empty spaces. In Townend's relatively spacious rooms, her few pieces of furniture were almost lost.

She could see now how small both High Moor and Allercliffe had really been. Again, she was acutely conscious of the sudden good fortune her father had made possible – and felt a sense of underlying panic.

Could she and Luke really manage to make something of this? They had virtually no capital and Townend demanded a type of farming quite outside Luke's previous experience. But, once again, she managed to ride out the worry. Of course they would manage – and they would do more than simply manage. They would make a real success of this!

'It's the chance we've always wanted – a dream come true!' Catt whispered to Luke, in bed that first night. 'Provided we work hard – and are sensible – I don't see how we can fail. For we're our own masters now – we're not dependent on other people's fads and foibles any more.'

In the lovemaking that followed, any doubts that either of them might still harbour were swept clean away in an abandoned outpouring which effectively submerged even those latent images of Charles Leyton.

It was indeed just as well, Catt often remarked over the next two years, that she and Luke had never been afraid of hard work. In that time, they managed to transform Townend from an almost empty shell into a pleasantly comfortable home. Rugs softened and brightened the stone floors – rag rugs, first, made by Catt and Kate, but later, when it could be afforded, these were replaced in the front parlour by a real piece of Wilton. In his rare spare moments, Luke knocked up shelves and simple clothes chests and tables. As the money began to come in from Catt's sale of eggs and chickens, and from the fine embroidery for which she had again found a demand in Pickerby, Catt was able to pay the local cabinet-maker to make her sets of chairs and a fine double kitchen dresser. She started buying a few pictures – there had been none at High Moor or Allercliffe – mostly scenes of children or animals, but she had one Bible scene, a sepia lithograph of Ruth's farewell to Naomi. This was Catt's favourite, and hung in the best position over the parlour mantelpiece. In a bitter-sweet way, it reminded her of her parting from Josh, long ago . . . Ruth had done well in the end, despite the sad farewells, she remembered – and so would she!

Each new acquisition seemed to justify all the efforts put into obtaining it. Catt would often sit working to complete a piece of embroidery by candlelight after her ordinary housework was done, from midnight well into the small hours, so that she would be going to bed just as Luke was getting up to start the milking . . .

In the parlour there was a place of honour for the little spinning stool which had been Luke's mother's. Catt remembered wryly the day at High Moor when she had come upon Old William chopping up the spinning-wheel itself for firewood, home-spinning having long gone out of use. She had been too late to save that, pretty though she had always thought it – but she had persuaded her father-in-law to let her keep the long-backed stool. Now, cleaned and polished, the dark oak gleamed and she thought it looked very pretty, old though it was – and she treasured it, even though she knew old country furniture was generally considered a sign of poverty nowadays, and she had no wish to be associated with poverty any more. She was less sure about Nell's copper-faced warming-pan; all the best people now favoured brass. But she could not bear to get rid of it; it evoked too many happy memories of Nell. So Catt waited until she could afford to have the old copper face replaced by a shining new brass one – and never guessed her descendants would one day mourn the substitution!

Luke proved himself as skilled at handling cows as sheep. Within the first year he was able to increase the number of milkers and employ a day-labourer, who also helped with the milk-round – which meant taking the churns of still-warm milk round the streets of Pickerby, which was expanding all the while and would eventually stretch right up to Townend and beyond.

When the need and means for an extra pair of hands first arose, Luke had consulted Catt. 'We're doing so well,' he began tentatively, 'and I know there's Will and Betsy up there in that tiny place in Gelling, with next to nothing now . . . I've been thinking, if we did a bit of work in that stone outhouse by the orchard we could turn it into a cottage, and they could move in and help us. There'll never be more than the pair of them now, and Betsy could give you a hand, while Will worked for me . . .'

His voice faded as he saw Catt's thunderous and incredulous expression. 'Never!' she cried, when able to find her voice again. 'Never! Not after what they did to us.' She tried hard to sound calm, to justify herself – only half-succeeding, as she herself knew. 'Betsy and I could never get on with one another. Even if being poor has taught her what hard work really is, I couldn't have her in my house . . . As for your brother' – and Catt made no attempt to hide her scorn – 'folk do say he's more drunk than sober, even though Gelling's got but one inn! So what do you think he'll be like here, with the choice of Pickerby's half-score? What would the children think, seeing a drunken lout about the place? And what real work would you ever hope to get out of him?'

Luke nodded sadly. No matter he knew Catt was right – hadn't John and Susannah, with far less of an axe to grind than Catt, said exactly the same? Even when they were children together, his brother had always bullied him . . . Yet, he thought, family was family. Now that he was prospering and Will virtually a pauper, he felt he had to do something, in spite of the past and all the hurts.

Catt read her husband's mind only too clearly. And remembered words, heard long ago in Leyton chapel, of the beggar sent empty away . . . She winced – partly in response to her long-standing loathing of Will and Betsy which Luke's pleas for charity had reawakened, but also because those old teachings regarding charity towards one's neighbours, and even one's enemies, had come back to haunt her. But it was no use being sentimental – her own family's happiness had to come first. That was far more important than compliance with old, forgotten principles. What was needed now was some compromise between the ideal and the practical . . .

Eventually, she allowed: 'We can never have them here, Luke. And I don't ever want to see either of them again. But if you want to give them something – make it a bit easier for them – well, that's your business. I won't stand in your way.'

So it was left – a tacit agreement that Luke would give his brother the odd half-sovereign now and then, if he 'happened' to go near Gelling village. Occasionally he would pass there on some business errand connected with Townend. But usually a visit meant taking a special journey by train up the valley, alone, for it was agreed that no child should ever accompany him on these occasions. At the beginning, Luke would try to give Catt an account of what he had seen, but as time went by, and she continued to show a total lack of interest in the subject, he gave up bothering. It was enough she had agreed he could make these visits at all.

Luke did tell Catt, however, that High Moor was now amalgamated with the Home Farm, and the Halliday house just a store-place. He was struck by Catt's obvious relief on hearing this – and saddened by it, even though he understood it, for, notwithstanding all the heartache and misery he had known there, Luke still regarded High Moor as his real home.

But these days, there was scant time to dwell on the past – the present was so busy. For Catt and Luke the days were never long enough for all they had set themselves to do. The children were brought in to help; in the autumn, especially, the whole family joined in the fruit-picking, and even Luke Charles was filling baskets of apples almost before he could toddle. Any spare moments Catt salvaged from the house-work, the hens, or her sewing, she would spend among the vegetables – weeding, watering, hoeing, picking. Townend sold its produce to local people, and, to begin with, Luke hired his own stall in the weekly Pickerby market. Then, as Pickerby grew bigger and more sophisticated, a Melchester man arrived to open a greengrocer's shop. After that, Luke gave up his stall, much to Catt's relief, for it meant she was released from helping with it – she could never take to such close encounters with people she hardly knew. From now on Luke sold direct to the new shop.

There came a time, too, when Catt could afford a girl to do the washing and the roughest of the cleaning; and when she and her daughters could go to the dressmaker and the milliner for their best gowns and bonnets, and Luke could have the tailor make him a new suit and did not have to rely any longer on the cast-offs of Nell's long-dead husband.

But such luxuries were some way off, yet. The first years at Townend were very hard ones. Catt and Luke were working all hours, and even when their children were not actually being conscripted to help, their parents – Catt in particular – had precious little time and energy to spare for them. It was left to Kate – plain, withdrawn Kate – to do most of the bringing-up of her sisters and brother, even to the extent of being often kept away from school to do so, such as on days when Catt was occupied with the market-stall.

Catt tried not to feel guilty. After all, I can help her catch up on reading and writing myself, as soon as I've got more time, she told herself. But she never did. Just as she never managed to find the time to coach Luke beyond the basic literary skills, despite all her original intentions.

One consequence of this was that Kate grew up barely literate. Nellie and Susie, on the other hand, had a proper elementary schooling, while Luke Charles was to create family history by winning a scholarship to Pickerby Grammar School. True, Kate was happy to act as unpaid family nursemaid; though she was intelligent, she followed her father in being intelligent but not academic. It was not this, but her mother's seeming lack of interest in her as a person in her own right, which went back indeed, to the day of her birth and Catt's taking her help for granted, that was to rankle with Kate unconsciously throughout her life. The dutiful Kate could occasionally be stubborn enough to wear down even strong-willed Catt, while her apparent acceptance of her present condition in fact concealed a passionate desire to get away as soon as she possibly could from her family – from Townend – from Pickerby – from everything remotely rural. Kate longed for the chance of an independent life in Melchester, which was now only an hour's journey from Pickerby with the coming of the railway link between the two places. Little did she know that her mother had once fled from it and could never think of it in terms of anything but fear and loathing.

Kate's stubbornness first surfaced in her attitude towards religion. At school, the Pickerby parson visited weekly to give Scripture lessons. Kate shone in these from the start. Though she was outwardly so prosaic and down-to-earth, the Bible opened up a wonderful new world for her; and though she never learned to write well, she could read enough to decipher great chunks of the Old and New Testaments. Catt watched, fascinated, and wondered what the cardinal would have made of his fanatically Anglican granddaughter! She told herself that Kate's faith would fade, as her own had done. But it didn't. Soon Kate was asking to be confirmed and persuading Luke to override all Catt's objections.

It was Kate's religious leanings which finally led to the

fulfilment of her material ambition, for the vicar's wife had a sister married to a Melchester doctor who needed a nurse-maid for a new baby. At fifteen, Kate left Townend for good, not even returning for her own wedding, but only when a family crisis demanded it. At the Anglo-Catholic church in Melchester she met a gentle young booking-clerk, ten years her senior, with the same religious enthusiasm as herself and married him there within the year.

When that happened, Luke travelled to Melchester with his son to give his daughter away. But Catt stayed at home once again, pleading that somebody had to look after the farm. After all, what was the point in going back to a place she dreaded, merely to witness the wedding, in a heretic church, of a daughter who really had been a stranger to her from the day she was born?

Alone that night in the silent farmhouse, however, Catt wondered uneasily if Kate were the only member of her family she scarcely knew. In the hurry and bustle that had been her whole existence since the acquisition of Townend, had she not grown apart not only from Kate, but from all her other children, and – most importantly of all – from Luke, too?

       ✻   ✻   ✻

All that was some way off, yet. For now, after the grinding, almost never-ending labours of the first couple of years, life started to get a little easier. By the time Luke Charles began going to school, Townend was prospering and the Hallidays had acquired a certain status in Pickerby. Their children were all well-behaved and well turned-out. Catt and Luke appeared the embodiment of a thriving, thrifty farming couple. They had a pleasant house, and the growing collection of brass and china ornaments adorning the parlour gave witness to their growing wealth; they had a fine herd of cows, an immaculate orchard and a healthy bank balance in their relatively new account.

But they remained something of a mystery. Their sudden purchase of Townend, when they had appeared only steps away from the workhouse, continued to be the subject of some gossip. Catt, too, was considered to be rather aloof and remote. It was known she was not a native of the area – not even of the county – and she made no move to make friends beyond her immediate family circle. In the early years, when she was so preoccupied with Townend, Catt's former intimacy with Susannah suffered in consequence, never to be fully re-established, as later Susannah grew increasingly shy in the face of the Hallidays' growing affluence. Of course, the Halliday children, following Kate's earlier example, now went regularly to Sunday school, and Luke was an occasional church attender. But Catt had never been known to enter any place of worship, though she gave generously to church and chapel charities whenever she was asked.

About this time, news reached Townend of Nell's death, some months earlier, in Canada. After that, communication between the Pickerby and Canadian Hallidays dwindled, and eventually ceased altogether.

'She was the best friend we ever had!' cried Catt. 'It was she who gave us our start in life together. If only she could have come back to see us – to see what we've made of things, just once!'

She and Luke mourned Nell long and deeply. To Catt, she would always remain a more loving memory than her own real mother, whose final rejection had largely wiped out her original feelings of affection.

Now Catt was horrified to realise that, notwithstanding her solemn promise made to Nell, years ago, that she would be sure to visit and tend Clarrie's grave in Whinborough at least once a year, she had not been near it since becoming mistress of Townend. And yet, I never once forgot, when I was poor, she told herself reproachfully.

In the old days, when she had been living on the moor, in poverty and comparative isolation, a journey to Whinborough had meant a complicated combination of a cart-ride and a train journey she could ill afford – and the added burden of fitting things in so that Luke could be on hand to watch over the children. Yet she had never once missed her annual pilgrimage then. Now, with Pickerby station a ten-minute walk away, and a return service to Whinborough several times daily that was relatively cheap and certainly well within her new means, she had put the matter right out of her mind.

Oh, Nell, forgive me! A remorseful and mortified Catt set out for Whinborough the very next day. In the past, she had gone carrying a bunch of heather from the moor and flowers from her cottage garden; this time she took a florist's arrangement of expensive lilies and roses. She hoped Clarrie and Nell, wherever they now were, would understand by this that she was trying to make up for her past forgetfulness.

As she tended the pathetic, neglected little plot in the churchyard high on the cliff above old Whinborough, Catt wondered uneasily what in the world had happened to her sense of values. How could she ever have forgotten this most sacred of duties? No amount of work or worry should have kept her away – she, who had always been so bitter and resentful when she herself had been let down, had now, in her new-found prosperity, proved equally careless of promises made to others.

Catt finished her tidying, got to her feet again and sighed. *Oh, yes, you'll forgive me, Nell – you always forgave everyone!* But the remembrance of Nell's perpetual generous-heartedness, contrasing as it did with her own incapacity to show forgiveness – to Will and Betsy, for example – only added to Catt's feelings of shame and unease.

Perhaps it would have been different – perhaps *I'd* have been different, nicer, even – if Luke had taken up Nell's offer, all those years back, and we'd gone with her to Canada. The thought struck her so forcibly, she fancied she heard herself speaking it aloud . . . She and Luke might have been even better off than they were now. That first little son might still be living, and almost grown-up – and there would have been no need to call on her father's charity, to admit her secret to Luke. And then these subtle, invisible barriers which now existed between her husband and herself would never have arisen.

Why didn't I try harder to persuade him? thought Catt. For

I'm sure I could have! He loved me so, he would have done anything I wanted, had I pressed him hard enough. But I was too much in love with him, too afraid I might lose him – so I stayed silent.

With what result? Years later, when she was older and made ruthless by desperation, she had gone ahead to bring her own dream to reality, regardless of Luke's most deeply held feelings . . . And, though material success had followed, something vital had been lost.

As she stood, brooding on the past and the might-have-been, Catt saw a woman in deepest mourning hurrying down the path towards her – a woman of about her own age, and with features seeming vaguely familiar . . .

'Annie!' cried Catt, stepping forward instinctively – but the woman bowed her head and moved on past her, heading for a grave beyond.

Of course, she had been mistaken, she was upset, not thinking rationally – Annie would have been unlikely ever to return to the town of her childhood . . . But the sudden vision, however flawed, of yet another memory from her past only added to Catt's agitation.

Almost without thinking, she found herself walking down into the old town, to the little house on the cliff where she had lived those happy months with Nell. She had not seen it since her wedding day. It was still there, still a boarding-house, if a little seedier than in Nell's day. The harbour district below it was fast turning into a mish-mash of attractions aimed at the growing numbers of trippers. There were fewer fishing-boats, and everything seemed to have shrunk and grown more tawdry. All the elegance and opulence was firmly on the South Cliff now. Catt was glad Nell had not stayed to see it all changed so.

On her return home, Catt threw herself into her household duties and her family with renewed and almost frenetic energy. Her Whinborough visit had stirred memories she would far rather have kept buried. Still, the past was over and done with, she told herself; there was no point in dwelling on what might have been.

202

Catt remembered how Old Will Halliday had clung to memories of a past, some real, some probably imagined – and how his present had been blighted and, in the end, his family's future at High Moor destroyed by them . . . No, one had to live for the present – and dream only of the future, never of the past. Only in so doing could one's ambitions be brought to fulfilment! And was that not exactly what she had been doing, and was continuing to do? She had dreamt of and worked for a fine future for Luke and her children, and now, she comforted herself, it was all coming to pass, just as she had hoped it would.

But was it? Were things really all that they should be? Cocooned in her dreams of grandeur, Catt resolutely closed her eyes to the fact that Luke never ceased continuing to yearn for the moors he loved so dearly. She brushed aside her neglect – amounting to virtual exploitation – of her eldest daughter. She refused to admit her own inner feelings of faith in the divine. She hadn't time to worry about such trifles! And it didn't matter, anyway; for the time being, for the present, the gloriously successful present, she felt impregnable within the well-guarded walls of her own little world.

Here she was in total control; here she could love Luke and further what she considered to be his best interests, in spite of anything he might think. Here she was utterly, utterly safe; nothing could penetrate here to harm her or hers, nor bar the future path she had marked out for them all.

22

Then tragedy struck. All Catt's dreams of a carefree, prosperous future were rudely shattered.

Susie – pretty, affectionate, effervescent little Susie, with Luke's golden hair and Luke's sunny nature – caught a spring cold, and the cough that had been part of it, remained when the cold itself had gone. As the weeks went by, it grew ever worse. Even when racked with coughing, Susie looked bonnier than ever; her cheeks acquired a new blush, her blue eyes burnt so brilliantly that at first one scarcely noticed that her face was growing thinner almost by the day.

'A consumption,' pronounced the doctor, and prescribed rest and a special diet. But when Catt pressed him to name a date when Susie would be well again, he merely shrugged and turned away.

For a while, Catt refused to believe the doctor's diagnosis. Consumption? In this clean, well-to-do house, where her children never lacked for anything? In the past, in the days at High Moor and Allercliffe, she might have understood it, but not now! Why, her efforts and sacrifices to move her family up in the world had been motivated, in part, by her desire to save them from the diseases which ravaged the poor, especially the children . . . and she was no longer poor!

She looked at Susie's flush and sparkle. The doctor's wrong, she comforted herself – and, as Susie seemed to rally – it's nothing by growing pains, surely . . .

But the doctor had been right. Before the year was out, Susie was dead.

Together with his three surviving children, a heartbroken

Luke stood around the little grave in Gelling churchyard. Catt was not there, however; she remained shut up at home, raging against the injustice of it. Her grief was compounded by a dreadful bitterness and fear. For what had little Susie ever done to deserve this? What had any of them done? In the grip of a terror she refused to admit even to herself, Catt wondered, as she had wondered before in times of crisis, whether this was the hand of God, punishing her for abandoning Him. But why should He choose to do this through her sweet, innocent little daughter?

Following Susie's funeral, Catt fought to keep her nightmare fears at bay by throwing herself into improving Townend with a vigour that verged on the manic. And, at the same time, Luke had to be rescued from his grieving; in his unhappiness, she could feel him slipping further and further away from her. Then she seized on what she believed was a brainwave.

'Sheep!' cried Catt triumphantly. 'We could have sheep again, now, love – and this time they needn't be the sort that keep you away from me.'

Luke looked doubtful; but in the end he gave way to Catt's enthusiasm and the couple put down most of the savings they had so far accumulated to buy a few extra acres, a mile or so from Townend, on the Whinborough road. They began building up a small flock there. But if Catt hoped this would raise Luke's spirits she was sadly disappointed. The fat, valley breed had little in common, in Luke's eyes, with the wild moorland flocks which had been his life for so long. And though the sheep were to be a financial success – nearly all Catt's farming ideas were money-spinners, these days – it was a project whose management really remained in her hands alone.

In any case, the new project paled into insignificance, all its therapeutic powers lost in the new calamity which fell upon the family. For hardly was little Susie in her grave than Nellie, too, began to sicken.

'She's simply pining for Susie – for they were almost like twins! It will pass, in time.' This time it was Luke who refused to face the truth, who struggled to quell Catt's anxieties. After all, the two little girls, with little over a year between them, had always been particularly close. Nellie had cried for days after her sister's death and for a time seemed almost inconsolable.

But soon it was all too clear that Nellie was suffering from the same illness that had killed Susie. There followed the same unhappy cycle; weeks of nursing, all to no avail; weeks of watching a happy little girl gradually reduced to a wretched, coughing skeleton. It was even worse this time, for the consumption took longer. Occasionally, Nellie would seem to improve; her parents would take new hope, would believe that, yes, the doctor really had been wrong this time. Only to be doubly shattered when the remission did not last. The end came inevitably, though Nellie did not finally die until sometime after the first anniversary of Susie's death.

Again, Luke stood in Gelling churchyard, to see Nellie buried in the same grave as her sister. But this time there were only two children to stand alongside him. And again, Catt raged at home in impotent grief and anger.

In vain, Luke, who remained outwardly stoical in his misery, for all his inner suffering, pointed out gently that there were children dying almost every day of the week, all around, from some sickness or other. They were not alone in their misfortune. Catt refused to accept it. She was convinced that she was being singled out for divine retribution, and, in her heart, she was afraid.

It seemed to Catt that she had only to love someone dearly to risk having them snatched from her before their time. First there had been little Luke, taken so early, and now Susie and Nellie, her two favourite children – though she would not admit to this. She had never been close to Kate, inhibited, perhaps by her eldest daughter's in some ways uncanny resemblance to her grandfather, Charles Leyton – and, by the quite unreasonable resentment (and Catt knew it was unreasonable, but could not prevent herself feeling it) that Kate had lived when little Luke had died. And although Catt adored Luke Charles, and had already made all kinds of plans for his future, she was slightly in awe of him, even from his babyhood. Beneath his outward charm, she sensed he possessed some of Kate's underlying aloofness – combined with a streak of ruthlessness that matched her own.

The deaths of Susie and Nellie meant that one more softening influence vanished from Catt's life. For a time, her dreams turned more often to nightmares, as she struggled to break free from the nagging belief that her own actions – the denial of her faith, so publicly expressed in that mad Bridestones ritual, right at the start of her marriage – had caused divine retribution to be brought down on the innocent. Oh, yes, whatever she might think she believed, or did not believe, Catt had indeed prayed long and often for her daughters, in her heart, in the silence of the sickroom . . . but should she have done more? Gone, perhaps, to the redbrick church her father had dedicated – and sought reconciliation, forgiveness, even? Would that have made things different? But this was nonsense! What need had she of forgiveness, anyway? For she had been far more sinned against than sinning.

Eventually, unknown to Luke, Catt made another visit to Henry Martin's office. 'I know I promised not to get in touch with my – benefactor,' she said, 'and in return, he agreed he would not communicate with me. I have kept my promise – and I always will. But' – and her voice shook and broke – 'would it, because of the way things have turned out, be possible for you to let him know that my two little daughters have died . . . and ask if a Mass could be said for their souls? I do not think he would object to that.'

Even as she stood there in her mourning gown, pale and very near to tears, Catt was inwardly reproaching herself for being so weak – for giving in to what she believed was mere outdated superstition.

But when the solicitor subsequently informed her that her request had been passed on, and fully granted, and that her benefactor shared her grief, Catt felt that a great burden had been lifted from her.

* * *

Was it simple coincidence that, after this, life seemed to take on a distinct turn for the better? Little by little, the agony of the family's grief begn to ease. The farm and the dairy prospered, while the plump vale sheep that Luke secretly continued to consider not real sheep at all even carried away prizes at the local agricultural shows.

Kate left to work at the doctor's house in Melchester. Though she would not admit it, even to herself, Catt felt more comfortable with her eldest child away, more in control of her own destiny. Kate's character, as well as some of her physical features, reminded Catt of things she would rather forget. Even Charles Leyton's gift to her of Townend, which had been the material making of the Hallidays, as she well knew, had exacted a heavy emotional price.

Luke missed Kate badly; they had always been very close. The letters that passed between Melchester and Pickerby were mostly between father and daughter – clumsy, badly spelled notes from two people, neither of whom was very literate. And it was to Luke, in due course, and not to Catt, that Kate first confided that she had fallen in love and wanted her father's consent to get married.

To outsiders, Catt and Luke appeared an exceptionally stable and contented couple – allowing, of course, for the sadness which had touched them with the premature deaths of their two little girls. In reality, however, unlike that earlier tragedy, when the death of their first-born son had served to bind them more closely than before, grief now only accentuated their fundamental separateness; no matter that it was a separateness others could not see.

Luke could still surprise and delight, by creeping up behind Catt, say, when she was hanging out the washing in the orchard, clasping her round the waist, kissing, murmuring the old endearments, or exclaiming how bonny she was looking this minute.

He loves me as much as he always did, Catt would tell herself at such moments – more, maybe – we've more time for

208

one another now, we've grown closer.

But she knew this was only half the truth. Love her still Luke certainly did; and it was true that she saw much more of him than in the early days. They were business partners now, and working as a team . . . Yet she could not help feeling that some kind of invisible wall had grown up between her husband and herself and that here they were, travelling along together but on opposite sides of it, in parallel but never converging. Though always in sight, they were condemned, in a sense, to be perpetually apart.

Their lovemaking, too, had lost much of its old passion – maybe this was to be expected, for we're both growing older, Catt told herself – but, nonetheless, there were still times when she desperately longed for Luke to turn to her in the night with some of his former abandon and blot out those old nightmares of hers that continued to haunt her now and then . . . She yearned to remind him of the strength of her love for him – was it not for Luke that she had always planned and laboured, regardless of the cost?

Catt could not bear to face the fact that Townend, and the circumstances of its acquisition, had opened a gulf between Luke and herself which the years showed no sign of diminishing.

It was time she became less introspective and withdrawn, she decided. So when Luke Charles delighted and surprised everyone with his scholarship to the grammar school, Catt seized the occasion to indulge in one of her rare bouts of public entertaining. Out came the rarely used best Wedgwood and the embroidered linen cloths; the brasses gleamed from extra polishing. The guests at the tea party included Luke Charles's future headmaster and the Pickerby vicar and his wife, as well as the entire Carter family. The grand finale was a toast to Luke Charles's future, in Catt's home-made elderberry wine, served in Waterford crystal glasses bought specially for the celebration.

That afternoon, Catt remembered, in retrospect, Luke had seemed particularly happy. His eyes glowed in the pride of his son's achievement. He was full of smiles and lavish in praise of

Catt – more relaxed and more like the Luke of bygone days, before Townend and his daughters' deaths . . .

When all the guests had gone, he pulled Catt to him, kissing her full on the lips just as he used to do – but so rarely did now. 'That was grand, love – really grand! I was proud of you – and of the lad, too, of course. I know it was his special day – but then, without you, none of this would have been possible.'

Afterwards, seated alone by the dying parlour fire, with father and son gone out to the cowshed for the evening milking, Catt dared to wonder wistfully if, perhaps, after today, she and Luke might be on the verge of yet another new beginning – in which they could retrieve some of their old trust and faith in one another.

She was still pondering on this, and feeling a sense of unaccustomed peace at the thought of it, when Luke Charles came rushing in, white-faced and distraught.

'It's Father! He's collapsed in the dairy!'

The momentary bliss of the afternoon's end was, in the days to come, quite forgotten. Catt could remember only the chilling moments when she had seen Luke lying unconscious on the stone floor of the milking-shed, a thin trickle of blood oozing from his mouth.

Once the initial shock had passed, the incident seemed, at the time, comparatively trivial. Luke came to almost at once, and was soon, half-humorously, half-shamefacedly, explaining it all away.

'That parlour's so close, and you'd built up a wonderful fire for us, Catt – it was as hot as an oven! And then I'm not used to so much elderberry wine – stooping over the cows so soon after all that drinking gave me quite a turn.' Luke smiled at his wife apologetically. 'We're not young things any longer, Catt, either of us, are we? *You* should be taking it easy, too, after all you've had to do today. Just leave me be awhile. I'll be as right as rain in no time.'

But Catt, by now thoroughly frightened, was having none of this. She swept all Luke's protestations aside and got him to bed. Then she got the hired hand to finish the milking, and sent Luke Charles for the doctor.

At first sight, the doctor's response seemed reasonably reassuring. He examined Luke thoroughly, diagnosed 'a bit of a fever' and prescribed a few days' rest. 'After all, we don't want this to lead to anything more serious,' he said.

But then followed a question which struck Catt as much more sinister. 'Did either of your husband's parents die fairly young?'

Fear – unreasonable fear, she told herself – tore at Catt's heart. 'Well, his father was almost eighty – and he'd lived hard and drunk hard – but his mother died in her forties . . . I was told it was some kind of consumption.'

'And then there were your two little girls,' the doctor said gently. 'So there's every reason why we ought to be careful to take things more easily for the present.'

Catt broke in swiftly, trying to persuade herself as much as the doctor. 'Ah, but there's no comparison. His parents' house was just a poor little place – right on the moor-top, and so damp and cold – and the place we had when the girls were tiny was damp and unhealthy too.'

The doctor's response was measured and cautious. 'No doubt. But you must understand, Mrs Halliday, that tuberculosis seems to attack some families more than others. It's not clear why – sometimes the wealthiest households are affected, while the poorest are not. Still,' he went on, sounding an optimistic note, 'I can find nothing fundamentally the matter with your husband at the present time. But it is as well to be on the safe side, given the family history. So I am simply asking you to be sure he works less hard.'

Much later on, after the doctor had left and Luke had fallen into a dreamless and exhausted sleep, Catt made her way out to the cowshed. She sat there on the milking-stool, leaning her head against the warm, comforting body of their prize heifer. She thought back to her early married life and how she and Luke had had but the one cow then, and so many slights and so much hurt from Old Will and Young Will and Betsy . . . And yet, in spite of everything, they had had, in those days, such a joyful love for each other that everything had seemed bright and good. So why was it that now, when they had relatively so much, that true happiness seemed always to elude them?

Ironically, neither Catt nor the doctor could know that it was this fine prize herd carrying its endemic but invisible disease, which had been the cause of her daughters' sickness and subsequent deaths. That same sickness which was, in fact, already beginning to attack Luke.

23

Luke appeared to make a complete recovery, and within a day or two, he seemed outwardly quite his usual self. But the incident had shaken Catt to the core, threatened the confidence she had had in their future, made her realise again what, in the bustle of building up Townend, she had almost forgotten . . . that without Luke, she was as nothing.

In the aftermath of his collapse, while Luke was still confined to his bed, Catt insisted on a number of changes. The hired day-labourer became a live-in hand, and in addition a boy came in daily to help with the milk-round and the sheep. As for the house, the woman whom Catt had formerly employed for only a few hours a week to help with the rough cleaning and the laundry now became virtually a full-time servant.

'I've been trying to get you to agree to these changes for years,' commented Luke wryly, when Catt told him what she was doing. 'But you always said we shouldn't spend the money. At least my fainting like that's made you see a bit of sense! After all, so long as we've enough put by to see to the farm and to Luke Charles's future, why shouldn't we spend a bit of what we've earned to make life easier – we shan't be here for ever.'

Catt tried to believe she had not heard her husband's last few words; though they echoed her own, hearing them said aloud frightened her.

For the first time in her life, Catt now had time for some of the things she had always longed to do – to read a few books, and to do some fine embroidery for herself and her family,

213

not just for selling to other people. She joined Pickerby's new circulating library – which had the effect of at once raising her status in local society – and even bought a few books of her own. The novels of Dickens and Mrs Gaskell were a start, and she began a family custom of reading a chapter aloud from something most evenings. She had originally planned this in the hope that Luke would be inspired to alternate the reading with her and so improve the skill she had started, but which had languished because they had both been too busy or exhausted to find the time to continue. Luke, sensitive to the presence of his clever young son, refused to take the turn offered and thereby risk showing up his own faltering efforts, though he was happy enough to listen to Catt or Luke Charles. And when she tentatively suggested taking up the old writing lessons, he rejected that, too, saying half-jokingly that he was now much too old to start learning anything new – and anyway, hadn't she already taught him sufficient to enable him to write to Kate and manage the farm business?

As for the fine embroidery – alas, there were no longer any pretty little girls in the household to wear Catt's handiwork. If only I'd had time when Nellie and Susie were alive, thought Catt sadly. Instead, her beautiful garments had all been worn by strangers. There was still Kate, of course, but she was in Melchester, and in any case had little time for elaborate blouses, preferring to dress plainly. Still, Kate was engaged to be married, so Catt was able to devote herself to producing drawerfuls of finely embroidered pillowcases, mats and tablecloths for her daughter's future home. But even as she sewed, she guessed her offerings would get little use. Yet again, it seemed, an opportunity had come too late.

But if reading and sewing did not give the pleasure Catt had anticipated, the new-found freedom which she and Luke now had, their release from the old routines, more than made up for it. For now Catt and Luke were able to spend whole days away from Townend together – something virtually impossible in the past, before they had live-in labour. And Catt determined to seize this opportunity to the full . . . even if she resolutely refused to believe that time was running out.

They would take the train to Whitcar or Whinborough, look at the shops, stroll by the sea, listen to the summer bands. Sometimes Luke and Catt would get off at one of the intervening stops and spend the day in some picturesque little village on the coast or in a moorland valley – almost all of which, Catt was to find out, had some connection with some Halliday ancestor or other. They went exploring Whitcar Abbey's ruins on the cliff-top – trudging with other trippers up the 999 medieval steps to reach it. 'They say people used to go up on their knees, as a penance, once upon a time,' said Luke. And then went on to look at the parish church next door, where Luke's parents and Aunt Nell and her husband had been married – with its graves and monuments to so many lost at sea. At Whinborough, they put flowers on Clarrie's grave, strolled on the promenade, and rode up and down the funicular railway, which had still been unfinished in Catt's days at Nell's. And on every outing, Catt bought a little Goss ornament, so that her mantelpiece became a kind of record of their expeditions.

To Melchester, however, she refused to go, even to visit Kate. Luke could not persuade her. Melchester still held too many awful memories, never mind that Kate clearly loved it as much as she had loathed it. Luke had to go alone to visit his daughter – or, at weekends or during the school holidays, with Luke Charles for company.

As the weeks passed, with Luke continuing to look so well, Catt's sense of well-being grew and those dark demons of fear ceased to plague her. Over a year went by with scarcely a ripple to disturb the even tenor of their lives. Kate's wedding was planned to take place in Melchester just before Christmas. Before that, with the coming of autumn, there was Luke's fiftieth birthday.

Catt had originally wanted to give a special party to mark the occasion, but Luke, who was still fundamentally as shy as ever, demurred. 'Parties are for children,' he declared, and refused to change his mind.

'Well, think of some special present I can give you then!' cried Catt. 'And it must be something very special, for a very

215

special birthday – your half-century! Though no one would think it, to see you.' She looked approvingly at Luke's trim figure and saw the ruddiness in his cheeks as proof that all her care and solicitude had succeeded. It was many months now since her husband had had to see the doctor.

But Luke's answer was not the one Catt wanted to hear. Indeed, it was not one she had ever considered.

'I know what I'd like best of all. For us to take one of our days out, and get the Whitcar train – but, just this once, we'll get off at Gelling Halt.' Luke stopped, seeing Catt's shocked expression, and explained: 'Oh, never fear, love, I don't want to visit anyone there! It'll be *our* day, and no one else's. But we could take a basket of food with us and walk up onto the moor from the station, and have a picnic there. That'd be far better than any party indoors! And there's one or two of the old spots we could visit – the churchyard, maybe – but nothing that you don't want to see.'

Catt nodded. She had made her offer, and it was impossible to go back on it now, she knew – even though she had been expecting Luke to ask for a watch and chain or some such thing, never, in a month of Sundays, had she thought she would have to be visiting Gelling again with him! Still, it was all a long time ago . . .

So to Gelling they went, on a fine, calm September day, bright and sunny. But as the little train puffed its way up the steep cutting which led up from Pickerby and out to the moors, Catt was seized with such a feeling of impending doom it was almost as though she had been physically punched. This was just one more product of her too vivid imagination, she told herself, connected with the bitter memories of the past. Yet, try as she might, she could not entirely shake it off.

By contrast, Luke was like a young man again, and bubbling with enthusiasm. As they went along, he pointed out old remembered places – the eighteenth-century folly at the top of an embankment, built by an eccentric parson, where he and Catt had sometimes walked years ago; the brand-new station at Newby, just below Gelling; and a mass of young fir trees

216

planted where Catt remembered only meadow, one of the plantations that were coming into fashion these days; and dominating everything, as always, the moors themselves, at the moment spread out in their fullest glory – a mighty ocean of royal purple, with the heather in full bloom, and picked out here and there by the harsh gold of the gorse.

As they stepped off the train, Catt could have sworn her knees were trembling slightly. It was the first time she had ever been on the station itself, though she had passed through it often enough on their excursions to Whitcar.

Luke stood still on the platform for a few minutes, watching the train pulling away into the distance. He took a long, luxurious breath. 'Why, there's nothing to touch Gelling air, is there? Why is it that it loses so much of its fizz by the time it gets down to Pickerby? Up here, a body can really breathe.'

He laughed delightedly, and took Catt's arm. She felt reassured then – but as they started the steep climb up the track from the station towards the village, he was seized by a sudden paroxysm of violent coughing. After this, they made slower progress; Luke seemed to have difficulty for some time in getting his breath back properly. In the end, they were forced to sit down on the bank by the roadside and rest awhile.

'It's old age, that's what it is,' said Luke, half-laughing. 'Don't forget, it's my fiftieth birthday we're celebrating. You can't expect me to run up these slopes like I did when I was twenty-five!' But Catt had noticed his heightened colour. The old, dreaded tentacles of fear began winding themselves around her once again. . .

At the fork, one way led to the village and the Horseshoe Inn, and the other, past the church, towards High Moor. 'I thought we'd not bother with the village,' said Luke, with a knowing glance at Catt's apprehensive face. 'After all, we never did go there much, did we? And we always gave the Horseshoe a miss – even if others didn't.' He had no difficulty in reading Catt's horror of being suddenly faced with Will or Betsy. 'But I would like to see the church again, and the

217

childrens' graves. Just one more time . . .'

Just one more time. What did Luke mean? But even as Catt stifled a fresh gasp of panic, Luke was already pushing open the lych-gate into the churchyard, holding it open for her. Catt stepped through like an automaton, still numbed by his last few words.

Stumbling through long grass still wet from the morning's dew, they came to the spot where Luke's parents lay buried. Catt recalled the legendary Whinny Moor and wondered if Old Will had managed to get across it yet. There was no gravestone: Young Will would not have wanted to waste any of his inheritance on that, she thought grimly. It had been different for her own dead baby; the stillborn were not permitted marked graves. Now she and Luke walked over to the place of little Luke's burial, near the north wall of the churchyard – and next to it, the plot, marked by a small stone cross, that held the graves of Susie and Nellie. It was the very first time Catt had ever set eyes on any of them.

She fell to her knees, setting in place the few sprigs of heather she had just picked from the moor. She shared them out between the two little graves. As she did so, she seemed to hear again the rippling laughter of her dead daughters – Luke's 'golden little girls'. Yet it was of the tiny dead son who had come into the world and left it without a single sound that she thought most deeply – lying here, alone, all those years, until joined by his sisters . . .

She was suddenly conscious of Luke's voice. 'Don't forget, Catt, this is where I want to be buried too, when my time comes. Here, at Gelling, on the moor's edge, along with my own.'

'Oh, Luke, love! Don't talk of such things. Not now – not ever. It frightens me so!' The tears danced in Catt's eyes. 'That sort of thing's years away – for both of us – and' she tried to calm her near-hysteria – 'when the time *does* come we'll want to be together, will we not, and there's no place for me here . . . there never has been, you know that.' And it's not just this church that's not mine – I never belonged on these moors either, she thought sadly, though for a time I believed I did.

They've brought me little else but grief. Aloud, she added: 'It was different with the children – I can understand you wanted them all here . . . but you and I, we're Pickerby people now, and in Pickerby cemetery we could both lie together.'

Luke took Catt by the shoulders, gripping her so tightly that she flinched slightly. He looked her straight in the eye; she had rarely seen him so determined. 'I want to be buried *here*, with my family,' he said, very quietly and slowly. 'I came from here, and I want to come back here at the last. And this time, Catt, it is *you* who will have to see it done. Promise me! Promise me that you'll not stay away on the day of my burial – like you have done for all the others!'

His grip seemed to become even tighter; had it not been Luke who was holding her, Catt would have struggled in fear to tear herself away, as from a menacing stranger . . . Then she realised that at this moment Luke *was* in fact a stranger to her – and that there was a part of him that always had been and always would be – because he was in some sense at one with the moors on which they were standing, as she had never been and never could be.

Almost mesmerised by the intensity of his stare, she could scarcely find breath to stammer, 'Yes, of course – I promise – if that's what you really want.' Then, as her courage returned, she added with spirit – instantly conscious of all the old taboos she was breaking – 'Everything will be done just as you want it done, and I'll be there in the church – in this church – with you, as I've always been with you. I swear it!'

Luke relaxed, and grinned – the familiar, placid Luke once again. 'Why, love, you've turned so pale! I shouldn't have held you so fast. I don't know my own strength . . . And this is much too sad talk for a birthday! Let's get ourselves out on the road towards High Moor and eat our picnic.'

The remainder of the day went by happily and uneventfully. Catt was surprised and relieved that Luke seemed almost indifferent to the sight of High Moor, viewed from some distance away and looking almost benevolent under the sunny sky. She suspected that he was affecting an unconcern for her benefit, trying to make up, in some measure, for their recent agonised conflict. Whatever the reason, he gave no hint of wanting to walk any closer. Even the Bridestones, seen from this safe distance, appeared less threatening than they had in days gone by.

Luke's outburst in the churchyard, and Catt's eventual positive response to it had, for a while, worked to bring husband and wife back to the intimacy of their early life together. For in a sheltered hollow deep amid the heather, far from the nearest track, Luke made love to his wife with a passion and fervour she had almost forgotten he possessed.

Afterwards, as she lay back in the ferns, looking up with rapture at the blue sky and her husband's bluer eyes, Catt felt she was the happiest person alive. All did, indeed, seem well with the world! Then the clouds started to come up, and the day turned cooler. Luke's face crumpled in a fit of fresh coughing, and after that Catt could think only of getting Luke away from this place, and its memories, as quickly as she could – and back to the safety and security of her adored Townend.

24

When she came to think back on life, in the long loneliness of her widowhood, Catt realised that Luke was never to look so well again as he had done on that birthday outing.

She failed to recognise the first tell-tale signs of illness. Her happiness made her blind to them – for, following that day on the moors, with lovemaking following hard on revelations, she and Luke had regained some of their former companionship and unaffected delight in one another's company.

Their business was going well, too; when Catt remarked that come the spring they might think of buying or renting still more land and increasing the sheep flock, Luke was as enthusiastic as she was, and for once did not make his standard wry comment that these were not what he thought of as 'real sheep'. Perhaps, after that last visit, that spell the moor had cast on him since birth was beginning to loosen, even just a little.

But as winter drew on, Luke's cough grew worse. Unknown to Catt, he went back to see the doctor – this time to have confirmed that the dreaded disease which had killed his two little daughters now had him in its grip, too.

To begin with, the doctor was fairly optimistic. 'You've always been a fit man – it's children and the very old who are most at risk. I've known plenty of cures – well, remissions anyway. Do as I told you before: take things easier. If you look after yourself this winter, come spring and the warmer weather, maybe you could leave your wife to run the farm for you for a week or two and take a real holiday at one of the spa towns – Harrogate maybe, or even Bath or Buxton.'

But Luke had no intention of doing any such thing. If his days on this earth were numbered, he wanted to spend every one of them with Catt. They had had far too many separations in the past. And, he promised himself, for as long as possible he would not tell her what the doctor had diagnosed.

So he said nothing, even when, just before Christmas, Kate's marriage took place in Melchester. Stubborn as ever, Catt refused point-blank to attend, pleading that someone had to stay in charge at Townend, even though she knew quite well that the hired man could have coped without her and Luke for a couple of days.

'You were always Kate's favourite, love,' she told Luke, 'and after all, the father's the essential one at a wedding – he has to give the bride away! Take Luke Charles with you – he'll be company for you and it'll be a treat for him and maybe he'll meet some lads of his own age there. It's hard on him, he's almost like an only child.'

Catt thought wistfully of what a picture Nellie and Susie would have made in their bridesmaids' dresses – even though she herself would still not have been there to see them, Kate's church being somewhere she would never, in any circumstances, have entered, she told herself. Later on, she was to reproach herself vainly and bitterly for wilfully depriving herself of Luke's presence for those two precious days.

Luke returned from the wedding, full of tales of the elaborate ceremony – quite different from the run of Pickerby church weddings, he said. The church had been filled with candles and crosses and statues and incense, even though it was Church of England – and Kate had worn a fine gold cross around her neck, a present from her new husband, plain though her dress had been.

Catt pursed her lips. This inscrutable daughter of hers seemed to be practising a sort of mock-Catholicism – it was as if the granddaughter of a cardinal was poking fun at the real thing, at the religion of her ancestors . . . but then, of course, Kate was sublimely unaware of her Catholic inheritance. Catt could not help wondering what her father would have said to it all!

222

At once she found herself being attacked by all the old guilt – guilt that she had failed to bring up her children in the faith of her childhood, never mind that she herself had cast it off . . . Why was it that that same faith still refused to let her go? It seemed that however much she rejected it, it would keep coming back, intruding when she least expected . . . and these intrusions would bring back memories of her father, and those in turn would revive emotions so shocking she would have done anything to blot them out altogether. If Luke's cage was now Townend, Catt's was something far less visible but infinitely more constricting.

Luke described how he had ventured outside the town centre to look at Miss Fredericks's house. 'I'd always wanted to see where you lived before I knew you. I even rang the doorbell! I would have liked to have talked to your friend Annie, if she'd still been there. But she wasn't. The old lady died years back, the present folk told me. It's all changed now.'

'I don't suppose St Agatha's would have changed,' commented Catt acidly, a little shaken by Luke's nerve at delving so deep into her past. 'It would still be the same cold, loveless place.'

Luke beamed. 'Not now – for I've done my best to put the love back in it! I went there, after I'd been to the house. It wasn't very different from Kate's church. I knelt down,' he went on, 'and said a prayer for all of us – but for you, especially, love! Oh, I know how you hated the place, having been so unhappy in Melchester – but I wanted my prayers to get rid of all those unhappy memories, once and for all – and when I got to my feet again, I felt certain, somehow, that they had.'

At this, Catt flung her arms around her husband and hugged him tightly. 'Oh, Luke! You're too good for me. Far too good. I don't deserve you!' She noticed with shock how thin he had become – her arms seemed to be resting on his actual bones. The old fear came flooding back; she clung to him still more fiercely.

'Don't ever leave me! I'd die without you, you know I would!'

It was small comfort to Catt to hear her husband's rejoinder: 'Nay, lass, you'd be all right. You're so strong! And what with the farm and Luke Charles to keep you busy – don't talk so! Why, it's *me* who couldn't manage without *you*. Where would we be now, but for all you've done?' Luke's face turned unusually solemn. 'I took on unfairly, Catt, when you first mentioned Townend – but I was quite wrong to do so. Of course, I know that now – but I'm sorry I acted as I did and said what I did. It's been a real godsend to us, and all thanks to you. When I see men I used to know, who were once shepherds like me, and now having to do casual labouring, even begging, sometimes – why, I could have been one of them, if it hadn't been for you.'

It was at precisely this moment that Catt knew instinctively that something was wrong. But she could not bear to face Luke, to hear what exactly it was. She went on hoping against hope that if she said nothing, it would all somehow go away . . .

In the end, Luke never even had to tell her. For as time passed, the dreadful truth became increasingly obvious.

Luke weathered the winter reasonably well, but in the spring his cough grew worse. There was no longer any question of his going away for a 'cure', even to relatively nearby Harrogate; he had not the strength to do so. He was now losing weight rapidly, his strength draining from him almost by the day. No longer could he hide from Catt – or from the rest of the world – the gravity of his illness.

Still, Catt refused to give in. She fought for Luke's life like a tigress, loading him with every luxury she could think of, trying to relieve him even of those few light tasks he could still manage. Luke could not be allowed to die!

In desperation, she even made her way to the Catholic church. It was evening, and dark, but in any case she was past caring whether anyone saw her. She progressed from the Lady chapel to the high altar, pouring out her intercessions. She lit candle after candle, until the church glowed as for a festival. When Nellie and Susie had been dying, she remembered guiltily, she had steadfastly refused to let herself come and do this for *them,* successfully persuading herself, then, that it was simply superstition and could do nothing to help . . . But now, she wondered, had she been mistaken? So, as she prayed, against all the odds, that Luke might recover, she interceded for her dead daughters, too. And for herself.

A figure emerged from the shadows. 'Is there anything I can do to help?'

Startled and tongue-tied, Catt could only shake her head and hurry away from both priest and church. But she could not help going back, again and again, though from now on she took care to stay at the back, ready to rush out of the door the moment anyone appeared.

On one of these visits she picked up a religious paper in the church entrance. It was filled with news of her father, of his visits to the poor of this city and that, of his meetings with royalty and politicians, of things he had said and written. She realised that Charles Leyton was an important person in society. But he was much more than that; as she had guessed at her last meeting with him, he had become a very good man, too.

And, of course, he had been so very good to her! Should she not now try to be more charitable and forgiving – and fully accept his regrets for the hurt of the long-distant past? In any case, she knew that her mother, Mary Jane, had never considered it a hurt, much more an honour! It was she, Catt, who had borne the real burden – and the main force behind this, she now realised, had been not Charles, but his mother, with the connivance of her own.

Then Catt read on that the cardinal was gravely ill at this very time, and that prayers were being asked for him. So it was that she, after all those years of hating, now came to add prayers for Charles to those she was offering for Luke and the girls and herself.

But, even as she did so, there rose up before her yet again that old, now almost-forgotten erotic image where Charles Leyton was transformed into her dream-lover. Catt shuddered uncontrollably with shame and self-loathing. Could she not smother that quite unnatural evil yearning,

225

even at a time like this, and in such a place? Surely, she must be a truly lost soul!

She flung down the paper and hurried home to the dying husband whose love always had been and always would be a marvellous and perfect reality. No dream, this – but the rock of her very existence.

Not for very much longer. In the summer warmth, Luke rallied a little. But it was merely the last, defiant flutter of a dying flame. By autumn he was permanently confined to his bed, almost wasting away before Catt's eyes.

Sometimes, his thoughts would wander. And Catt, constantly at his bedside, would hear him speaking of his childhood, and of High Moor – and then of herself, as she had been in those early days, before her ambitions and dreams had come between them and she had grown hard and ruthless . . . And then she would mourn for herself, that lost, innocent self, as much as for Luke.

Then winter came round again. On the first anniversary of Kate's wedding, Luke still clung to life, though the thread was growing weaker.

Luke was very lucid and calm on this particular evening. He moved his head on the pillows to look at his wife with eyes so brimful of love that Catt longed with all her heart to drown in them and die along with him.

He asked her to draw back the curtains for a moment. It was a fine, moonlit night and frosty. The whole landscape sparkled. The rise in front of the farmhouse – the rise that marked the start of the climb up onto the moor – lay spread there before them, bathed in silver.

The moor was beckoning. Luke could feel it drawing him irresistibly towards it. 'You'll not forget your promise, love?' he whispered. His fevered hand clasped hers even more tightly. 'You'll be there to see I rest in Gelling?'

Catt nodded. At first, she could not find the strength to answer. When she did, she cried: 'Of course I will! And I'll see to it that I come and lie beside you, Luke. We'll be together there – always.'

She saw Luke and herself, young again, running through

the heather, up on High Moor top, all cares vanished, and become a part of the earth and the sky around them, loosed from the fetters of old prejudices, and united, for ever and ever. No longer were they blighted by the dreams for whose fulfilment she had sacrificed her own soul and Luke's happiness. In this final, most glorious dream of all, Catt and Luke were fused into one eternal pulse of everlasting love. Nothing could ever come between them any more.

Catt looked down, and saw that Luke was dead, and her dream dead with him.

The world felt suddenly cold and she all alone in it.

1893

Catt remained dry-eyed and stony-faced throughout the funeral service. The words of grieving and of consolation flowed over her, but she remained untouched by them. She was held fast in the dark world of her own overwhelming sense of guilt and of remorse.

It was because of the sins she had committed, she felt, that all her dreams had turned to dust and ashes. She had no Luke now, no Susie, no Nellie – who would be taken from her next? There was no one left except for Luke Charles – and Kate. And as for Kate, I have never really known her at all, she mused.

Everything I did, I did for Luke. And what I got was no more than I was owed – *he* owed it me, didn't he? It was only simple justice that I was demanding . . . And then Catt recalled that fearful moment when Luke had first made love to her, and even as she had cried out with excitement and delight, it had not been Luke's face she had seen before her, but that of her own father . . .

He never touched me, she told herself – and I have known for a long time now that he never even *wanted* to touch me. It was all fantasy, a creation of my own imaginings, and yet I feel so – tainted. Permanently. It is not fair that I should feel so! It is not fair that I should have loved him as I did – before I knew who he really was.

I'm trapped. Trapped forever, thought Catt. Trapped in a web I have made myself. And yet, whatever I've thought, whatever I've done, whatever my mistakes – and, God knows, there've been plenty – I have loved Luke throughout it all. He

228

gave me everything. I did what I did because I wanted to give him something, something in return – to get him away from his wretched past, as he had got me away from mine, to push him forward into the fresh start he couldn't or wouldn't make for himself. Townend was done for him, as much as for me . . .

But, of course, it was High Moor I should really have set out to get for him, even though I hated it. It was what he really wanted, and I knew it. But who would have thought it would be in Townend that so many of us would die? It was as if it held a kind of curse . . . Maybe it was God's way of punishing me – for thinking such forbidden thoughts, not to mention my deserting Him the way I did. But why did He have to do it by destroying the good and the innocent, and leaving me behind?

Catt was scarcely aware that the ceremonies inside the church were drawing to a close, of processing, with Luke Charles close by her side, into the churchyard, of casting the ritual handful of earth into the grave.

It was the sight of Betsy and Will, hovering on the edge of the mourners, that brought her back to reality. Momentarily her grieving gave way to triumphant practicality.

I shall have a memorial stone put here, determined Catt, that will be the finest in the churchyard. It will tell the world that Luke belonged to High Moor! And there'll be a space for my name on it, too, just as there's a space for my body down there beside his.

Then they were back in the carriage, heading once more for Townend and Pickerby. As they dropped down from the moor, Catt noticed the St George's flag flying at half-mast from the Catholic church.

Her father, the cardinal, was dead, too, she guessed. Dead, just as Luke was. *So my prayers for both of them were unanswered . . . as the prayers of the damned would be . . .*

Suddenly it seemed the most natural thing in the world that both the men in her life should have died so close together. Catt wanted to weep for each of them, but the tears would not come. She felt as if she herself had died too – and that only Luke's arms around her could bring her back to life . . . But

229

was it really *his* arms she wanted?

She shivered slightly, then drew herself up. She turned to look at her son. And resolved to quash the doubts and regrets and desires once and for all.

There were still the two of them! Together, she and Luke Charles would carry on, just as Luke would have wanted. There was so much that needed doing. Work would help lessen the sting of their loss. By the time Luke Charles is ready to wed, vowed Catt, I'll have got the size of our holding doubled. It's utter nonsense to think of being condemned to perpetual damnation! Life's not over, not by a long chalk. On the contrary – a new life's about to begin!

From now on, she determined to put the threats of the past firmly behind her – the threats which the Bridestones had come to symbolise. Why, even today, those wretched, evil stones had forced themselves upon her – but it was to be the very last time they did so. She need never set eyes on them, nor think of them, ever again!

So it was that Catt arrived back at Townend, strangely elated and happier than she had been for many months, for her head was once more full of dreams. Expansive, ambitious, happy dreams.

No hint in these dreams of tragedy yet to come: no thought that young Luke Charles might, some twenty years from now, be choking to death in the mud of Flanders, just as his father had choked to death in his own blood: no premonition of Catt herself, dying only days later from influenza and a broken heart, an old, defeated woman at the last, and afraid of the dark and the unknown, yearning for that old, safe faith, yet unable till the very end, to find it again.

Just before she died, Catt cried out: 'Jesus and Mary have mercy!' This would remain a perpetual mystery to the surviving child at her bedside – who had always believed her mother to be quite without religion.